THE GLITCH

HANNAH JOCK

authorHOUSE®

AuthorHouse™
1663 Liberty Drive
Bloomington, IN 47403
www.authorhouse.com
Phone: 833-262-8899

Published by AuthorHouse   09/30/2021

ISBN: 978-1-6655-3583-0 (sc)
ISBN: 978-1-6655-3584-7 (e)

Library of Congress Control Number: 2021917231

Edited by Patti Wahlberg and Jan Wilson

Print information available on the last page.

Cover Designed and Illustrated by: Tracy Bywater

This book is printed on acid-free paper.

CONTENTS

Chapter 1   Welcome to Katroia 1
Chapter 2   We Come across a Tear in the Fabric of Time....8
Chapter 3   Everything Turns Black and White 20
Chapter 4   We Give Ellie's Idea a Shot.................................... 29
Chapter 5   We Get Busted 35
Chapter 6   We Chat with the Enchanter 44
Chapter 7   We Hit the Road 52
Chapter 8   We Dig into a Mineral Cove 60
Chapter 9   I Go Calamity Mode 64
Chapter 10   Welcome to the Fallen Realm 75
Chapter 11   We Hire a Fourth Recruit 85
Chapter 12   The Fallen Fortress Welcomes Us with
             Open Arms 88
Chapter 13   The Way of the Fortress... 96
Chapter 14   The Beans are Spilled... 104
Chapter 15   The Fortress' Idea of a Mirror Maze................ 112
Chapter 16   I Die 119
Chapter 17   Welcome to the Edge..124
Chapter 18   We Are Backed Up 134
Chapter 19   We Are Offered a Trust Exercise 145
Chapter 20   The Final Raid Begins 155

Chapter 21   We Kick Some Serious Butt 158
Chapter 22   I Find My Way Home 167
Chapter 23   We Prepare for the Void 177
Chapter 24   The Cavern of The Void 183
Chapter 25   Ellie is Kidnapped by Slime 188
Chapter 26   Welcome to The Void 195
Chapter 27   And so, Our Final Battle Begins 204
Chapter 28   Two Down, Two to Go 215
Chapter 29   I Teach the Dragon a Lesson 219
Chapter 30   A Vision of Victory 226

Chapter 31   Welcome Back to the Overworld 228
Acknowledgements 237
About the Author 239

For Mom and Dad,
Who never doubted me
And have encouraged me every step of the way

CHAPTER 1

Welcome to Katroia

It was a ravishing spring afternoon, when the Sherberry Cherry Blossoms were barely clinging to their buds and the velvety grass cast short, skinny shadows over the earth. The sun's final golden rays began to tuck away among the trees of the forest canopy, projecting a camouflage pattern along the ground. Fleecy moss caked the surface, hugging around rocks and damp tree trunks, while blanketing the coarse, moist dirt.

Wild birds sang a chorus of harmonious songs within the husky canopy. Most of the time, their hymns were scattered and isolated. But sometimes, if you really listened closely, you might just barely hear their songs blend together into one massive, wild symphony. Other sounds of the forest sometimes joined in – the little skitter of rodents' feet across stone, pebbles clattering and rolling along with the flow of a stream, and the gentle whispers that were carried in the wind.

On most days, my mother would run off with me into the woods. I would follow her as we hopped over rocks, leapt across narrow streams, and wandered and wandered and wandered until we got lost. Then she'd turn around to meet my eyes and put on her brave, wild grin.

"Oh! Listen, Kaila. Do you hear it yet?" she would beam.

We would stand in silence and listen patiently as we slowly began to notice the wild symphony coming together. Then, my mother would sling an arm around my shoulders and titter delightfully, "All of the individual sounds of the forest will *always* seem to work together to form an orchestra – even if you don't hear it at first." She looked down and smiled at me again. "Only if you wait patiently and listen, everything will make sense in the end."

I would smile back at my mother and then glance up at the horizon, which was now painted with rich sunset colors. The late, golden sun now seemed to reach out toward the sky, longing to grab its way back up to the top. Despite its efforts it only sunk down further and tucked itself away among the trees of the canopy.

We would stand for a few more minutes in the clean, forest-scented air, and then hear a male voice shouting commands from the onset of the woods.

"Maya! What are you doing? Your shift is not over for another hour! Get your little behind down here and get to work!"

Mom dropped her head and managed a giggle.

"Coming, Will!" she promised. Then she winked down at me. "See ya for dinner, my little Kaila Bear."

And after that, she would take off, apologizing to Will for ditching him in the forges and promising an extra thirty minutes of her shift.

I could never help but smile back at her. I loved her so much.

Shoot, I then would think to myself. *I forgot to pick up Ellie from her hunting lesson.* At that, I would leave the forest and head back for my little sister, who was determined to be a hunter like me and Mom.

Same drill today. Every morning, at around two o'clock (I'll give an explanation for that later), Mom would take my sister and I out in the woods, just to escape and enjoy the fresh air. Now that Ellie was doing one o'clock lessons, she could join us when we escaped into the grand Sherberry Forest. Then at some point, Will, the owner of the forges, would yell at Mom from a mile away and she'd go sprinting back to work. She was too nice of a lady to be fired, and she was an incredibly smart and strong worker.

At around lunchtime, the three of us were reunited and continued the conversation we were having in the woods that morning. We were usually joined by our... well, we call him our friend, Luke. People can't usually imagine him to be just about *anyone's* friend, but Mom decided he needed a home.

When Luke was around ten, his home was lit ablaze and burned to the ground right in front of him. He barely made it out alive, being the only survivor. What was surprising was that he wasn't even sad when it all happened – when he'd lost his entire family, leaving him parentless for the rest of his life. Instead, he was angry. As he stood outside his burning home, his eyes didn't even water. Though the fire was just reflecting in his eyes, everyone thought they were burning up in anger. Nobody really knew why he was so mad when his house was reduced to a pile of charcoal, but one thing we knew was it had something to do with the *fire* specifically.

After that day, he'd built a reputation for grouchiness. He wasn't particularly a bully or anything, he just always walked around with either a scowl on his face or a dead-serious expression. Only since Mom was the nicest woman in Katroia, she was able to break through Luke's hard shell of anger and capture his trust. It's been hard, not going to lie, but Luke really seems to trust us now. Mom had even sometimes been able to cast a smirk or, more rarely, a smile on his face.

Luke usually joined us for lunch to listen to Mom's jokes and entertaining stories. He sometimes smiled and even laughed, but usually his face looked dead serious.

Right, I promised you an explanation for something. I would expect you to think that being awake at two a.m. would be kind of ridiculous, but time here in Katroia isn't the same as it is in your world. You see, us Katrins live inside a 'video game'.

Not exactly sure what that's supposed to mean, but that's what we've been told by the players. Most of them just rudely walk past us and mutter something under their breath like, 'Stupid villagers' or 'Katrins – so annoying'. And I'm not goanna lie, they smell like wet, sweaty socks sometimes...

I know what you're probably already thinking: I'm about to go on and on about how weird and different your race is from ours – and I would if you weren't the ones listening to my story -- but I'm not trying to make enemies here, so I'll decide to skip that part.

Honestly, you guys don't seem so bad all the time. Rarely, players would stop by and talk to us. A few times, we'd been told that we lived inside a video game. Players said they came from another world – apparently a more *real* one. There were twenty-four hours in a day--weird, and no specific hours for night. Like, apparently, they wake up at some random time within those hours and decide to take a nap whenever needed. I mean, come on people, at least have a designated time dedicated for sleep!

Whatever. There were more details, according to the players. *So complicated.*

Here in the land, or game, of Katroia, we have about four hours to be awake, and two hours to sleep or to fight hostile spawns that come alive at nightfall. We Katrins don't require more than three hours of sleep in a week or so, which gives us energy to defend the village pretty much every night. Here the

Hannah Jock

sun has a certain time that it rises and sets. What the sun's up to in the 'real world', I have no idea. I guess it just pops up and says *hi* and then dips back down at random times. Just a wild guess.

Mom works at the village forges from one to two-thirty a.m. There, she works on molding weapons and armor for battle. I don't know about your world, but at night, monsters rise from the ground and threaten the village with their weak little growls. That is when we Katrins gear up and fend them off to protect the village best we can. If we don't, well, let's just say they can cause quite a calamity. They aren't the best fighters, but they sure can tear things and shred them to slivers, no problem. Usually, some of the hostile spawns get at some of the village property, but the refurbishers can easily fix that up during the day.

Sorry if I am making this feel like history class. I'll begin the actual story for you if I'm boring you to death.

By the way, my name is Kaila Kinsworth. That probably should've been the first thing I said.

Also, this pork sandwich I'm eating right now is totally five star.

"Sorry about this morning," Mom said before she took another sip of her beef stew. We sat at a thickly glazed, maple log picnic table around the Center Fountain, which sprayed pure spring water in all different directions, forming an impressive design. A dozen picnic tables encircled the fountain, creating a most delightful dining area. Before us, a party-sized deli lunch was spread across the table, most of it half-eaten. The sun hung high in the cloudless blue sky and the air was still and smelled like the cherry blossoms that lay on the ground around their home trees.

"I had quite a load of work today and couldn't afford to come outside." Mom made a crooked smile. "Guess it's not something to apologize about because Will seems quite happy with me." Then she chuckled. I always loved to listen to her spirit-lifting laugh. It reminded me of silver wind chimes ringing in the wind.

I couldn't help but smile back at her.

"It's totally fine, mom. I got to watch Ellie do her hunting course while you were gone. She was a beast!" I said and nudged my little sister on her shoulder. "Why don't you tell her what you achieved?" I suggested, a sudden wave of pride creeping into my heart.

Ellie's face lit up like she was just offered a fresh-baked cookie straight from the village bakery.

"Oh, you'll never guess!" she beamed. "Captain Freya gave me my very own golden sword! She said I am ready for the prep tests early!"

A wide full-toothed smile spread across Mom's face like butter.

"Really? Oh Ellie, I'm so proud of you!" She wrapped her arms around my sister and squeezed her tight.

"Yeah... Watch the ribs please, Mom," Ellie squeaked.

"Oh sorry." My mom sat back and gazed at her daughter through loving eyes. "I knew you would be the best in the class. I wouldn't be surprised if you got your hunting license early too!"

A rare smile played at the corner of Luke's mouth. Usually, this would be a surprising experience, but I wasn't all that astounded. I mean, Ellie's been training for hunting since two years ago when she was ten. I also wouldn't be surprised if he was only glad he didn't have to drop her off every time she had to go to the training range.

I gave Ellie another lighter hug. "I'm proud of you, Sis," I chirped. "I swear, you'll be one of the best hostile hunters in the village one day."

Mom brushed the grease off of her hands from her work in the forges and stood up. "Well guys, since we never went for fresh air this morning, why don't you say we just go now?" she advised. "I don't have any more duties for the rest of the day."

"I'm out," Luke announced as he dismissively waved his hand and left the table. "I'm going out to the forges to repair my sword."

Mom said goodbye to him. Ellie and I looked at each other, holding a silent conversation in between our heads.

"So are you suggesting we go now?" I finally advocated.

"I don't see why not." Mom slung her sword scabbard over her shoulder. "Let's hit it then, shall we?"

I stuffed a last bite of pork sandwich into my mouth and rose from my seat, uttering a response through stuffed cheeks.

Mom laughed and grabbed my hand. "Sounds good, Kaila."

CHAPTER 2

We Come across a Tear in the Fabric of Time

The rest of the day went by relatively smoothly. We ended up going for a nice long walk through the woods, getting lost a few times, but eventually coming back just in time for dinner. In no time, we were back at the picnic table chowing pork stew that Mom had personally spiced. Gotta admit, Mom is an incredible chef.

After dinner, we hit the drill. All of the hunters of the village (which was approximately twenty Katrins) grouped together in the armory to gear up for combat.

When I entered the building, I found the group buzzing around the armory like a hive of bumble bees, in a slight rush to find their gear. When I walked through the door, straight ahead was a twelve-foot long wall packed copiously with dozens of personalized armor sets. Katroia is known for a ridiculously wide variety of materials and organisms. For instance, there are approximately fifty-four different species of animals, twenty-nine types of minerals, and thirty-five plant species.

On the right and left walls, benches and tables lined the fourteen-foot rigid stone wall, where hunters could hang around and prep themselves for two hours of combat.

"So Mom, how long until Ellie can join?" I inquired of my mother that night.

She shrugged. "Most graduate a year after they get their golden swords, but I predict Ellie will breeze past that last bit."

"Probably."

Mom smiled at me and headed off to find her steel armor that hung among thirty sets. I took my place next to her and scanned the wall for my platinum armor.

"And for your information," Mom added, "I've already got a thin opal set for her to use when she is able to join." She found her set and picked it off the wall, waving me to sit next to her on a bench that hung off the left wall.

As I strapped on my platinum armor, I could practically feel my sister's gaze upon me through the window. Normally, her cheeks were bright red and she had on a welcoming smile that could brighten up a room. But she glanced around the armory with mild jealousy in her eyes. Weird.

I slung my opal sword over my shoulder and headed over to the window where Ellie had her head poked through the window.

"Hey, Ellie," I greeted. "What's up?"

Ellie shrugged. "Just watching you guys gear up and all." She looked into the armory dreamily, like she was trying to give me an obvious message.

"You wish you could hunt with us?" I guessed.

Ellie nodded sadly. "The trainings are nice and all, but I really wish I could actually go out and hunt with you guys like a warrior."

I put on my brave smile that I had inherited from Mom. This smile always seemed to cheer Ellie up.

"You already are a warrior, Ellie. If only you could see yourself sometimes... You swing your sword around blindly and somehow destroy any enemy in your path!"

The bright red color began to return to Ellie's cheeks.

"I'm telling you, Ellie, once your hunting courses are over and you can be an official hunter, you'll be right up there with the best of us! No doubt on that," I gushed.

Ellie was just blushing now. "You really think so?"

"I know so."

Ellie's blushing then turned into a wicked grin that made me think, *uh oh*.

"Hey Kaila, you're a mischievous one, right? You like stealthy tricky stuff?"

I knew this one quite well. "What do you want?"

"Well..." Ellie began, fiddling with her fingers. "If it can be our secret, maybe I can tag along in the shadows and secretly try my skill. Like, I'll be the ninja warrior hiding behind houses, jumping in – *WHACK* – and jumping out to look for another victim. See what I mean?"

I knit an eyebrow. "I don't know, Ellie. That's kind of dangerous..."

"Since when did you ever care about *dangerous*? It's literally your middle name!"

Well, she got me there. My name is literally Kaila Danger Kinsworth. I'm sure Mom intended for me to live up to that name – and I was, if you asked me.

"I mean, if you get found out, do you have any idea how much trouble we'd be in?" I deflected. "Also, if you were to get hurt..."

"Come on, Kaila. I'm not some weak little girl who needs constant protection!"

Hannah Jock

I hoped my ears weren't as pink as they felt when I processed those words. I guess she had a point. I had always been that overprotective sister to her and had never really considered that maybe I was annoying her.

"Uh… I-"

Ellie blushed again. "No, sorry. That's not what I meant."

"It's fine," I demurred. "If you really feel like we can pull this off… I don't know… just maybe…"

"Oh, thank you, Kaila!" Ellie reached through the window and gave me a big bear hug. A few people stopped to look at me. My cheeks got so hot they must have been cherry red, and my forehead was beginning to bead with sweat.

"Oh, sorry. Ellie, you shouldn't be in here." I gave a weak smile to everyone. "Sorry guys, I just offered to go mining with my sister tomorrow."

Everyone shrugged and got back to work.

Ellie shrank back out the window and said, "Sorry."

"Way to be stealthy," I deadpanned. "Now go home and get geared up, little ninja hunter. Don't forget to put on black," I whispered after her. She nodded and put on her puckish grin as she bolted back toward the house a few trails down the main village branch.

I immediately regretted the decision on her behalf, but I knew this would make Ellie feel privileged by her older sister.

It wasn't long before all of the hunters were ready to file out of the door and fend off hostile spawns from our village. The sun was dipping down below the earth and monsters began to reach their way out of the ground – a wide variety of zombies, skeletons, ogres, and all those kinds of monsters that should have been scary. We were so used to fighting these things every night that we didn't find them all that hard to disintegrate. Plus, there weren't really any blood and guts that would make us nervous to slice through flesh. The monsters we killed just sank into a pile of glowing blue flakes.

"All right hunters! Everyone ready for hunt number one thousand, nine hundred seventy-two?" Captain Freya of the hunt announced. There was a dim round of agreement among the hunters. "Ok!" She twirled her gleaming topaz sword between her fingers. "File out!" Freya opened up the doors to allow everyone to flood out of the armory and into the perilous night.

I drew my sword close to my chest as I began to range the village. Before she could offer we stick together, I dashed out of Mom's sight, silently apologizing for breaking such a rule for the entertainment of my sister. I marched down the trail that led to the central area a dozen yards away. There, the black tourmaline fountain resumed its function, the moon shimmering through its loops of water that poured into the base, which cast short beams of light to riddle across the central area.

A dozen picnic tables formed a circle around the tourmaline fountain. A few yards further out, a ring of buildings surrounded the central area. Ten dirt-packed trails led off in different directions from where I stood in the center.

I cautiously meandered through the central area and down the *Birch Wing,* where our house was perched. Twenty yards down the trail stood our glazed birch log house. An oak log roof sat on top, smoke escaping its brick chimney. Crystal-clear windows exposed the well-lit indoors. An illuminated deck hung out front, holding a few rocking chairs and flower vases.

As I could see through the door, Ellie was watching out the window patiently, waiting for my cue. She had on golden armor that she borrowed from the training course, and her new golden sword hung on her back, wrapped in a leather scabbard. When she saw me, a grin crept across her face.

I gave her a thumbs-up signal without thinking. If I did think, I would hesitate, but I knew that if I let her do this, I would be that awesome older sister that let her do dangerous stuff -- and this was her chance to prove to me that she was a worthy hunter.

Ellie leapt to her feet and did a jumping-jack before crawling to the back door of the house, her golden sword bouncing on her back. It was a bit big on her, but I knew she could handle it just fine.

A few seconds later, she reappeared around the corner of our house, holding her sword. It gleamed faintly in the moonlight and seemed definitely balanced in her hand. She held it like she'd been doing this since she was three.

"Okay," I whispered to her. "Remember, stealthy ninja. Jump in, disintegrate target, jump out. Got it?"

"Got it," Ellie confirmed. Then she tip-toed back behind the house. "I'll follow you. Don't worry about me."

I didn't need to be asked twice. I drew my opal sword and began advancing into the battlefield – right where I was standing.

A small group of three zombies crawled up from the ground in front of me. Their torn rugged clothes hanging off of their shoulders and their smug, listless expressions would've intimidated me if I hadn't been slicing them up every night for two years now.

I almost shrugged as I slid into action, rolling under the first zombie and slicing its legs clean off, which just drifted to flakes. I stabbed it in the back before it got a chance to growl in pain and I came up just in time to see the second zombie's arms up to strike me. I easily sidestepped and toppled it over with the end of my sword.

Zombie number three looked just about ready to flee and destroy the village instead of me, but I just threw my sword straight into its back, causing it to sink into the ground as usual. The sword dropped to the dirt with a clatter.

I slid to pick up my sword and kept jogging through the night.

Nearby, I heard zombies' growls and gold slicing through flesh. I looked over to see Ellie swinging her sword around, blindly cutting zombies in half. I couldn't help but shake my head in pride and smirk at her. I loved watching my sister fight so fiercely for such a sweet little girl. There was a sign written on her adorable face that read '*decoy*,' but only I saw it.

Suddenly I felt the tip of something sharp pierce into my back. I winced and waited patiently for the pain to pass. One benefit about fighting in Katroia is that if you get pierced by something light, if you could wait a second, the pain will eventually crumple away – and getting shot with an arrow in Katroia isn't very painful.

I spun around to see a fully armed, seven-foot ogre knocking an arrow into its bow and taking aim at me. If the thing had been more intimidating, I would have been pretty ticked off. But ogres and their crooked, warty noses and yellow teeth make it impossible to take them seriously.

I let it shoot it at me with an expression on my face that clearly said: *Do it. See what happens.* Unfortunately for him, ogres don't have very big brains.

The monster shot his arrow at me, which I easily warded off with my blade.

"Do it again, fatty," I snickered. Not to my surprise, he did. I was thinking about laughing until seven more fully armed ogres and a few skeletons stepped out from behind buildings.

"Hey Ellie," I called. "Maybe a bit of help would be nice."

And in a moment, my sister was by my side.

"What's the challenge? Bring it on!"

I seriously loved her spirit. "Careful on this one, but I know the two of us can totally take it."

"Definitely."

And we sprang into action. I started off by clashing my sword against solid iron. Sparks flew from the ogre's chest. The ogre guffawed thunderously and balled its fists.

"You cannot destroy me, little Katr..." I ignored the warty monster and dashed around it to slide my sword into a chink in its armor.

Then something from behind drove a train into my back – or so it felt. I barely had time to let out an "Oof!" before I was sent flying against a building.

"*Kaila!*" Ellie called compassionately and she was immediately in front of me.

The wanted ogre loomed over her, holding the most humongous platinum sword I have ever seen.

My sight started to blur as the pain in my back deteriorated and then began to shrink. "Ellie, you should really find another monster," I warned through a hoarse voice, knowing that the pain would pass within seconds and that I could chop up this monster no problem.

"Listen to your friend," the ogre laughed. "It's your best bet."

"She's my sister," Ellie announced. "And no, are you honestly convinced I'm about to walk away from my sister after you've just sent her flying against a wall? I want a turn!"

Half of me wanted to make her leave this to me, but my other half wanted to let Ellie stand up to this ogre and show him who's boss. Like seriously, it would look dumb to stand up all brave in front of your sister and then walk away because she told you to.

The ogre guffawed again and swung its ten-ton sword straight at Ellie. She ducked just in time to parry the nasty blow. Then she pounced on top of the ogre, wrapping around to its back and bringing the edge of her sword to its neck. I almost winced as she sliced its head clean off, even though only flakes came out as it disintegrated into the dust.

"Yeah! That's a little bit of *Ellie* for ya!" I crowed as I stood up once the pain left me. "There's my little ninja warrior in action!"

Then I noticed another ogre aiming an arrow in Ellie's direction.

"Oh wait! Ellie, hit the deck!"

Without even seeing the threat, Ellie dropped down just in time to miss an iron-tipped arrow that whizzed overhead. The archer ogre aimed another arrow at her.

"Roll!" She did as I asked, again just in time to dodge another arrow, "Now roll again!"

Ellie did as she was told, but this time, an enchanted opal sword from behind sliced the ogre right in half. As the monster reduced to glowing blue flakes, my grinning mother walked out from behind it, her hazelnut hair tied back into a high ponytail, and the blue moonlight reflecting off of her radiant skin...

"Mhm, always doing the mischievous, dangerous thing, aren't you, Kaila?" she grinned.

"Named me after it."

Mom laughed, lighting up the whole village with her first chuckle.

"You let Ellie into the hunt?" She gave my sister the stink-eye. "Why am I not surprised?"

"Sorry Mom," Ellie confessed. "I just thought I could be like you guys."

"Hey, it's fine. You *are* like us." Mom put on her brave smile again. "Plus, you followed my inherited example. Welcome to the hunt, Ellie."

Ellie blushed, as usual. "Wow, then. I guess we should start off by clearing this set of ogres and skeletons, shall we?"

We found ourselves again fighting as a family down the Birch Wing. The three of us cleared the set of monsters in no time. At some point in the middle of the battle, I spotted Luke leaping across the rooftops. He stopped to look down at us – well, specifically at Ellie. I could have sworn I sensed a hint of a grin sneaking along the corner of his mouth before he shook his head and continued his patrol. Our secret was safe with him.

Once we were done brushing up this group, Mom suggested we patrol along the edge of the forest. This was easily agreed upon and soon, we were ranging the woodside.

As we walked along the onset of the woods, we bulldozed though a few groups of hostile spawns. While we weren't mopping up bad guys, we even found ourselves in a conversation about farming hacks and funny stories about us attempting to ride mad cows. But at one point, Ellie randomly stopped dead in her tracks.

"What is it, Ellie?" Mom queried.

Ellie's eyes narrowed toward something in the village. "Do you see that?"

I tried to follow her line of vision. Then, I noticed a faint glow in the ground near a spruce house.

"Yeah, I see it. What about you, Mom?"

Mom shook her head.

About twenty yards away from us was a relatively small gap that seemed to be filled with a blue light. I couldn't see the bottom of the gap from where I was standing, so I wasn't sure how deep it was. A yellow mist accompanied the bland light and began diffusing around the area.

"Whoa," Ellie exclaimed.

"Want to check it out?" I asked.

Mom's eyes widened. "What in Katroia… yeah, ok, let's go check it out."

We walked cautiously toward the strange glow with our swords drawn for some reason. "Oh my goodness, that's…

whoa, that's totally a tear!" Mom gasped. She was so in awe that she didn't even remember how perilous it was.

"Ellie, it's extremely dangerous," I warned. "Don't walk any further."

Ellie didn't seem to get the message.

"That is so cool! I wonder what's inside." She kept walking toward the death trap.

"Ellie, stop!" I commanded.

"Elliana!" Mom shouted after me.

"What?" Ellie turned around too late. She had walked straight in the range of being sucked into the Tear in the Fabric of Time.

"Ellie! That will destroy you!" Mom cried frantically as she threw herself toward my little sister. Ellie had just enough time to scream before Mom grabbed her around the waist.

An immense tidal wave of colors detonated from the Tear. Long yellow arms thrust out of it, aimlessly swaying around, trying to snatch up another victim. One of them was wrapped firmly around Mom's waist, another drawing near Ellie. Terrifying beastlike roars and rapid *shiiiing* noises pierced our ears and rang off our ear drums about a million times.

"MOM!" Ellie yelped as she grabbed onto a broad branch of the nearest tree with one hand, while clinging to Mom with the other.

"Help! Somebody, *please!*" I sobbed as I fell to my knees, knowing that trying to save them would only suck me in too.

Actually, Mom *had* run into the Tear to save my sister, so maybe if they had another hand... I leapt to my feet and began sprinting toward them before Mom screamed, "KAILA, STOP!"

Blinding colors exploded everywhere. A thick blue fog spewed into the air all around us. Ellie's screaming was blotted out by the piercing sounds of the Tear shrieking.

Freya, Luke, and a few other hunters dashed out from behind a house. A few of them passed out and Freya turned pale as an onion.

"MAYA!" she spluttered.

Freya ran to help. She fearlessly leapt up to grab at a branch of the tree that Ellie was clinging to and reached down into the thick blue fog.

"Maya, where are you?" she cried.

Somewhere in the fog, Mom yelled, "Get Ellie out of here!"

Freya did what she was told. She snatched Ellie by the wrist and threw her out of the threat, straight into my arms.

"Oh, Ellie," I cried as I embraced her in a trembling hug.

"GET MY MOM!" Ellie demanded.

"Can't you see I'm trying?" Freya roared over the horrific sounds of shrieking *shiiiing* noises and diffusing mist.

All I heard was a terrifying scream from Mom and the Tear shattered. Freya was sent flying ten feet from the eruption and slammed into the side of a building. An overwhelming ray of colorful lights rolled into me and Ellie and sent us tumbling up against Luke, who then toppled over by the impact. The rest of the hunters lost their balance and collapsed backward. Everybody ended up flattened up against the walls of the group of houses around us. If it weren't for those walls, we'd all be on the moon by now.

And as quickly as the ruckus came, everything went dead silent.

Everyone was completely frozen. A few more hunters had been knocked out, including Freya. The rest of us sat or lay on the ground in a daze. Nearby, crickets chirped peacefully, and the stars shone silently down on us.

The first thing that moved was a salty tear that rolled down my cheek. "Mom...," I croaked, finally breaking the terrible silence.

CHAPTER 3

Everything Turns
Black and White

Ellie curled up on my lap and cried. The wail was brimming with such unbearable sadness that all of wildlife seemed to close in and try to comfort her, but there was nothing that could cure her brokenness. I had tried to contain my tears as best I could, but it was only a matter of seconds before I began bawling, salty tears and snots running mercilessly down my face.

The hunters were tearing up as well. Luke looked down at me and my sister with so much pity.

A group of hunters rushed around the corner also, their swords and bows drawn, ready to dissolve any threat in the way. When they saw us, however, they lowered their weapons.

"What happened?" One of the high-ranked hunters, Richard Cort, inquired in a soothing voice.

Freya moaned piteously and rolled to her side, clutching her head. "A Tear in the Fabric of Time…" She lifted her tear-filled eyes up to Richard. "We've lost Maya."

Richard went almost as pale as Freya had when she'd seen Mom in the Tear and leaned against another hunter for support.

"It just *had* to be Maya? You're serious?"

He noticed Freya wasn't up for saying it twice.

"I'm so sorry," Richard lamented.

My clothes were beginning to soak in Ellie's tears.

"Mommy," she bewailed.

I tucked my head into Ellie's shoulders and let the painful ball in my throat drop. I forgot about everyone around us as I let myself cry. I couldn't see past this night. I didn't want to think about how much terrible sorrow I would have to experience in the future. I couldn't imagine my mother being gone for the rest of my life. I feared if I did, I might fall into a million pieces and let myself die from sickening sorrow.

I just wanted to go back in time a few moments and warn Ellie of the death trap earlier. Ellie's arm was within reach when I remembered how dangerous The Tear was. I could have grabbed it and spared her and Mom. I could have helped get them both out. Instead, I just sat back and watched my only family get sucked away. If only I had done a few things with some common sense, I could have lived out the rest of my life with a loving mother keeping our spirits high and caring for my wants and needs.

But no. She was really gone for good. Ellie and I would be orphans for the rest of our lives.

We are all taught about Tears in the Fabric of Time sometime in our young childhood. They are extremely rare – only point six percent of Katrins get to see one. We are taught that if you get really lucky – or unlucky in some situations – you just might be able to spot one.

But never, ever go near or it, or your death has been perfectly prearranged.

Once you get close enough, the Tear will drag your body into the fabrics of time. You will be ripped into a quantum realm of past and future memories folding around you and overwhelming your body until it is shred apart from your soul. The Katrin body simply cannot withstand such power coming directly from the system. The Tear is a gap in the protective wall set up to shield us from the overwhelming power of the system. Once your body slips through the membrane, waves of color strike into you as time overlaps itself and gets you caught up into it. Eventually, your soul will be reaped and shattered to pieces. Nobody has told us what happens next. It must've been too terrible to break to us.

And my very mother…

I began to choke on the razor blades that felt like they were caught in my throat. The thought was too painful. *Don't think about it,* I repeated to myself. But the thought of Mom's half-shredded body sprawling through a clot of memories as her soul is reaped and shattered was too hard to avoid. And my sister's awful, choked sobs only made it harder.

I was afraid this night wasn't going to end.

But fortunately, it did. The hunters told Ellie and I to go to sleep while they kept up the hunting. Nobody even scolded Ellie for sneaking out to hunt. They just said to get some rest and take some time to think.

Unfortunately, I didn't feel up for *thinking.* As I lay in my bed, I began to *choke* when I tried to think. *What would Mom say?* I thought. *Something like, 'What happened today is enough for today. Get some rest, my little Kaila Bear. Tomorrow will bring its own worries.'*

But when I tried to think about it rather than hear it come from my Mom's mouth, another lugubrious sob slipped out. My eyes wouldn't stop flooding tears, and my throat refused to open up for steady breaths. I tried so hard to imagine Mom snoring softly in the bed next to me so I stood a chance at sleep, but even with all the tears, I wasn't physically able to perform such a miracle.

Hannah Jock

I'd already decided that I was never going to find joy again. I almost didn't *want* to without Mom.

I never fell asleep that night – It was only two hours after all.

After what felt like three millennia, the dull sunrise peeked through the window, causing me to squint. I realized I'd somehow survived the terrible night, regretting I had. I didn't want to get up. Didn't want to see anyone. I didn't want to deal with Luke. I wanted to stay in bed forever and rot, hopefully putting myself out of my misery at some point.

But it wasn't long before Ellie dragged herself over to my bed and hugged me so tight I found myself gasping for air. I let out another sob and twisted in her grip so that I was holding her instead.

Her warmth mixed with the sunlight peeking through the window slowed my sobs. Not enough to make me want to get up, but enough to make me want to hug Ellie and love and comfort her. Of course, the comforting part wasn't an option. But weeping together in my bed made the love part possible.

As the day went on, Ellie and I never left the house. We spent most of the day in my bed crying, but every hour or so we would sit up, sniffle, and search for food around the house. Food always made everything better – especially chocolate.

Nobody stopped by our house that day. Everyone seemed to respect our space for lamentation—though I *was* expecting Luke to swing by and give us some cookies instead of a scowl just to let us know he cared. Maya technically was *his* mother as well.

I wouldn't be surprised if Luke ran away to curl up under a tree and cry either. He'd never really showed any emotion since we'd found him the day his house burned down. Maybe he just wasn't up for showing his tears to people who didn't think he had feelings.

Eventually, after a full day of tears and sniffles, the sun

began to dip back down below the trees. And this time, I found myself exhausted when night came back around.

Ellie sat at the marble table that hung off the wall in the front of our house. Our home was constructed in a really fat L shape. Counters and windows lined the longer side of the house, with a door on the right side of the end. Our three beds sat at the shorter end, one massive window overlooking them.

"I think I might be able to sleep tonight," Ellie sniveled. "I'm totally drained." She watched the sunset with glassy eyes, looking like she might just fall forward on her face and begin snoring. "We haven't slept in two days, either."

I nodded and fell back into my bed. "I'll try," I croaked, approaching another round of unstoppable tears. With my lip still quavering, I rolled over on my bed and pulled my blankets over my shoulders. "But I'll need your help."

"Okay," Ellie agreed and crawled onto my bed, slipping under the snug, fleecy covers.

The second night was a bit easier, with the help of the exhaustion of tears and Ellie's arms around my waist. And within the first fifteen minutes, I let myself shut down and get a nice long, dreamless sleep.

***

The next morning, I woke up late, because I couldn't even see the sun through the window, meaning it must be midday. Ellie had twisted around and was curled up against me, still snoring away.

I decided that I was going to deisolate myself today and try to face the world. I was going to shove the thought of Mom's death to the back of my head and pretend that she was just working away in the forges, forgetting to take off with us into the woods…

I choked back a sob at that thought. From now on, there

would be no more running into the tranquilizing woods with Mom every morning. No more sunshine. No more joy. No more rolling streams and green grass and velvety moss…

No more listening patiently at Mom's side for a wild orchestra to come together every morning. No more embracing her outgoing, creative personality for hours every day.

Stop it Kaila, I chided myself and promised I'd one day regain my sanity.

It wasn't long before I sat up, my hair a birds' nest, and rubbed my sleepy, crusty eyes. My head felt like it weighed twenty pounds – I had probably given myself a fever from building up so many tears. Light spilled into the room, causing all of the different colors to appear warmer and richer.

Then I glanced over at Mom's bed, half expecting to see her sleeping soundly in a curled ball. I wanted so badly to see that, but unfortunately, the bed was still made from two mornings before.

Suddenly, Mom's bed looked like a coffin. Everything in the room lost its color, like a cloud had crept over the sun and the light had gone out. I remembered again what had happened two nights ago, unable to block the terrifying memory from slipping into my head. I gasped back tears and pressed my palm into my forehead, trying to shove the memory out.

I shook my head. *Don't think about it,* I screamed at myself. *I made myself a promise last night not to think about it. Mom is alive. She's with me. She is just invisible.*

To my surprise, that actually worked for a few minutes. I forced myself to walk outside toward the central area to sit down for lunch. The news about Mom had spread surprisingly quickly. The baker showed me a look of pity when I stopped for some food. He even gave it to me for free.

The picnic table was pretty much soundless. Ellie soon joined me to sit in silence while we munched miserably on mixed fruits. Luke did something really abnormal that would have made my day under normal circumstances. When he spotted us, he stopped by and told some of Mom's jokes to cheer us up. To be honest, he made me crack a smile a few times when he repeated the really good ones. But nothing could genuinely make me happy.

Ellie didn't crack a smile, though. She was totally miserable.

"This is all my fault," she kept saying. "If I hadn't come, nobody would have noticed the Tear. She threw herself in for me. I should have died." I tried to comfort her, but it was hard since I was broken in the same way.

After breakfast, Will gave me a box full of Mom's forging stuff and some of her hunting supplies. He said I could use it and do anything I wanted with it. I almost screamed and threw the stuff back at his face, but I decided maybe I would recover one day and appreciate some memories of my mom.

As I was carrying the mementos back to the house, I realized that containing my sadness in public was harder than I had imagined. As soon as I entered the house, I collapsed over the box and just fell into pieces.

"*Why* is this happening to me?" I wailed, stomping my foot on the ground, hoping it would cause an earthquake and split the earth in half. I *seriously* wish there was such a thing as a time machine in this game. Then I could go back in time, stop Ellie from walking into the Tear earlier than I did, and I would be eating lunch with Mom right now.

I let out an angry wail as I grabbed a chunk of gold from Mom's supply box and chucked it at a window across the house. As I watched it shatter, I felt my heart do the same – except it hurt way more. I found myself doubling over in pain, clutching my chest as I tried to keep my heart in one piece. But every time a shard hit the floor, more of my sanity broke off.

I was getting kind of sick of crying, but suddenly, it just felt so *good* to feel tears rolling down my cheeks one after another. I wanted to bathe in them, drown in them, let them take over and

Hannah Jock

never let them go. I wanted to live out the rest of my life drifting away into my lake of salty tears, regretting every second I spent watching my sister and mother being snatched into a Tear.

I let myself blubber away on the floor, hugging Mom's supplies like they were the only thing in the world that mattered anymore. There was always love and color and joy in my life while she was here with me. Now all of that color had entirely drained out. It is as if Mom was my lens of joy and color. And now that my lens was gone, I would for the rest of my life see the world in black and white.

Soon enough, Luke had appeared in the doorway. He began to say something as he walked in, but when he noticed me crying helplessly on the floor, he stopped in his tracks and shut his mouth. He kind of just stood there awkwardly, like he wanted to say something to comfort me, but there were no words that had that kind of power.

"Sorry," I sniffled as I stood back up and wiped tears from my eyes. "It's pretty hard to control that."

Luke didn't exactly answer. He just eventually did what he had to do in the house and stepped back outside. I think I heard him say he was sorry somewhere in there before he left.

I was just about to leave to go to the farms to tend the animals as I was supposed to every day. Then I decided I was going to skip it and wander into the woods like Mom always did.

Only if you wait patiently and listen, everything will make sense in the end. I could remember Mom's words of wisdom.

Well, I needed a little bit of sense right now.

So I set off into the woods. As I wandered deeper, memories of my time with Mom came flooding back to me with every step. This time, instead of sobbing like a baby, I noticed tiny pigments beginning to return to the world. I could almost feel Mom's essence in the woods, like she really *was* right there next to me, and it wasn't just me trying to imagine it.

As I leapt over streams and skipped over rocks, more and more color came flooding into the world. My joy tank, which had been completely drained, was beginning to feel a little bit of life again – although not enough to actually make me happy.

Then, as I scanned the glades ahead of me, I noticed the vibrant color pink within the shades of green and brown. It wasn't a small, ruby-shaded pink flower, but a – yeah, a bright pink sleeveless shirt. The one Ellie always wore.

As I approached closer, I saw my sister's little head turn around and find my eyes. Her light, caramel brown hair was a bit of a mess, but I thought she looked cuter that way. She also looked a bit dazed, as if she were recently in deep thought.

To my surprise, Ellie seemed to be acting herself again.

"Hey, Kaila!" she greeted cheerfully as I approached.

"Hi Ellie, what are you doing out here this early?" I asked, trying not to sniffle as I said it, but I couldn't control my voice right now.

"Running from chores."

"Same."

There was an awkward silence. I groggily strode over to the rock she was sitting on and plopped down next to her.

"So Ellie," I swallowed a lump that attempted to cause tears. *Not now,* I told it. "Why so… happy?"

"Why not?"

I suddenly felt guilty for breaking her impressive streak of hiding sadness. I managed to crack a smile.

"You're right, Ellie. Why not?"

Ellie looked down at the mossy forest floor.

"I guess you deserve to know why I'm really acting so… normal."

I looked up into her brown eyes hopefully. "Why is it?"

Ellie put on her brave grin – not Mom's brave grin, but *her* brave grin. In other words, her grin that meant she was up to no good.

"Because I have a crazy idea," she proposed.

CHAPTER 4

We Give Ellie's Idea a Shot

Before I reveal the plan, let me remind you that it wasn't my idea. Just try and keep that in mind.

"Ok, Kaila. Here's my idea," Ellie began, signaling me to begin holding my breath.

I was honestly scared of what might come out of Ellie's mouth because she said it might have something to do with getting Mom back, which was impossible. But I listened just to hear what she had to say.

"So, you know the Enchanted Library that everybody is forbidden to go near?" Ellie drawled.

"Absolutely not, Ellie," I replied. A minute earlier, I was willing to hear what Ellie had to say, but at that one sentence – *nope.* "This is not a rule like 'nobody who doesn't have a hunting license can hunt.' This is a serious charge."

"Just listen," Ellie told me. "That Library is notorious for having hundreds of texts that can tell you anything. I can promise you that it has at least *one book* that explains every detail on Tears in the Fabric of Time." She looked down as if hesitating.

"And?" I prodded.

"And you know how nobody has told us what happens next – after you get sucked in? Just take a guess as to why. You never know, maybe they go somewhere that is reachable and it's just really dangerous? Maybe they just didn't want people to find it out and spread the news, causing half of Katroia to attempt to save their loved one and die."

I shook my head. "Ellie, why don't you go and review what you've just said." I waited a few moments for her to fulfil my request. "There are about a million possibilities that could've happened to Mom."

Ellie dashed her eyes around frantically as if she were trying to think of something to say to that.

"Hey! So what if I'm wrong?" she said. "Might as well find out if there really *is* a way…""And if there's not? That's a *really* big problem. That place's security is the best in Katroia. And given how incredibly amazing security gets in Katroia, I'm going to guess that's pretty spankin' good. If we get found out and don't even get any good information out of it… I'm not even going to try and imagine the consequences!"

"But it's worth it for Mom, isn't it Kaila?"

Whelp, she hit my weak spot.

"You know what, Ellie?" I looked into her deep brown eyes with piercing emotion, "You have a tendency to persuade me into doing really dumb things sometimes. I don't know why I always give in to your perilous ideas, but I do, and they *always* come with consequences. What happened when you persuaded me to steal cookies from the bakery for Mom's birthday? What about when you made me go fishing in the pond of lost souls?"

I had so many other examples off the top of my head that I decided not to bring up. "Ellie, what happened when you convinced me to let you join the hunt two nights ago?"

Ellie stared at the ground in silence.

"But those were just silly little ideas for entertainment. This time, it's a gamble for Mom's existence…" I hesitated before saying this bit. "So, I guess we don't have a choice," I concluded.

Ellie's face lit up. "Really? So, you're in?"

I grinned back at her. "Mom didn't name me after danger for no reason. Now let's go get her back… Or see if we can. Don't get your hopes up."

Ellie pumped her fist in triumph. "That's the flexible, amazing, dangerous big sister I've always known I had!"

My head spun. *Why am I doing this?* I thought.

And yet again, I found myself back at the house, grabbing different supplies that might be necessary for a highly secured break in. I packed a small knife to pick the lock with, a flashlight, and a small bag to keep things that I might use. Ellie just packed a dagger and left the rest to me. There isn't really much to bring to a break in.

For the rest of the day, we kind of just hung out around the house and waited for night to settle. We chowed on some snacks that were lying around the house and ran into some normal conversations--only about seventy-five percent of them concerning Mom.

Some of me believed that there was just a little bit of hope that would follow this crime, but most of me knew the truth – there is no getting Mom back. I'm just doing this to break the rules and lose our membership in this village.

"You know what, Ellie?" I began, but then hesitated when she looked up at me with a reassuring smile. "Yeah, never mind."

I went through that cycle about a million times that day until finally, the sun began to dip down below the horizon. There was no turning back now – well, maybe there was – but I wasn't going to. This could be my only chance to get my beloved mother back.

As I stood next to Mom's bed, the sheets still made, but a little crumpled from sitting like that so long, I felt my eyes brimming with tears.

No, I'm not backing down, I promised myself. *If there is any possible way to get Mom back, anything is worth it.*

But I knew for a fact that there *was* really no way.

There was a heavy knock on the door. I almost jumped, but I kept my hands over my mouth. Ellie quickly stuffed her dagger under her sheets, and I followed her lead.

"Hey, Kaila," a female voice called from outside.

I meandered toward the door and creaked it open.

Freya stood outside the doorway, fully armed and holding her enchanted topaz sword in her hand. "I'm really sorry about what happened..." She dipped her head low and stared at the ground. "I totally get it if you're not up for hunting tonight."

I sighed. "It's not your fault, Freya."

"It's mine," Ellie muttered from the corner.

"No," I said. "It was nobody's fault." I took a deep breath. "But uhh... I do think I could take the night off, Freya," I told her through a hoarse throat. "Thanks."

Freya nodded sadly. "I hope things work out for you guys." She glanced around the house. "I should get going to the armory."

And with that, Freya slowly turned around and jogged down the Birch Wing.

I swallowed down a tear and closed the door.

This is it, I thought. *No more crying like a baby from now, until I find out there is nothing I can do.*

I swung around and twisted my frown into a brave grin. I could feel my cheeks turn pink as they tried to hold the expression.

"Well, Ellie? Let's hit the road."

Forcing back hesitation, the two of us weaved through the shadows between the houses. Hiding ourselves from the hunters wasn't an easy job, but we seemed to manage. Ellie and I were both super light on our feet.

Overhead, I heard pounding on the rooftops. "It's Luke," Ellie whispered as she flattened against the side of a house. I followed her lead. We both held our breath as we waited for Luke to stop by and stare at us suspiciously.

We were lucky not to be noticed because we even saw Luke's shadow pass over us, yet he didn't stop to acknowledge us.

As soon as Luke was out of sight, I leaned over Ellie's shoulder.

"Let's keep moving," I whispered.

As we kept jogging through the alleys, we had to sneak by a few fights. Just seeing the ogres and zombies and skeletons threaten my fellow hunters made me want to jump in and disintegrate them back into the ground where they came from. Now I knew how Ellie felt every night.

In no time, we had slipped past the onset of the woods, and under the shadowed canopy. Other than a few rays of blue moonlight that occasionally peeked through the leaves, I could hardly see a thing.

So, I flicked on my flashlight, surprising myself at how different the forest looked at night. Sure, everything was in the same place that it had been during the day, but something about the essence of the night made the forest look like an entirely different environment.

"Hey, Kaila! Look dead ahead!" Ellie murmured over my shoulder, after we had jogged through the woods for a few minutes.

And there it was, maybe fifty feet ahead, our lustered destination arrogantly stood upon a moss-coated rock. At the base, roots twisted together into a semi-circle shaped cottage. Precious stones mixed in with the rooty base and worked their way up to a fire opal second floor where all of the most important enchanted books sat on shelves and lecterns. Around the building, fireflies buzzed through the air. Wait – *were* those fireflies? Or just flecks of magic radiating off of the building? I didn't even know.

There were a half-dozen guards standing outside, their eyes peeled. They all wore camouflage armor and black boots, holding enchanted bows and swords. They were looking in different directions, giving Ellie and me time to dash behind a boulder.

"So," Ellie whispered so quiet I wasn't sure if that's what she really said. "What's the plan?"

CHAPTER 5

We Get Busted

Ok, this is definitely going to be a *lot* harder than I imagined. Ellie and I just sat there in the dark behind a boulder, trying to think of a way to break into the library. We both stared in different directions silently, to prevent risk of being noticed.

So far, we got nothing.

Why hadn't we created a plan beforehand? Like, I dunno, maybe a little plan A, plan B, or at least an idea to start us off? We had an hour to sit around in the house before we left anyway!

Honestly, I was okay with sitting here for a while. What we were about to do here was extremely perilous. I needed some time to take a breath before being thrust into a stressful situation again.

While sitting here behind the rock, I could hear the delightful sounds of nightfall that were echoing off the trees. I had always thought of nighttime as a dark, dangerous time when monsters claw their way to the surface and put our village at risk.

Sure, all those things are true, but besides that, the night is just as beautiful as the day.

And while I sat there and listened closely, just as in the day, new instruments of the wild orchestra begin to fold in. Crickets sang in the tall grass, owls hooted away in the canopy...

That's it! The canopy!

"Ellie," I whispered, "I've got a plan A."

My sister turned and waited.

"No plan B?"

"Who needs a plan B? If plan A fails, we're toast."

Ellie waited a moment, as if hesitating. "Ok, I have a plan too, but let's hear yours first. It will probably be more reasonable."

I took a deep breath.

"Ok Ellie, listen up."

I almost laughed, but then I remembered that more than a whisper could cost our citizenship in Sherberry Village.

"Literally," I said. "The owls hooting overhead are pretty loud, aren't they? Not to brag, but you and I are probably the best tree climbers in the village. If we could get up into the canopy and be as light on our feet as possible, then maybe if the guards hear a bit of rattling overhead, they'll probably suspect it's just noises of the wild, if we're not too loud. Plus, the *real* wild noises will probably drown out the sound."

Ellie just stared at me. "Yep, definitely better than my plan." She looked up into the trees. "Branches look pretty thick, so I wouldn't guess there would be much rustling in the leaves... Hey, Kaila, maybe we really *can* pull this off!"

I grinned at her and held up a fist. "Hey, the two of us can pull anything off."

Ellie drove her fist into mine. "Definitely. Now, we need a small distraction so we can get up into the trees."

I picked up a rock from the ground, "This'll do."

I felt like a big fat bonehead doing this, but I chucked the rock precisely on the thick branch of a tree on the other side of the library, creating a low *thump* sound. Surprisingly, all six guards spun around and knocked an arrow into their bows.

Ellie and I silently leapt into the tree above us like agile squirrels. I grabbed the most stable branch in sight and used it as a gymnastics bar to fling myself onto another thick oak branch.

"Who's there?" one of the guards bellowed. I almost squeaked in fear until I noticed the guard was talking toward the tree I threw a rock at.

Ellie gave me an ecstatic look from the branch next to me. I mouthed, '*it's okay*', and pointed up to signal, '*climb higher.*'

"Come on, Ken, something fell from the tree, you idiot!" another guard scolded.

"What if there really *is* somebody there?" Ken asked.

One of the guards looked at Ken with compassion and then back at the guard who scolded him.

"Hey, give him a break, Toby. It's only his first day doing this!"

"Oh sorry, Lucy, for insulting your *boyfriend*," Toby taunted.

Lucy's cheeks turned pink. "He's not my boyfriend!" she said.

"Guys, stop fighting!" another guard yelled from behind the library. Toby snickered at Lucy and stood back in attention.

Meanwhile, Ellie and I were climbing across the canopy toward the Enchanted Library with record soundlessness. A few times we rustled the leaves a bit, but the guards didn't seem to care. They just argued with each other like siblings while two kids leapt right above them toward the library.

It was a relief to see that the top of the library was pretty much flat, except for a few roots sprouting from the rim.

Without a noise, I leapt off of my last branch and on top of the roof. Then Ellie jumped on after me.

I easily spotted a trapdoor in the roof and started walking toward it, my dagger unsheathed to unlock the hinge when I heard a small click under it.

I heard muffled voices from under the trap door, but only one word echoed into my mind. *Busted. With a capital B.*

The trapdoor creaked open and two more guards crawled out, but before they got to their feet, they both froze.

"What in Katroia..." one began. "What are you doing?"

"Sorry!" Ellie squeaked as she grabbed a glass bottle from her bag and unscrewed the cork on top. Purple mist swirled into the air and into their nostrils.

The guards gritted their teeth in pain and dropped to the floor... or the ceiling.

I glared at Ellie with a flabbergasted expression. "Why didn't you use that earlier?"

Ellie dropped her eyes to the floor.

"It really hurts when you wake up. I wouldn't do that to six guards if it wasn't completely urgent."

I let myself smile at that.

"You're such a sweet girl, Ellie."

Ellie smiled back, but it eventually turned into a smirk.

"We should probably get moving," she whispered.

"Probably."

And before I could hesitate again, Ellie and I had crawled through the trapdoor and into the Enchanted Library.

Hem, hem. . . Let me repeat that. Ellie and I easily broke through the impossible security of the Enchanted Library and slipped right into the floor of the most valuable enchanted books, no problem.

And *wow*-- this place was gorgeous!

Ellie and I stood right inside an immense glowing membrane of fire opal, one of the most rare and precious materials in Katroia. The walls were lined with oak bookshelves fashioned of twisted roots and precious stones lodged into them. Lecterns of the most valuable books were scattered among the room. Long, tattered, ancient scrolls hung off the ceiling strung up with copper wire, and a huge red circular carpet caked the ground and covered most of the rooty floor. An expanse of golden speckles hung in the air like the golden mist that diffused the room.

"Wow, this place is more beautiful than I expected," Ellie marveled.

"Sure is," I agreed. "Now, let's find that book." I wasn't wasting any time marveling over the building when a guard could storm in at any moment and arrest us.

Just a few minutes earlier I was sure that this risk contained no hope. Even now that we were in this sacred room, rustling through the bookshelves and examining scrolls, a helpless sense of doubt hung over me like the mist that filled the room.

And yet, I still scavenged the floor for an ancient book about the Tear. Since the rows of books weren't labeled, I found myself having to read every book title in floor two. Meanwhile, Ellie paced around, checking scrolls and lecterns that scattered the huge open space in the middle.

I began to feel a headache crawling in as my eyes dashed between the sides of a million hard-cover books. *Pond of Lost Souls... The Fallen Realm... Tear in the Fabric...*

Tear in the Fabric of Time!

"Hey Ellie," I called over my shoulder to my sister, who was currently gazing at the *Hunting Groglins* scroll. She immediately blinked up at me, the hearts in her eyes fading.

"What? Did you find it?" she asked eagerly.

"Yeah. Come check it out."

Ellie made a joyful sound under her breath and came bounding over to my side.

I tenderly closed my hand around the side of the book and wriggled it out of the shelf. No traps?

I stared down at the brown book lined with silver and spread with a film of dust. I let out all of my hesitant emotions with one long, heavy breath across the sheet of dust settled over the cover. But as I watched the particles slide off of the hardcover, the hesitation came flooding back.

For a moment I couldn't even open it. I just stared at the brown and golden cover, hoping that looking through this wouldn't only make things worse.

"Well?" Ellie prodded.

I closed my eyes and sighed, "Okay," before folding open the sacred, enchanted book that hadn't been touched, probably for decades.

The pages were a bit crusty and heavily tinted brown, but everything was clearly readable. On the front page was the general description of what The Tear is in poem form:

> *The game's membrane of time is placed in an orderly set;*
> *But in a glitch, a malfunction, it's not perfect I bet.*
> *Most players will go about their days;*
> *Without seeing or believing a nearby Tear is ablaze.*
> *When you see one or hear one you are best to run*
> *For if not, if you stay, you'll be pulled into that one.*
> *The Tear in the Fabric of Time will consume you inside;*
> *Time of the past; of the future will come and collide.*
> *Lost and afraid, your soul will be*
> *As time overlaps into you, you will see.*
> *As your body tears and your soul is reaped;*
> *Your final breath will be a howl of pain down deep.*
> *Confusion takes over and kills you overtime*
> *And eventually, the Void will take you inside.*

I flipped the page, blinking back tears and found…
Nothing.
I blinked hard several times.

"What? That's it?" I could feel my brow furrowing already. "That can't be it!"

I swiped through the pages of the book furiously. The only other things inside the pages were pictures of the Tear and Katrins being sucked in. It showed the inside, of a million different images of time overlapping into a huge chasm of emptiness surrounding a poor soul.

That Katrin caught up in all that today... was Mom!

"No!" I cried. "Tell me about the Void!" I scrambled through a few more pages – a dictionary of Katrins that were consumed by a Tear.

And in the very back, a golden name was etched into the page, still warm to the touch:

"Maya Kinsworth," I read aloud through a choked sob.

I tried to swallow down the bowling ball in my throat that offered tears, but salty water just came flooding down my face anyway. "What the *heck* is the Void? Why doesn't it say? Do I want to know?" I bewailed, slowly dropping to my knees and hugging the useless book.

"Uhh, probably not," Ellie said, holding up a shaky arm to the right wall.

I looked up at her. "*You* know what it is?"

Ellie let a tear roll down her cheek. "I think so," she managed to choke out.

She led me around a few hanging scrolls and lecterns toward a silver engraving on the right wall. Right at the top was carved two words:

The Void.

Ellie held a hand over her mouth, closed her eyes, and turned away as I began reading down the description engraved on the fire opal wall aloud.

"The Void is a dark, eerie chasm where Katrin souls go to die;
Helpless and lost, too confused to cry.
There they spend eternity, gone and forgotten
In the darkest chasm, they spend forever depressed...

"Stop telling me about dark, depressing, confusing chasms where the soul is tortured!" I wailed. "I don't want to hear it!"

"Kaila, keep reading," Ellie said.

"No!"

"Just the last few lines!"

"Why?"

"Trust me!"

I grunted irately but turned around to face the engraving anyway. I tried my best to skip over all of the non-helpful lines, but then I came across a few lines toward the bottom:

But after years of death and endless mourning
A brave Katrin shall rise and take on an impossible journey
Through the Fallen Realm they shall travel;
And to the edge of the Edge, the Void will unravel.
At the onset of the Void, a dragon stirs
And a chance to regain what once was yours.
But beware fellow Katrins, of the impossible journey ahead
For one to take on this task is a foolish airhead.

I snorted. "A foolish airhead," I repeated.

Ellie didn't find it funny. She examined my eyes like there were three of them, waiting for a response.

I didn't think this would occur to me today, but I had a feeling that this was going to be my lucky hour. I had totally won the war of tears in my eyes and razor knives in my throat.

The Enchanted Library didn't lie.

There really *was* a way to get Mom back!

"Ellie, we're going to the Fallen Realm," I said, finally feeling a hint of hope stir in my soul. "Pack tomorrow morning, leave tomorrow evening." Then I put on my brave grin that helped shove back tears. "All in favor?"

Ellie's grin went down the puckish direction.

"Sounds good to me, Kaila."

For a moment we just stood there smirking at each other until it began to get awkward. I shuffled my feet and took one last glance around. I still couldn't believe our good fortune. I pinched myself to make sure I wasn't still dreaming.

"So, do you think we've got all the information we need?" I asked Ellie, breaking the silence.

"No, that's pretty much all you need," a middle-aged sounding male's voice echoed from another room that I hadn't even noticed was there. Sure enough, a fire opal door sat open and a man in black and blue robes stepped into the Library. Behind him, I could only make out a golden desk freckled with rainbow radiating balls that seemed to be made of condensed mist. Beside that, I saw a wave of colors surrounding certain enchanted books and unwritten scrolls laying meaninglessly on the ground.

The man stepped into the room, his clanky black shoes clapping onto the ground with every step. Long black and blue robes hung off his shoulders and dragged on the ground as he meandered toward us, and his intimidating crooked smile was hard to miss. Dark walnut hair crowned his head, and all around him, a glowing blue membrane radiated off of every surface.

I found myself just barely standing on my two wobbly legs, trembling in the seal of our certain death.

The man put his hands on his hips and gave me and Ellie the world's scariest glare.

"I was going to ask what brings you here, but I already know. You see, I'm the very Enchanter of this Library – The owner. And you two are *totally* busted."

CHAPTER 6

We Chat with the Enchanter

The first official sentence I was able to create in my thoughts was, *'We're dead.'*

Ellie and I just stood there in the middle of the second floor of the Enchanted Library, terrified out of our minds. Neither of us dared to move, much less pronounce a single word.

The Enchanter studied us silently, mostly focused on our expressions, but I could tell there was more to it. It almost felt like he was sticking his nose into our thoughts.

"Oh boy, what should I say to this?" The Enchanter scratched his head. "I think you two are busted... However, I think I'm feeling quite merciful right now, especially concerning your reason for being here. Noble purposes have a soft spot in my heart."

My mouth twitched. *We're dead; I'm dead; Ellie's dead,* I chanted to myself until I processed what had just come out of the Enchanter's mouth.

"Wait, what?" I responded, with perplexity in my voice.

The Enchanter sighed and then glanced around into space, seeming to be lost in thought.

"Okay, follow me, you two." He waved his hand beckoningly and walked straight toward the wall. Before he walked into it, however, he held up his palm right in front of it and a space opened up into another enormous room.

I could feel my jaw starting to unhinge and my legs turning to rubber, but I ignored my body and wobbled over toward the Enchanter, my mind entirely blank.

Ellie and I followed the Enchanter into one of the most immense rooms that had ever met our eyes. The walls were black and seemed to be made of shiny pure flint. They were smooth and layered, occasionally glistening whenever a random magical wave of light flashed over them.

The floor was made of the darkest shade of wood I could ever imagine. Fifteen feet up, blood-red curtains draped overhead to make up the ceiling. Vines of precious stones hung from what seemed to be thin air above the curtains.

But the most dumbfounding part about the entire room was the enormous glowing sphere that spun leisurely in the center of the room. It was mostly shaded navy blue, but little scenes materialized all around the globe. They all looked like important events in life such as intense battles, weddings, deaths, et cetera... Blue bolts of energy seemed to strike at the ball from all different directions, holding it in place in the air.

The entire room felt like a magic container. Strange clouds emitting colorful light drifted about, the fog getting thicker and thicker the closer it got to the ball.

My legs still trembled as I walked, but now it was mostly because I felt so powerless in this place. I suddenly seemed like some baby worm inching along the ground of a grand rainforest, not even deserving of legs.

The Enchanter eventually stopped walking. I was expecting

some huge ceremonial speech about our stupid actions or something, but the Enchanter just watched his ball, as if he had forgotten about us already.

It was an uncomfortably long time before Ellie whispered in the smallest voice possible, "Um, Mr. Enchanter?"

"I apologize, Elliana," the Enchanter sighed and turned back toward us. "I'm sorry if this is freaking you guys out. Now that you're here and know information you most certainly should not, you must know everything. Try not to space out; this is information you must know now. Agreed?"

I am proud to say that I had the wits to nod my head. This guy was nicer than I imagined, but I was still terrified of the consequences.

"No need to worry about consequences, Kaila," the Enchanter promised, causing my head to blow off my shoulders. "I will try to minimize punishment. You are two nice girls, and the reason you are here right now is of a noble heart. That is hard to punish someone for. Plus, you both just suffered a devastating loss – you don't need any more hardships to deal with."

"How do you know...what I was just thinking...," I squeaked.

"And how do you know why we're here?" Ellie finished.

The Enchanter smiled at us like he was delighted to share about his talents.

"You see, I can see important events that occur around Katroia, as you can see on this sphere. When I saw your mom... what happened to her, I knew you two were going to do at least *something*. I've seen some of the stupid things you've done and couldn't imagine either one of you just accepting your mother's death without getting into *some* kind of trouble. So, I kept a close eye on you two since then. I wasn't exactly surprised when you daredevils agreed to break into one of the most secure and

Hannah Jock

sacred buildings in Katroia." Then he winked at us, just to keep in mind that he wasn't angry about that at all.

"As for how I *'read your thoughts,'* Kaila, when somebody is in at least ten feet of my range, I tend to be able to know what people are thinking. So, I didn't actually *read* your thoughts. I just had a good idea of what was going through your head," he explained.

I made a crooked smile.

"Good to know that I'm being stalked. Now what were you going to say in the first place?" I just wanted to set aside the subject before he started bringing up stupid thoughts and actions of my past.

"Oh please don't get me wrong, Kaila. I'm not stalking anyone! It is my job to make sure the game stays in order. When things seem to get boring, I write something interesting that could be added to Katroia and it becomes reality..."

"Wait a minute, smarty pants," I chided, anger suddenly brimming over my fear. I didn't know how I was able to feel *anger* in the presence of one of the most powerful men in Katroia, but if he was the reason behind Mom's death, I was ready to start planning an assassination. "Are *you* the one who created The Tear in the Fabric of Time?"

The Enchanter sighed.

"Technically, yes. I tried to make something different, but it didn't work at all as I expected."

I kind of just stood there, my arms folded over my chest, trying not to think of the time when Mom was sucked into an eternal, dark, depressing abyss where her soul remains in broken, confused, lost pieces. Then, I practically doubled over at the fact that I'd just chided the Enchanter of Katroia. A terrified squeak escaped from my lips.

"I'm very sorry, you two," the Enchanter consoled, and I could hear the sincerity in his voice. "Even the Enchanter can make mistakes... Ones that can cost hundreds of lives." He let the sentence settle as he stared at the ground. "Well anyway, I don't stalk people. I just check around to see if there needs to be any updates."

"Updates?" Ellie prodded.

"It's just a change in the game to make it better," the Enchanter explained. He glanced at both of our expressions, probably to see if we were out of questions, then he said, "All questioned out? Great. Story time -- Listen carefully."

The Enchanter waved his hand in front of his sphere. Instantly, the view of Katroia-wide events faded and a big black spot appeared in the middle.

"About six decades ago," the Enchanter began, the black spot on the sphere beginning to swirl into colors, "there was a man who had lost his wife to a Tear..."

"Oh that's cool," Ellie marveled, but then when she saw the Enchanter's expression, she blushed. "Not that the guy lost his wife – it's just your sphere. It goes to the story." She pointed at the globe, which showed a pixelated man hunching over a colorful crack in the earth, a ragdoll woman flailing under it.

The Enchanter raised an eyebrow.

"Anyway," he drawled, "this man had the same risky heart as you girls and broke into this Library just as you two had. Here, he realized that there was a way he could get back the one he loved most." The image on the globe shifted to the man flipping through books and nodding.

"I let him go on this little journey that led to death anyway, not knowing he had a really big mouth. Of course, he had plenty of friends who had lost loved ones also. He shared the knowledge with all of them. Those friends eventually shared it with their other friends who shared it with their other friends... and the news kept going down the line." The image shifted to an assembly line of people, who turned toward each other, whispering a message down the line like they were playing a game of telephone.

"One by one, everybody eventually set off to the Void to save those whom they'd lost-- about a thousand in count." The Enchanter looked down at his feet sadly. "Yes, a thousand men attempted to save their lost loved ones... But not one of them returned alive."

Behind me, I heard Ellie gasp. "Not even one?"

The Enchanter shook his head. "Most of these people were grown men. I give you the free choice whether or not to go, but I'm only saying, you *will* likely die."

"Whelp," I mumbled. "Thanks for the heads up. We're still going. Or, I'm still going."

"I'm going too," Ellie joined in.

I gave a concerned look at my sister. "You sure?"

"Yup." I could tell Ellie didn't want to think this through and was just trying to force herself into it. "I would rather die while trying to rescue Mom than live the rest of my life in a *living* void."

"You would go to the Void if you died anyway," the Enchanter warned.

"It can't be as bad as suffering Mom's loss forever. Plus, in the description, it said 'you're too confused to even cry', which means I won't have to lament over Mom anymore," she said.

The Enchanter bit his lip. "I guess, if you're seriously willing to die..." Then his eyes turned serious. "But Elliana and Kaila Kinsworth, the two of you have to *swear* not to tell anybody this. *Nobody,* you hear me?"

"Ok," I agreed.

"I mean it. Not one soul."

"Ok, I promise 'cross my heart and hope to die."

"Good, because you will." The Enchanter took a deep breath. "I know you've been notorious for breaking rules and all, but I know enough about you to know that this is the kind of rule you're not going to break. I'm trusting you with this. You have no idea how big of a risk this is on me."

I felt my cheeks warm up.

"Thank you, Mr. Enchanter," I whispered. "We won't let you down."

The Enchanter sighed, fidgeting with a small sphere with a button in his hand – probably some kind of memory-wiping device. "You know why the description of the Void is so important on its wall?" He paused a few seconds, probably waiting for one of us to say *do I want to know?* But eventually, he continued.

"I think this line was already imprinted on the script, but… every *single* time a Katrin dies, it goes to the Void, was that clear to you?" The Enchanter asked us.

My head spun with the overwhelming amount of things I'd learned today. I could feel a lump climb up into my throat that I was thankfully able to push back. "*Every* Katrin?"

"Yes, so living out the rest of your days would be easier on you than dying so fast and entering the Void so soon."

Of course I was still willing to go on whatever journey that would get Mom back, but I still knew the stakes were *way* unfair.

"But… why?" I asked, struggling to keep tears at bay.

"Why?" the Enchanter echoed. "Because we live in a video game, Kaila. Players who die respawn and get infinite chances at life. *Katrins* who die are simply deleted from the game and are lost and forgotten. Humans don't believe we have souls, so they decide not to do anything about us who die. It is not within my power to perform an update to spare lost souls – once something is deleted from the game, it cannot be restored.

"But listen well, Kaila and Elliana." He enunciated our names like they were about to become legends. "If anyone were to make it through the Fallen Realm, to the edge of the Edge, and defeat the Dragon of the Void to rescue their lost loved one, not only will they be brought back, but the Void will be no more.

"A new portal will open up – the portal into a new Spirit Realm. All lost souls will wake there. They will no longer be lost, or confused, or afraid. Portals to this new Realm will emerge from the ground and offer a chance for Katrins to meet with those whom they'd lost. Souls cannot exit The Realm, but Katrins can freely warp in and out. It will be, hands down, the happiest day of Katroia. Every lost soul will be restored to joy, and it will be all because of some Katrin who journeyed all the way to the Dragon of the Void.

"You see, the reason I let you take this journey is because you could be the hope for the Void -- a legend, the heroes of Katroia," the Enchanter finished, tipping his chin up in shallow pride.

Then, there were a few seconds of silence while we let that sink in. "Yeeeaaah… So, all we gotta do is walk through some portals, beat up some bad guys, and we're the 'heroes of Katroia'. . . Sounds easy enough," I said, nudging Ellie's ribs. "Think we can do it?"

Ellie nodded stiffly.

After another long silence, Ellie and I decided we should head out. The Enchanter had ended up being a much nicer guy than I had expected him to be. I thought he would be all like *'Who art thou that invadeth thy Enchanted Library?!'* I guess that was one of the bright sides of the break-in.

So I thanked the Enchanter for being so kind and hospitable (even though he'd just told us we were going to die), and he let us walk out freely. I was half expecting him to yell *'SIKE!'* and then have his guards surround us and stone us to death.

And another bright side, even bearing the news I had just received about the terrible pain and loss we were about to face, I was brimming with joy.

There really *was* a way to get Mom back!

CHAPTER 7

We Hit the Road

It was the first time in two days that I wasn't thinking, *what in Katroia am I doing still on this planet?* We may have been walking into a death trap, but at least we had a solid plan.

Today we were going to pack our essential supplies. Both of our armor sets could use some serious repairing, we needed to grab extra food and elixirs, and our inventories needed to be filled with extra supplies that seemed necessary to bring to a death-run.

But first things first--the box Will had given me contained some pretty good materials for upgrading armor.

So, we stopped by the house to pick up Mom's box of forge supplies and made our way out to the stone-iron building down the Steel Wing. Since the sun had just risen, some of the forgers were on their way also. Most of them gave us looks of pity, but I was already feeling confident that their looks weren't going to touch my mood.

I hadn't been to the forges in so long that I had almost

forgotten about the smell. The air reeked like greasy iron, hot sparks, and – was that lava?

We wandered into the main opening to see a few Katrins buzzing about, carrying hot items with gloves and newly repaired swords. When the Forge Master, Will, noticed us, his eyes turned sad.

"Uhh… Hey guys. What are you doing here?"

Ellie forced a smile. "We're just repairing our stuff. You know, reclaiming Mom's workspace."

Will tossed his eyes back and forth between Ellie and me. "Well okay. You guys are allowed here whenever you want, by the way. Just don't go into the furnace room. Everything in there will give you a third-degree burn."

"Sounds good," Ellie chirped. "Come on, Kaila."

We wandered through broad hallways that had dozens of rooms branching off of them. The walls were made of cobblestone, except for the room at the end of the hallway. Lava flowed down the walls of the room, and large iron boxes contained raging white fire. Heat radiated off the walls even two yards away from the room, yet still, Katrins worked in there, carefully dipping weapons and armor into pools of lava. Then they slipped the weapons back out, dashed toward an anvil and immediately began pounding their items with huge sledgehammers.

The furnace room, I thought.

Soon enough, Ellie stopped in front of a messy room lined with singes along the walls. A dozen workbenches hung off the walls, supporting all kinds of stuff – from chunks of metal to long, sparkling bismuth swords. A sign in front of the doorway read, *Maya Kinsworth.*

"My goodness, this place is so beautiful," Ellie beamed as she entered the room. Along with the workbenches fastened to the walls, half a dozen swords of different materials were

strapped to the wall from iron handles. And don't even tell me –
okay, Mom seriously had been hiding a huge stash of different
types of armor! There was so much *opal* and *amber* and *sapphire*
and *topaz* . . .

"Kaila!" Ellie called from across the room. "We don't even
need to repair our weapons! We can just use one of these!"

She stood in front of the sword stash, gaping at each one like
they were made of pure diamond – the rarest gem in Katroia.

I strode back over to her side and examined the wall as well.
She was right. Our swords were juvenile compared to these
things.

Ellie and I tried fitting pretty much all of the swords. None
of them were completely balanced in my hand, but they all
looked pretty. Most of them were too light or too heavy or just
didn't fit in my grasp right.

And then I saw it.

I gasped. "Oh my! Is that spirit-gold? Spirit-gold is only one
of the most precious metals we have here in Katroia! And Mom
had a sword made out of it??? Where has our mother been? My
goodness gracious. . ."

The sword was double-edged and looked majestic and
powerful. This one actually *glowed*. It didn't just seem like it;
light was radiating off of it. The hilt was fashioned from petrified
oak, but the rest of it was solid spirit-gold! Jackpot!

I grabbed the double-edged sword by the middle and held it
out in front of me in a horizontal line. It was perfectly balanced
in my hand, a little heavy, but totally manageable. My eyes felt
like they were about to pop out of my head in the shape of hearts.

"Can I try?" Ellie asked.

I didn't want to let go of it, but I nodded and dropped the
five-foot long sword (two-and-a-half feet per blade!!!) into her
hands. The sword obviously felt to her like a block of concrete.

"Whoa!" she blurted, as her arms sunk down with the sword.

She looked like a toddler trying to lift a twenty-pound weight at this point, causing a giggle to escape from my lips.

"That's pretty heavy," she squeaked. "Hurry, take it before I drop it."

I gladly did as she requested.

"This is *so* my sword," I decided confidently.

There was only one issue – Its scabbard could only hold one side of it, which meant I would be walking around with the tip of my sword dangling over my head.

I slid it into its scabbard to see if it at least looked okay, but it did something I definitely didn't expect – which only made my day more manageable. One side of the sword slid down into the other side magically, leaving just the hilt to stick out of the top so that it looked like a normal sword. I didn't even believe my eyes until I blinked about a hundred times.

Where did Mom get this? Did she make it?

Those questions were left unanswered. All I knew was that it was *my* sword from now on.

Ellie stared at the sword in the scabbard so dreamily that I was afraid that if it *were* light enough to balance well in her hand, she's snatch it, stroke it, and hiss, '*my precccciousssssssssss*'

"That's... did Mom do that?" she beamed instead.

"Apparently--she was a clever girl."

We both stood in silence for a few seconds, staring at the ground and remembering Mom's crafty personality.

"Anyway, have you chosen a sword yet?" I asked Ellie, trying to switch the subject before it hung too long in the air.

"Yeah, I think this Sphalerite sword is good," Ellie said, as she picked a silver-white sword off the wall. She waved it around in front of her eyes. "Fits good, not too heavy. This feels like the right sword for Ellie."

"Great," I agreed. "Now before we waste our entire day picking out swords, we should get packing." Ellie nodded, her smirk returning.

So, we left the forges and headed back home. As soon as we stepped outside, the air smelled cleaner than ever before, now that it wasn't polluted with fiery scents. For some reason, we didn't see Luke wandering around yet today, but I was sure he'd pop up and stare holes through our heads sometime soon.

As our house came back into view, I almost didn't recognize it. The flowers were still lush and perched outside the windows and the same deck with the same rocking chairs hung in front of the house, but...

I tried not to let any more of those feelings creep back into my head and trigger tears to start swelling, but I figured the more I missed Mom, the more I would be motivated to journey to the Void.

So, when we swung open the doors, I felt sure of myself that I was not going to live out the rest of my life without Mom. I was either going save her along with everyone else lost in the Void or go down fighting.

As soon as we stepped inside, we went straight to work packing. I grabbed everything I could possibly use in any situation until I thought, *this is ridiculous,* and started putting some things that seemed unnecessary back. By the end, I was packed to the brim of my inventory with more food than I'd probably eat, a number of different elixirs that I was probably not going to use, and tools that probably wouldn't be needed either. As I was packing all of the random things though, I decided that I'd rather be safe than sorry. Besides, when you put something into your inventory it becomes weightless, so what's the difference anyway?

Somewhere in the middle of our packing, I heard a heavy thump of booted feet behind me.

Ellie squeaked. I swung around to see a tall, slim teen standing behind me, brushing off his arms.

"That was tough, holding myself up there for so long . . . was some serious upper-body strength right there."

I gasped and covered my mouth with my hand.

"Luke? But how…"

"So," Luke interrupted. "What are you guys packing for?"

"Uhh…" I couldn't think of an excuse off the top of my head.

"No need to lie, by the way," Luke added.

Yes, there was a need to lie, I thought. The Enchanter made us swear not to tell a soul about the Void.

"I can't tell you," I blurted, hating my tongue for being so impulsive. "I mean, . . . oh, man."

"Let me guess," Luke said, "you broke into the Enchanted Library to find out if there was a way to get Mom back and the Enchanter let you go, making you promise not to tell a soul about it."

I looked intently, "How did you . . ."

"I've been stalking you," he replied. "Well, I watched when both you and Ellie wandered into the woods, knowing you were going to come up with *some* kind of crazy plan. I just climbed in to see what dumb ideas your tiny brains could come up with."

I looked at him with an inquisitive stare. "That's what the Enchanter said about knowing we were going to break in."

Luke chewed his lip. "Yeeeaaah . . . so you guys are going on some long, treacherous journey to get Mom back, I'm guessing?"

I nodded, realizing that Luke hadn't said *your* mom, but just, Mom.

"The Enchanter made it clear that it was likely that we weren't going to come back alive, but I'd rather die than live the rest of my life in misery."

"Cool. That means I'm coming."

Luke blinked up at me and Ellie, watching our expressions. He must've been satisfied because my jaw had finally reached the floor after all these hours and Ellie turned paler than Freya had when she saw Mom in the Tear.

"You're *what?*" Ellie managed to choke out.

"Hey, if you guys die, we all probably will. I can't believe I'm saying this, but if you two are gone too, I would have nobody. Nobody likes me, you know."

I found myself just kind of standing there next to my bed, an apple in my hand a foot from my bag. I wanted to tell him that if he died, he would end up in some dark depressing abyss for eternity, but another part of me wanted him along. He would be helpful. He was a great fighter and was also really, really smart. If anyone were to get us out of a tricky situation with an awesome plan, it would be Luke, even if he was grouchy the whole time.

In my head, I was thinking *bring him along,* but my mouth wasn't cooperating.

Bring him along, echoed a voice inside my head. Literally. I *heard* that voice – I didn't just think it. It didn't sound like my voice either – wait, did it even sound like *anything*? *Did* I hear it?

You won't regret it, the voice beckoned again. I felt like I remembered it from somewhere, like I should remember it just fine, but I couldn't seem to sort out that voice. It was like the memory was at the tip of my tongue, but the harder I thought about it, the more distant the memory felt.

"Kaila, you okay?" Ellie asked me when I noticed I'd started to sway. Her eyes were full of concern, and she looked ready to catch me if I collapsed.

"Yeah, I'm fine. Luke, you're coming," I decided.

Luke looked surprised.

"Really? Wow, I thought it would take all of my willpower to convince you."

I shrugged.

"Great, now let's go get you packed before I change my mind." I gave him a look that read, *you'd better hurry.*

"Oh, I'm already packed, so I guess that means we're ready," Luke said. "Kapeesh?"

I noticed the look in Luke's eyes clearly said, *please don't ask any more questions.*

"Luke, is there something ..."

Luke shrugged.

"Nah. Come on, we've gotta save your mom. We don't have time to waste."

First off, Luke sucked at keeping secrets. But it was impossible to make him tell you anything, so I decided to save it. Besides, he was right. Every second that Mom spent in the Void was painful.

"Ok then. Should we hit the road?" Ellie smiled up at us, setting the new mood.

"Yeah, I guess we should," I affirmed. "No turning back now."

CHAPTER 8

We Dig into a Mineral Cove

"**O**kay, **so our plan is pretty straightforward**," I said, as we walked through the forest in a single-file line. "We find a good place to mine, collect some Falleotite, build a portal to the Fallen Realm, go into the Fallen Realm, find our way to the portal to the Edge, go into the Edge…"

"Very straightforward," Luke muttered.

"Yes, very. Anyway, we're going to find the portal in the Edge that leads to the Void, and then slay the dragon in the Void. Sounds easy enough, right?"

"Kaila, you said that in the Enchanted Library--" Ellie began, but she never got to finish that thought.

"Yes, and?"

Ellie sighed, "You're right. This is going to be easy as cake."

"Cake is very hard to make," Luke reminded her. "That's a human idiom."

"Cake was easy two days ago," I said. "They gave it to us for free."

After I said that, Ellie stayed quiet. Luke began muttering things to himself just to keep away the awkward silence, but I took care of that.

"So, if either of you see any kind of cave or anything, let me know. That's step one to getting Mom back," I said.

Turns out, I made it sound *way* easier than it was. We'd been walking for about a mile before anybody said anything. I wasn't sure if anyone was keeping an eye out for mines anymore, because I really wasn't. We kept walking around the forest in search of a cave or a mine until Luke called out that he saw a big hole in the ground.

"Guys, hello, there is a ten-by-ten-foot hole in the ground about two yards to the right. It's kind of hard to miss," is exactly how he put it, but he was right. A few yards away from us was a huge hole in the earth.

"It doesn't look like a normal cave," I said. "Think we should go check it out?"

I kind of regretted saying that sentence again. Last time I had suggested to check out a strange feature in the ground, the outcome wasn't exactly wonderful. But Luke and Ellie seemed to agree and began moving toward it.

As I followed them toward the divot, I kept repeating the sentence over and over in my head: *There is no glow; There is no glow; There is no glow.*

But when we advanced close enough, I realized that it probably was a cave – just a very abnormal one. Strange.

Before any of us said a word, Ellie began to crawl into the carved dirt tunnel that led down into the ground. I was contemplating either saying 'it's not safe,' or, 'wow, let's check it out', so nothing came out of my mouth before Ellie turned around and said,

"Well, you guys coming?"

I didn't argue. After Luke shrugged and crawled in after Ellie, I kept my mouth shut and entered as well.

I wondered what was down this tunnel anyway . . . It could be someone's house, or a monster hideout, or . . .

I let out an astonished breath. The place was . . . it was . . .

"Beautiful," Ellie breathed. "Absolutely gorgeous!"

The place was a huge sanctuary fashioned with ornate stone walls. Dozens and dozens of precious stones burst out of the sides, sending beams of vibrant light off of each one. The whole place was beaming with colors. A few halls were jetted out from the sides, leading to who knows what.

"Look at all of these precious stones!" I marveled. I was about to take off and start grabbing jewels that we might need, but suddenly I heard a loud, alarming *click*, and chains cranking.

I immediately sensed danger and turned toward the exit of the cavern, but that was when I noticed that the exit was where the clicks came from.

My vision threatened to black out when I realized the reality.

I'd done it again. I'd suggested to check out a strange hole in the ground, putting everyone in danger. Now, we were left trapped inside a huge sanctuary of precious stones. Soon, something terrible was going to happen and we were all going to die.

Good one, Kaila.

I reevaluated the situation when I heard groaning and moaning echoing off the dark walls of the cavern. The only light provided were the beams of light that shone off the precious stones.

It was still dim, but all around me I could feel the essence of undead souls lurking in the darkness. The moaning grew louder and louder until a few dark figures came into sight.

"Ellie," I gasped, and reached for my little sister's hand, but she wasn't with me. Luke was gone as well. "ELLIE!" I yelled frantically, but I realized yelling wasn't going to get my sister back. "LUKE!" wasn't going to change the situation either.

About ten dozen grey, undead monsters emerged from the shadows, and two hundred forty groggy red eyes flashing in my direction.

CHAPTER 9

I Go Calamity Mode

I screamed for my life as I braced myself from the undead, grey figures dashing toward me. I could hear them shrieking in joy as their intimidating, red eyes flashed brighter.

"STOP!" I spluttered as I dropped to my knees, covering my head with my arms.

I wasn't going to look at those things with their bright red eyes and undead features. Their skin was so entirely *gray* and *pale* and *bloodshot* and . . .

I shivered just thinking about what they looked like – which was why I refused to look up at them.

They were running after me, their long, snakelike tongues lolling out of their mouths. They were hungry. I was their dinner – and there was nothing I could do about it.

I braced myself and let out another terrified wail when a thick sense of hopelessness settled over me. I'd given so much fury and determination in setting off to rescue Mom. But as soon as we'd met the first and easiest trial, I wimped out, and now we would all die. The Enchanter was probably watching me right now. But honestly, I didn't care who was watching me. Nobody could wipe out a hundred and twenty terrifying, undead creatures...

I'm so sorry, Mom, I cried in my head. *I tried.*

A pathetic try—we'd only barely started this trip—and already, weak 'ole Kaila Kinsworth curls up into a wimpy ball and lets herself die. I willed the big bowling ball stuck in my throat to roll up into tears. This would be a dumb way to die, but I couldn't escape the situation. This will be at the top of the list of *Dumb Things Kaila is Notorious for Doing.* I'd done it again, hadn't I?

'*Let's go check it out*'. Well look what I led us into this time. Now we all get to die.

What are you doing, silly girl? The same voice I'd heard earlier at the house echoed in my head. *Stand up to them and fight, my little Kaila Bear!*

Time seemed to slow down. My eyes were still squeezed shut, but I lowered my hands away from my head, and willed my lips to stop trembling. I felt energy beginning to prickle through my veins, starting from my feet and rising up through my shoulders.

Stand up and fight, my little Kaila Bear!

I felt like smacking myself repeatedly for three days straight. That voice that had whispered inside my head back at the house wasn't some long gone memory—it was my very mother's, whom I'd only lost three days ago! She was trying to talk to me through the Void and I hadn't even realized it was her!

My eyes flicked open, and I glared at the grey monsters with a wild expression that read, '*go on, ninny, hit me.*'

Watch the mood swing ladies and gents...

The energy was now rising to my head.

"Okay, Mom," I agreed, a smile playing at the corner of my mouth.

A strange thing happened. My body flickered for a few seconds into purple and blue shadows before I went numb. I was paralyzed for a second while the energy in my body brimmed over. And then, without thinking, I drew my sword, which immediately extended a second blade on the end, and dashed toward the mob of ten dozen grey monsters with empty-threated red eyes.

I began with a wide slash across four monsters, reducing them effortlessly to grey dust. I then mopped up a few more. I spun around and devoured the dummies easy as yesterday's cake. I didn't stop at all to take a breather. I even spun again and swung wide, exhaling this terrifying, eardrum-banging laugh that echoed off the walls way too many times. Half the monsters backed off at the sound. Even I was kind of startled at my own wicked laugh, but I didn't hesitate a second to contemplate whether or not that noise had just come out of my mouth or not. I didn't even feel myself inside my own body. My reflexes took care of every attack I made.

Wow, I can't believe how far I've come from the beginning of this battle. This was *fun!* Apparently, all I needed was a little kick start from Mom. Apparently, without her, I am nothing. Now I found myself laughing hysterically in the thrill as I wiped out dozens of monsters at a time. For once in a very long time, I was feeling completely and utterly unstoppable.

And, before I knew it, I was standing in the middle of a junkyard of grey dust. Every single rock-grey monster that once lurked the dark halls of the sanctuary were now all reduced to the ground. Red flakes drifted in the air, all seeming to gape around me like they were the audience and my victory had not been expected.

The red flakes blew together by a whisper of wind that came from the hallways. More flakes trailed in from them along with the breeze.

As I felt my limbs return to my control, I began to gain consciousness of what the flakes were doing. They were clumping together to form some kind of shape – two humans and another small figure at their feet materialized from the red flakes. One human had long hair, one had short—a girl and a boy. The boy was older than the girl . . . and they both seemed *really* familiar.

Once all three shapes had completely materialized, color began to spread across them, starting at the feet.

My heart did a double backflip.

"Ellie!" I burst, as I flung my arms around my sister, who had just taken form from red flakes. "Ellie, I thought you were . . . you were . . . I didn't know what happened to you!"

Luke arched a frown. "Good to see you too, Kaila."

I left Ellie and gave Luke a big Kaila Bear hug as well.

"Luke, I was so scared something happened to you, too! You risked everything to come and help us, and if anything happened to you . . . I would never forgive myself!"

I could feel Luke warming up a little inside. He didn't really say anything to that and when I let him go, I noticed he was blushing.

There were a couple seconds of silence. Then, Ellie began gushing out comments like, "Oh my goodness, Kaila, YOU SHOULD HAVE SEEN YOURSELF! You were like, EVERYWHERE, smacking and slicing at those terrifying ghosts! And then you flew around and slashed everything in sight, and spun around again and scared me with your guffaw, and . . ."

I laughed and embraced Ellie into another big bear hug.

"Kaila, I thought you were going to give up and die at the beginning," Ellie added. "Then, all of a sudden, you whipped out your spinjitzu and unleashed your inner Hulk!"

"Spinjitzu?" I repeated. "Inner *Hulk*?"

Ellie laughed. "Never mind, just some players sharing about

their world. What . . . exactly happened, Kaila? I want to hear the whole story!"

The next five minutes I spent gushing my story, beginning with my feeling of hopelessness, then Mom's voice. I explained how the energy brimmed over and caused an explosion inside of me. My reflexes took control of every action and wound up my skill level about a million notches. At certain parts of the story, Ellie and Luke filled in the awesome parts, like me slicing eight monsters in half and chopping two heads off with either end of my sword at the same time. Honestly, I didn't remember which parts they were referring to. It all felt hazy, like I was in a dream.

After I was finished, Luke explained how he'd felt his body vaporize and all he could do was spectate the brawl and hope I survived. He wasn't sure if he'd come back, even if I won, but he was still on the edge of his seat . . . even though he'd had no rear at the time.

Soon enough, the cavern became our cafeteria. Everybody began chewing down food like hungry pigs, considering Ellie and I hadn't eaten since lunch yesterday.

I soon noticed that the exit was revealed again, so we weren't in any known danger anymore. I tried to talk to Mom in my head, but she stayed silent. It was probably hard for her to make such communication. *It's okay, Mom,* I told her, just to make sure she wasn't feeling guilty about not being able to respond to me.

It wasn't long after that when I had completely let the reality settle in. Mom was dead in the Void. Her soul was supposed to be shattered and lost forever—but somehow, she was awake. And she was talking to me through my head. This wasn't supposed to be possible.

That idea sparked up a whole new conversation. Nobody could even take a guess on how Mom was conscious right now. The Enchanted Library had specifically told us that anyone sucked into a Tear has their soul reaped and shattered into pieces to be forgotten in the Void. There was really no arguing that.

But Mom must've found a way around it—heck, she always finds a way! Why do I even doubt her anymore?

After lunch, I was thinking about suggesting we leave the cave and find another one, but I immediately realized that was probably a dumb idea. The cave was copiously dotted with precious stones that would be more than enough to support our entire village. Of course, it contained at *least* enough Falleotite for one portal.

So, when I suggested we take a look around now that the threat was exterminated, nobody argued. We spent the next ten minutes exploring the place. Even after those ten minutes, we'd found no threat, nor anything out of the ordinary—well, except for the precious stones that freckled the walls. So, I decided the cave was now considered safe. Most of the halls led down to a Labyrinth where we continued to get lost, but we hadn't traveled so far that we could not make it out.

At one point, I suggested that this was useless. We'd walked into this place to almost be killed by some grey, undead monsters and there was nothing here but a ton of mazes. We didn't exactly need all of the stones, and there was no Falleotite anywhere, so this cave wasn't useful for the portal.

I had another hopeless feeling, like it would take days upon days to even find even a little Falleotite. Mom was waiting in the Void for us, and we couldn't even find any Falleotite to travel into the Fallen Realm.

But of course, it was worth it, at least. It's not like we were going to go home, so we had to keep at the first step until we found the next.

Kaila, Mom's voice echoed in my head again, causing me to stop dead in my tracks.

"What is it?" Ellie asked when I didn't say anything.

Kaila, the only way to make it through this is to completely and utterly believe you can. This is a Falleo Cove—it is based upon belief. If you genuinely believe you can find the portal, you will within seconds.

I squealed with joy.

"What?" Ellie repeated.

"Guys, let go of all hopelessness. Trust me. Just make yourself believe that we're going to get through this easy, peasy."

Luke gave me a look between annoyance and frustration.

"That's not an easy thing to do, smarty pants."

"Just do it!"

Luke's expression leaned toward the annoyed side, but he closed his eyes, as if deep thought.

"Okay, this is going to be *so* easy, and we're just going to open our eyes and find a portal to the Fallen Realm."

His tone was brimming with sarcasm, but when he opened his eyes, his face went pale as a cloud.

"What the heck? Why is the portal just *there?*" he said.

I followed his eyes to see what he was marveling over. I had a feeling that by the end of this trip, nothing was ever going to surprise me anymore.

Apparently, Luke had been serious about what he had said, because all the walls in the maze turned transparent. I could only see a tiny tint of blue where they should have been.

Through a few walls of the maze, there sat a twelve-by-twelve-foot room made of ornate stone and Falleotite . . . *Falleotite!* An entire, good-sized room fully constructed from it!

But that's not even what caught my eye. Installed on the back wall of the room was a frame constructed from Falleotite. It almost blended in with the rest of the room, except for the fact that red flakes swarmed inside of it. The entire wall around it was fashioned with incredible care, rubies and sapphires forged into the walls. The entire ground around it was made of crimson mold, and bloodred vines hung from the ceiling.

Just one look and my heart flung out of my chest.

It was an unignited portal to the Fallen Realm, just sitting there in the middle of a maze.

It didn't take much conversation for the four of us to begin jogging through the hallways of the maze. Luke, Ellie, and I could see straight through the walls and now only had to navigate around them to reach the portal room. We wove through the hallways, which were getting darker and darker by the second. Red flakes from earlier drifted through the columns. I wondered if the portal was the source of the flakes and if they had all been blown down the halls to reassemble Luke and Ellie.

In no time, the doorway to the room of the Fallen Portal loomed before us. I didn't give any hesitation before shoving open the heavy double doors and flooding into the room.

As soon as I entered the room, I could no longer see through the halls of the maze. The walls were almost pitch black, except for a few sparkling spots produced by the Falleotite. The portal radiated off just enough light for me to see Ellie and Luke.

"The next step is right in front of us," I breathed, eyeing the portal in awe.

The place was a twelve-by-twelve-foot room. As my eyes adjusted to the gloom, I noticed a fireplace set on the right wall. On the left wall, two wooden tables stood against the Falleotite. They were both big enough to fit all of our stuff.

"It's a little dim in here," Ellie noted to the obvious. "Can I light a fire, Kaila?"

"Sure," I said. I was thinking about reminding her to be careful, but I figured every step Ellie took was careful after everything that had previously happened.

Luke grunted and slung his bag off his shoulders and slumped it onto a table.

"Well," he sighed, "now what?"

"Now, we take a water break and enter the Fallen Realm, Luke," I said.

Luke rolled his eyes at me, but I could tell he was expecting it. He grabbed a water bottle from his inventory and began sipping.

In a matter of seconds, Ellie had a fire going on the right wall. The flame illuminated the room, lustering it up so I could see everything just fine. The light in the room flickered as the flames played in the fireplace, which added a cozy, mellow feel to the room.

Ellie sat down and began pouring water over her head, shivering in delight.

"Ahh, that feels so good!"

"Ellie, you're going to need that water," I reminded her, "there is no such thing as H2O in the Fallen Realm."

"Yeah, I know," Ellie sighed, biting her lip probably at the fact that there was no water, nor life, in The Realm ahead.

"I brought four extra water containers. You've got nothing to worry about, Kaila."

Her reassurance made me smile. I don't think I've seen much of her sweet side since Mom died. But soon we would get her back and everything would be back to normal.

I waited for something to congratulate me for being hopeful, but all I got was another feeling of doubt. How were we going to light this portal?

"Don't worry Kaila." Ellie smiled at me like she was reading my thoughts. "When we were at the Enchanted Library, I read in the Fallen Realm book how to ignite the portal. We just need some flint and steel."

Now I felt like I got all of the bad luck out when we were attacked by those grey monsters in the cavern. I just wished it could be like this for the rest of the trip.

"And you couldn't have lit the fire any other way," I grinned. "Take it away, Ellie."

And without another word, the three of us hovered around the frame. Ellie stepped up to it, her two igniting stones in her hand. She looked back at us, her smile cunning and her eyes wild.

"Buckle up, kids," she grinned and swiped the flint across the steel. "'Cause we're about to go on a *crazy* adventure!"

And that was all the frame needed.

Suddenly, a gust of red wind collapsed off of the Falleotite walls and caved in over the three of us. Loud, terrifying shrieks of an unknown creature echoed off the walls as we found ourselves caught in the middle of a crimson hurricane.

I stifled a scream as the wind forced me to my knees and a wave of blood red terror raced into my eyes. The loud wail of the rapid wind began to screech louder and louder as the red flakes were dragged into the circle.

Then, there was a sudden eruption that made me jump so hard I almost kneed myself in the eye. The huge crimson cloud burst from the portal frame, sweeping into me so hard I found myself rolling across the Falleotite ground for several feet.

And, even faster than it came, everything stopped—the noises, the red flakes, the terror—all vanished, as if nothing had happened.

Except for the fact that the portal had been ignited.

Inside the Falleotite frame, a thin sheet of red haze swirled alive and produced flaky tendrils to dance off the edges. Some sort of magical force swept into my thoughts and taunted me inside.

"Geez, did it really have to be that loud and sweep us off of our feet like that?" Luke mumbled as he pushed himself back up to his feet. "Like, maybe a little bit of effect would be cool, but I think the creator went overboard."

I grunted and brushed off my arms, wincing when I discovered a new bruise on my forearm.

"Agreed."

Ellie scratched her head and rolled to a kneeling position.

"Wow," she breathed. "I mean, when we left the village all confident and all, you know how we managed to push our hopeless feeling aside? Well, you know, that feeling is kind of crawling back."

I bit my lip, trying to find a way to be encouraging in a genuinely hopeless situation. "Well, we got all the way here–are you really contemplating going back?"

Ellie took a deep breath and tried to still her shaking hands. "I guess not."

"Well then, if you're not going back, the only direction we're left with is forward," I shrugged. That was the best motivational speech I could come up with in this situation.

"Yeah, but . . . a thousand Katrins attempted this—and most of them were grown men!"

"Yeah, but they didn't have moms whose souls were alive in the Void. They couldn't switch on Calamity Mode. Remember how many monsters I'd just wiped out with Mom's help?"

I couldn't help grinning as I said it, still not fully processing what had happened then. All I was excited about was the fact that Mom was awake in the Void and could watch and help us.

Ellie nodded, her courage returning.

"Okay, okay, I guess you're right. Let's go show the Fallen Realm who's the scary one."

Luke and I nodded, wide grins stretching across our faces.

"That's right, Ellie. *We're* the scary ones. We've got Maya Kinsworth on our side," I decided, placing my hands on my hips.

And the three of us rose before the beckoning portal. I laced my fingers through Ellie's and squeezed her reassuringly.

And then Team Danger stepped through the portal, hand in hand, daring anything in its path to step aside or face a perilous end.

Hannah Jock

CHAPTER 10

Welcome to the Fallen Realm

Things went wrong almost immediately. Here's how I thought it would work: The three of us would travel through a purple veil, holding hands, and pop out on the other side in a matter of seconds.

Here was the reality: As soon as we entered the glassy veil, I felt every nerve in my body drop and my spirit chasing after my body as it plummeted into a bottomless abyss with no walls, no floor, no ceiling. Piercing darkness swallowed me from all sides, leaving me no escape.

Ellie wasn't with me anymore. Neither was Luke. I began to fall slower and slower, until I was floating aimlessly in the abyss, the darkness slowly suffocating my consciousness. My thoughts began to get fuzzy, and if things could even get any blacker, I think I blacked out.

I squeezed what I was pretty sure were my eyes as tight as they could shut. I knew for a fact that I was going to get through this. The Fallen Realm was going to meet me soon, and my body would return . . .

Then a red blur in the distance came into sight. I heard a faint shrieking noise—the one I'd heard when the portal was in the process of being activated.

Then a crimson veil tore through the darkness and collapsed over me, ripping me out of the terrible Void.

My consciousness faded for a second before my ears popped and the shriek rang through again. Then, I was hurled out another side of a portal and dumped onto the ground like a sack of potatoes.

Things were still fuzzy around the edges, but the two primary colors that I could make out were red and black. But of course, I was only looking at the ceiling.

A few feet away from me, I heard gasping from my little sister.

I immediately rolled over and sat up, examining her to make sure she wasn't injured. Of course she wasn't, but her eyes were full of so much terror, they were hard to meet.

"Kaila," she croaked, and clung to my shirt like it was a life vest in the middle of an ocean. "Kaila," she repeated.

"You're okay, Ellie. The journey between realms is tough," I reassured her. "It's over now."

She sniffled back another gasp and scanned the place we would be spending the next, who knows how long—maybe until we died.

The whole place seemed like an immense cave with walls sixty feet high and canals eighty feet wide. Each surrounding surface was carved from a mix of red mud and Falleotite. The ground was unlevel. Stalagmites sprung from the uneven ground and stalactites hung from the flaky ceiling above. Some of the immense stalactites even reached down and touched the floor.

The air reeked of fresh lava, undead creatures, and other

metallic scents I wasn't familiar with. All around me, I could hear the groaning and wailing of all different kinds of unknown monsters. I could probably remember a few of them from the textbooks I'd studied in the village library, but I didn't take the time to memorize every monster lurking these parts. I didn't think I'd ever come here.

"*Wow,* this place is awesome," I marveled, trying to cover up the underlying fear building up inside of me.

Ellie gave me a terrified look. "Say that again?"

I smiled down at my little sister.

"Hey, Ellie, quit looking on the downsides, and think of how cool and complex this place is! Think about all of the awesome battles we'll claim victory over!"

Ellie's expression softened, as if realizing that I was just being over-optimistic again. "Okay, I'll try."

As if on cue, a loud, horrifying wail echoed off the walls of The Realm. My eyes flashed upward and I searched the canal for the threat and immediately, I saw it.

The monster wailed again. A massive black shadow stirred overhead, long tentacles extending off its back side. It didn't seem to use its tentacles to grab things, but to simply propel itself along. I stood there amazed while watching the way it pushed against the air. It didn't look at all like an octopus or a squid either; the abnormal shape of the body sealed that fact, but it was definitely bigger and *way* more dangerous.

"Fun," Ellie whispered, and immediately left my side.

Good idea. I chased after Ellie, hoping I was fast enough to outrun whatever the monster was about to hurl at me. I tripped over almost every step, but so far, I hadn't been harmed.

"Wait . . . where's Luke?" I cried, quickly scanning the massive canal for my friend . . . or, I guess, my brother. He definitely treated me like I was an annoying little sister, but I loved him anyway.

The monster—or the Rechicast, as I remember from one of the Fallen Realm informational textbooks—puffed out a fireball in my direction.

It took me a split second to realize that my life was in danger before I dove out of the way, barely missing becoming a Fried Kaila Bear—exclusive one night special. My first instinct was to draw my sword, which instantly extended a second blade on the end.

I seriously need to find a name for this sword, I told myself. *It seems like the kind of sword that needs a name.* When the Rechicast blew another fireball at me, I decided that I would publish that later.

I rolled again and scanned The Realm for my sister. I spotted her crouching behind a stalagmite, glaring at me through desperate, fear-filled eyes. I decided not to draw attention to her. I began to run around the Rechicast, drawing its attention as much as I could. *Now,* I really wished I had thought to pack a bow—what was I thinking? Of course, there were things that I would need to fight with a projectile weapon! I doubted that this thing was going to dip low and say, *Here's your chance! Run up and slash me with your sword!*

So there was always the option to run and leave the thing alone. But come on, how boring would that be? If Mom really was watching me right now, would she be proud to see me run from a fight I could possibly win?

Well, she probably would rather me be safe and not die, I thought, *but it would make her proud to see me destroy something that was a bit over my ability level.*

And plus, we were going to encounter much worse things on this road, so we might as well get a warm-up.

I slid across the ground the next time I was targeted by a fireball. I began advancing closer to the monster, my sword drawn, and I suddenly realized that trying to reach it with my sword was useless.

The Rechicast blew another fireball at me, which I easily rolled from.

"Kaila, what are you doing?" Ellie cried from behind her stalagmite.

What *was* I doing?

While my attention was divided, I was delivered another blast that I didn't have time to react to. All I could do was hold up my sword in front of my face, hoping for the best.

I could have sworn the flame hit me. It was inches from my face when I closed my eyes, but I wasn't at all affected. Then, I heard a wail from the Rechicast. A painful wail, not a taunting one.

I opened an eye to see what I'd done and found myself frozen at the sight.

The Rechicast was squirming in pain while a flame crawled up one of its tentacles. Somehow, I must've deflected the flame with my sword or *something*. I glanced at Ellie to see if she looked flabbergasted. She did, which meant I probably *had* deflected the blow.

I wondered if one of spirit-gold's properties was deflecting fire.

And there you have it: I'm naming my sword *Falethropis*, which means *Flame deflector* in ancient Katrin.

Of course, while I was distracted mid-battle, The Rechicast shot another fireball at me. I easily deflected the flame, but it wasn't before I heard the flapping of flame behind me that I realized this wasn't the only Rechicast in the Fallen Realm.

I didn't have time to raise my sword, but luckily, something else slammed into me and sent me rolling out of the fireball's range.

When I finally decided on which way was up, down, left, and right, I noticed Luke hopping back onto his feet.

"Pay attention, Kaila," he said, before fleeing off with his bow in his hand.

I was going to thank him for saving my skin, but he seemed already busy circling the enemy, sprouting arrows from its face.

A smile played at the corner of my mouth. Good to have him on the team.

Once Luke had finished off the Rechicast, he nodded me on.

"Your turn," he said and trotted off around a corner of the canal, searching for another match.

I turned to face the second Rechicast.

"All right, buddy, it's just you and me now. Show me your worst."

I spent the next two minutes circling the monster, taunting it to hurl a fireball at me, which I would easily deflect right back to its face. It didn't seem to learn its lesson. It just kept trying to blow fire on a deflecting sword.

Just as I noticed the Rechicast getting really weary and just a few blows away from death, I felt a searing wave of red-tinting pain wash over me like a tsunami. I wailed in agony, but I could tell my voice was trailing behind me. I was in the air.

"Kaila!" I heard Ellie cry from a few yards away, her voice traveling further from my ears.

Then I hit the ground.

I must've been twelve feet in the air when I had been blown by the inflaming poison to have landed this hard on my back. I rolled helplessly on the ground, until a stalactite that touched down on the ground caught me by the stomach.

I moaned piteously as I trembled on the ground, hugging my arms around my stomach. I could feel the burning pain on my back spreading to other limbs at an alarming speed.

I heard the Rechicast shriek in delight from a few yards away and it blasted a big chuck of fire in my direction. I didn't bother to look up. All I could do was swallow down a spike lump in my throat. I knew if I rolled out of the way, I would just die from the pain of the poison spreading through my limbs—so I shakily reached for my sword and found it almost impossible to pick it up. How had the poison spread so fast that I could barely pick my arm up?

But, precisely two feet before the fireball swallowed me up in flames, I saw a flash of brown, navy blue, and gold in front of my face.

The gold was in the form of wide dual swords. The navy blue and brown took the shape of a Katrin's clothes. Then I noticed another color: dirty blonde. I lifted my eyes to see a head full of coarse, dirty blonde hair. It seemed an inch overgrown, like he hadn't been to a barber in a month or two, but I thought it matched his style, looking at his adventurous clothes.

When the fire ceased to curl off the edges of his swords, the boy stood and turned to look at me.

"Man, that was a nasty hit. You okay?"

My bottom lip twitched. I was so confused I almost forgot about the searing pain tearing at my nerves underneath my skin. This boy had intense blue eyes, and he wore brown pants and a navy-blue T-shirt with black printed letters on it that read, 'Sherberry Forest Forges'. Two long steel swords hung off of his back, attached to a black strap that crossed over his chest. He wore light brown hiking boots made for climbing mountains.

"I'm, uh, you know, kind of poisoned," I managed to croak, "but thanks for saving me." The poison was now spreading to my lungs. I could feel it.

"Oh, I'm sorry," the boy said, and immediately bent down. "I think I can help you out here." He retrieved a glass bottle from his inventory. "Where'd the poison hit, your back?"

I didn't have time to say anything. I grabbed the nearest ground-touching stalactite and nodded desperately, while barely heaving myself to a sitting position.

The boy popped open the cork on the bottle, and light blue smoke diffused out the top and drifted to my back, where the pain was most intense. I closed my eyes and hugged the stalactite as the elixir worked into my back.

"Kaila!" Ellie cried as she jogged over to my side. "Oh, thank goodness, you're . . . alive!" She gave the boy crouched next to me a surprised look. "Who . . .?

"Oh, I'm again sorry," the boy laughed, scratching his head. "My name is Asher. And . . . um, in case you're wondering, what hit you was that Strablin over there. He pointed to a pile of golden flakes. "Those things are wicked dangerous. Seriously, Kaila, are you okay?"

For a moment, all the pain in my body compacted into one place, which was the most painful thing I've felt in my life. I gave a yelp and accidentally punched Ellie in the thigh, making her jump back.

Then, all the pain drained out of my back, and the light blue mist that depleted the pain from my body turned green and blew itself back into the bottle that Asher was holding.

Without command, my lungs let out the longest relieved sigh I've ever heard. It was satisfying to feel excruciating pain cripple away in a matter of seconds.

"Jeez girl," Ellie grunted, rubbing her thigh. "Glad my face wasn't there."

"Sorry," I said. Then I looked up to Asher, who was still waiting for an answer. "Yeah, I'm . . . fine—Thank you."

Asher grinned. "No problemo! Now, what in Katroia brings you to this horrid place?"

That question seemed to change the mood of the conversation.

Ellie's eyes dropped to the ground.

"We're here to get our mother back from the Void," she said. I kind of gave her a look, telling her with my eyes, *Thought we weren't supposed to tell anyone.* But Asher deserved it, so I didn't say anything.

Asher looked surprised. "Really? So am I—well, except for me, it's my family. Not just my mom."

The entire Realm went silent after that. Asher looked so sad, I felt like our situation wasn't so bad anymore. He sighed and continued.

"My house was burned down. I had a mother, a father, an older brother . . ." His voice broke. "And a little sister. My father and I were the only ones who survived. And even though my father physically survived, it's like his heart and soul died that day. I haven't fully gotten over it yet. I don't know that I ever will."

The bowling ball in my throat began to roll back into place. "I'm so sorry."

There were a few seconds of silence after that, that I wished would break. My wish came true the hard way.

I heard Luke giving an angry battle cry as he shoved his way onto Asher, toppling him over onto his back. He drew his sword and held it up to Asher's neck, breathing viciously.

"Whoa there," Asher said, lifting his hands in surrender. Then, his eyes narrowed to Luke's, whose face turned murderous. "You . . ."

"I'll give you two seconds to cry for mercy," Luke shouted. "Then off with your head."

"Luke! Let him go!" I cried. "What is *with* you?"

"This freak burned my house down!" Luke hollered, pressing his steel blade against Asher's neck.

"You killed my family!" Asher accused.

"That doesn't make it right to kill mine!" exclaimed Luke.

Wait, what?

"Speechless, eh? Now off with your head!" Luke pressed his blade deeper into Asher's neck, but before he was cut, Asher tried to hold up the sharp end with his bare hands.

"Stop!" I yelled. Now that I had my limbs back, I crawled over to the two boys and grabbed Luke's shoulder.

"Don't even try to spare him! He's tricking us into trusting him, then he'll attack us all at once!" Luke snarled.

"No he won't! *He* spared *me*!" I deflected and pulled Luke back. "He saved me before I died of poison!"

Asher scrambled back and brushed his fingers across his throat, his chest heaving unevenly.

"Look man, I'm sorry about what I did two years ago-"

"See? He is being suspiciously kind after he was almost killed!" Luke spat and wriggled his shoulders out of my hands.

"Violence is not the answer," I snapped before Luke pounced back onto Asher. He hesitated and sneered at him, squeezing the hilt of his blade tight in his hands. I waited for his face to soften from a murderous glare to an expression like, *I'll kill you later.*

"Okay?" I resumed, trying not to break through the thin ice separating Luke's mercy and his ruthlessness.

"I hate you," Luke seethed. At least he wasn't trying to kill him.

"Great!" Ellie smiled. "Now, what in Katroia is going on?"

Hannah Jock

CHAPTER 11

We Hire a Fourth Recruit

It took a minute or two to get Luke to chill the fumes.

"Luke, I *am* really sorry about what I did two years ago," Asher tried, but Luke wasn't ready to hear it.

"Save it," Luke snapped. "You want to know what in Katroia is going on, Ellie? I'll give it to you. This loser burned down my home, wiping out my entire family two years ago . . ."

"You left out the first part of the story," Asher said. "You apparently got bored and wandered into the Sherberry woods to burn down some random Katrin's house and ruin his life."

"I told you to save it. *Gosh,* your mouth is as big as the entire Sherberry Region!" Luke exclaimed. "Are you kidding me? *You're the one who* got bored and burned down *my* house!"

Asher gave Luke an irritated look. "Look, man, I'm not sure *who* you think you are for ruining my life, and then blaming *me* when I simply took revenge. You crushed my entire life before my eyes when I was just twelve, and I was terrified! What would you expect I would have done?"

"Stop it you two!" I interrupted. "I mean, it would be great to have another teammate, somebody else to watch your back on the most dangerous journey a Katrin could ever travel!"

"No! He'll kill you! That's why we've got to kill him first." Luke reached for his sword again.

"Hey, I didn't even *ask* to come along with you," Asher said. "I just saw your ... uh, friend dying over here and helped her out. I don't have to come with you guys if you don't want me along ... And, for your information, Luke, no, you can't kill me."

Luke's face transformed into tomato as he snatched his sword and dashed for Asher, who easily sidestepped, unsheathing his two swords like he'd done it six thousand times.

Luke spun back around and flung himself at Asher again, but this time I didn't stop him. Something told me that this guy knew what he was doing.

While Luke lunged at him, Asher stood like he wasn't going to do anything. His swords were lowered, and he stood straight up, not even in a fighting position. Seeing him standing at full height, I could estimate him being five foot six—probably an inch over me.

And just a second before he was hit, Asher held his sword up parallel to Luke's, and then twisted his blade into his adversary's in a way I've never seen anyone do. Luke's sword fell from his hands and clattered on the ground in front of him.

Half of Luke looked angry, while the other half looked actually impressed. He realized that he had no weapon, so he took a step back and stood straight.

"Come on Luke," I begged. "Look at his level of skill. If you were standing in front of a mob of six ogres, who would you wish were here?"

Luke huffed in frustration. He looked around the group with pure anger in his eyes. He wasn't really afraid of Asher rebelling against us. Luke just had such a deep hatred toward him that he couldn't even stand Asher being along, even to protect us.

But as Luke looked around at the three of us, he began to notice that this was a three-against-one situation, and he had lost.

"Yeah, whatever," he finally said. "Fine."

Ellie's expression lit up. "Yes!" She beamed and jumped to her feet. She held her arm out and pretended to knight Asher on either shoulder.

"Asher whatever-your-last-name-is, I gladly welcome you to Team Danger!"

Asher laughed. "Team Danger?"

"Team Danger!" Ellie shouted.

Then we were off with me in the lead, followed by Ellie, Asher, and Luke to keep watch in the back. We wandered straight through the mega corridor of the Fallen Realm to plow over anything that got in our way of saving Mom, and now, Asher's family.

CHAPTER 12

The Fallen Fortress Welcomes Us with Open Arms

As we walked through the Fallen Realm, the mega corridor split off a few times. We decided to always take the right turn, since Ellie decided that right was always right.

Man, we ended up in a lot of battles involving several Rechicast, skeleton warriors, corpses, and tons of other unidentified organisms.

While we were safe—or the safest the Fallen Realm can get—we mostly walked in silence, except for Luke muttering unflattering comments from the back and Asher sharing a few jokes to lift the spirits.

Honestly, a few times I wondered how over a thousand people came here, and all died in the Fallen Realm. All of the battles we'd run into were relatively easy. But then again, we were in search of the Fallen Fortress, which was where the real danger probably was.

It wasn't until my legs began to feel like rubber when Ellie shouted, "Go left!"

I had been busy staring at the flaky black and red ground so I hadn't even noticed that down the left corridor, The Realm opened up to a larger section, as if the corridors could get any bigger.

They could.

The closer I got to the clearing, the wider my eyes stretched.

Okay, this wasn't an immense hallway anymore. This was an endless cascade of cliffs and lava and spikes and—what were those–Fallen Trees? They looked like trees, except the trunks were black and purple and the leaves were like cherry blossoms of crimson flakes. These tree-like things were everywhere. They grew in little clumps, like tiny forests scattered around.

When I looked up, I couldn't see the ceiling of The Realm. A hundred feet above, a thick haze hung in the air, ending the line of sight. There could have been a ceiling, there could have not. When I looked far enough, the haze thickened so I couldn't exactly see the walls on the other side of the opening.

The terrain was *definitely* not flat. Lava somehow drooled from haze above, landing in huge lakes of the searing-hot molten rock. Cliffs dropped off everywhere–not just along the walls. There was no way you could reach the haze on the other side without climbing at least sixty cliffs.

"Gosh," Asher marveled. "Somebody grab me a paper bag."

Luke strained his eyes into the haze across The Realm. "I think I see—I don't know, it's kind of faint . . ."

"What?" I asked.

"I don't know, Kaila," he repeated. "There's only one way to find out. Come on guys."

We all followed Luke into the clearing. He led us down a small cliff, around a lake of lava, up a cliff, around a cliff, and then Ellie held up a hand and stopped us, hugging her knees.

"Wait up, Luke," she wheezed. "Can we, like, take a break, maybe?"

Luke turned around, his expression grim. "You need a break?"

I could sense shallow anger in his voice, but I didn't say anything. Man, bringing Luke to the Fallen Realm just isn't the best combination when you're trying to keep everyone's spirits up before possible death.

"Yeah, can we eat lunch or something?" I suggested.

Luke began to stare a hole through Asher's head, but he shrugged, and said, "Whatever."

Then he sat down and retrieved some food from his inventory. So cool how it worked—you could just stick whatever you wanted into your pocket, no matter the size, and it would become weightless. Then later, you could simply pull anything from your inventory that you stuck in there from earlier. Never really understood the science behind that, but apparently, not all of the laws of science apply in 'video games.'

Ellie sipped the rest of her water and unwrapped a beef grinder that she had been given for free from the village deli. I began to munch on some fruit and berries from the 'Sweet Garden'.

We didn't eat for long. I began to notice what Luke had been talking about—the side of a crimson-colored brick wall. It looked about forty-five feet tall with a balcony off the roof. In front of it, a narrow river of lava flowed into another lake at the bottom of a lavafall. A drawbridge was lowered over the river, seeming to be where the entrance loomed, but I couldn't see that side from our angle.

"It's the Fortress," Asher said. "The Fallen Fortress. If we can survive long enough to find the portal to the Edge there, we can leave the Fallen Realm."

"And into another realm?" I sighed. I was so done with

realms, even though we hadn't even been in the Fallen Realm for too long. I missed the sunshine. I wanted to get out of this deep, polluted cave of death and back into the woods with Mom.

"Yep, realms are fun!" Asher quipped. "Besides, then we'll officially be one-third done with this stupid journey."

"Well then," I asked everyone, "did you all get a good breather?" Ellie smiled and Asher nodded. I figured Luke would be ready soon. "Great. Now how do ya'll feel about taking a trip to a death fortress?"

Asher grinned. "Sounds like a blast!"

This time, Asher led the group. He went a bit slower than Luke did, which left us some room for a breather when we needed it.

The four of us sliced through a few groups of monsters, climbed down a few cliffs, and walked halfway around two or three lava lakes.

Finally, we spotted a faint trail of red flakes that wound around a few cliffs and lava pools. It required a hike up a relatively small hill and then curved around to the entrance of the Fallen Fortress.

At the bottom of the hill, I could hear Ellie's breaths getting shorter and choppier. She grasped my hand for reassurance. I wanted to tell her it was okay, but I really couldn't make such a promise. Over a thousand grown men had died here, inside this fortress. I didn't expect us to get out alive, but at least dying here would be better than having to live the rest of my life without Mom—besides, I didn't *have* a life besides Mom.

I squeezed Ellie's hand and gave her a smile.

"We've got this," was the only thing I could think of. Of course, it was a lie.

We hiked up the hill as slowly as possible.

Finally, we trembled before the terrifying entrance to the Fallen Fortress that loomed arrogantly over us. The opening looked like the huge mouth of some awful monster. Red flakes peeled off the beefy archway surrounding the glowing stalactites that impaled the ground like teeth. A horrid black mist hung in the air all around the entrance, as if to clearly articulate, *This place is a death trap. Don't say I didn't byou.*

I got the warning. Every nerve in my body told me to turn back and run home, but I refused to go back without Mom. I was going to face this . . . Even if it meant losing my life.

I grabbed Ellie's hand and puffed up my chest.

"Well?" I prodded. "Who's ready to go kick some butt?"

The Fortress got the message. An alarming rumble echoed off the walls of the Fallen Realm and shrieked back into our ears. Thick dark mist detonated into the air, swirling together to form a huge hurricane around us. Then, six long red and black see-through arms sprouted from the sides of the building and flailed around like an angry toddler.

"AS YOU WISH," a thundering voice burst from The Fortress. The mega toddler arms extended in our direction, its palms facing us, and its fingers readily arched.

***

We weren't given time to scream before the four of us were snatched up into the arms of certain death. The force was cold around my body, sending shivers up my spine.

"Let me go, you sorry excuse for a . . ." The arm crept up to my mouth before I could finish my tantrum. I could hear Ellie trying to scream under the enormous hand covering her mouth. I twisted my head around to see Luke and Asher struggling in the grasp of the Fortress's version of a welcome mat.

"*I warn you again that most of the situations you will encounter inside will be just as perilous as this—except they will gladly kill you,* the voice boomed.

After what felt like eons, the arms that held us in the air flung us straight through the monster mouth entrance of the Fortress like little pebbles into a well.

I heard a lot of grunting and groaning as the four of us rolled across the cold, hard brick floor of the Fortress. Luke was gutted by a stalagmite. Ellie and Asher tumbled for a while until they were both stopped by a stalagmite in different ways—Ellie grabbed onto it to end her tumble, but Asher was struck in the head by it, significantly *slowing* his roll. I overestimated the roll and dragged my sword along the ground to reduce the roll, ending up yards closer to the entrance than everyone else, who'd ended up groaning and doubling over.

I could hear the taunting laugh of the Fortress dim out into silence, and the black mist that diffused the room, began to withdraw.

I almost cried when I recalled the Fortress's last sentence: *Most of the situations you will encounter inside will be just as perilous as this—except they will gladly kill you.*

"Kaila," Ellie wailed, "we're goanna die."

I was about to say, *I know,* but luckily, I stopped myself. Why did I bring my little sister with me? This is no place for sweet, little, eleven-year-old Elliana. She deserves to be at home in the arms of her mother, rather than facing this horrid chance for a painful death.

I squeezed Ellie close. "Don't give up, okay? Never do that."

"Okay," Ellie sniffled, but she didn't say anything else. She could probably sense I had nothing more reassuring to say.

We all lay sprawled in the middle of some massive cylinder, colosseum-like building with a diameter of probably a hundred feet, and a height of two hundred. Twelve grand doorways lined the walls. In between each of the doorways, a ten-foot staircase rose up to a second row of identical doorways. Through each of those doorways, it seemed like there was another room with even more rooms branching off.

This was ridiculous. We had to somehow find the portal to the Edge in this giant maze of, what seemed like, thousands of rooms. Plus, every room held some dangerous monster that gave us a slim chance of escape? Jeez, whoever constructed this place *really* knew what they were doing if they were trying to keep us Katrins out.

Nearby, Asher moaned and rolled to a sitting position, holding his palm over his head where he was hit.

"Gosh, I feel like I was just inflamed by a blowtorch."

Luke rolled his eyes at Asher and crawled to a stand, hugging his stomach. He looked like he wanted to throw an insult at Asher, but he kept it to himself this time.

"Well?" Luke gibed, "we just gonna sit here and complain for the next few hours, or act like big kids and get up to face more torture? Your choice."

My eyebrow creased. "You gonna continue to hurl insults at us for the next few hours and get us all fed up with you? Or are you gonna shut up?"

Asher whistled. Ellie looked at me and took my hand again.

Luke's face boiled over. As I stood slowly, he stormed over to me and stopped so close to my face, I found myself practically inhaling his angry breath.

"You know what, Kaila?" he began, but I wasn't eager to listen to this guy bark at me for the next ten minutes.

"*YOU* know what, Luke? We didn't have to even take you along in the first place. We could have just said no and avoided constant negativity. *You said* you wanted to come because you didn't want to live life without us." I regretted every word coming out of my mouth in that moment, but I decided maybe Luke should know how I feel. He should know that I have feelings and am not just a dummy for insults. "Luke, if you really cared about us that much, then maybe you should treat us like it!"

That got Luke to shut his mouth. I could feel Ellie trembling at my feet and looking up at me like I had six eyes. For years, we'd tried so hard to keep in our emotions and endure Luke's attitude. I had never let my emotions out on him before, but at this point, he left me no choice.

Another awkward silence for the next minute.

"Sorry to interrupt . . . uh, the spirit-lifting silence . . ." Asher tapped a spot on his arm where a watch would go. "But we've got some families to save . . . so, I, uh . . . I beg your pardon . . . We should probably hit the road . . ."

"Sure," Ellie agreed, trying to sound chirpy to seal the end of the previous mood.

Nobody else argued, but nobody else agreed, either. Of course, nobody really wanted to hit the road, but we kind of had to—even though it had certain death written all over it. I think we missed the neon sign hanging over the entrance that read in bold: *For dumb people who can't sound out the word D-E-A-T-H.*

And yet again, we found ourselves navigating the endless rooms and hallways of the Fallen Fortress.

CHAPTER 13

The Way of the Fortress

We were halfway across the diameter of the room
before Ellie gasped and said, "**Stop.**" All four of us stopped
dead in our tracks, ready to face whatever monster was in
lurking the shadows, but there was no threat. And if there was,
Ellie probably wouldn't have said 'stop.' It more likely would
have been, 'run'.

"What is it?" Asher asked.

Ellie pointed to the ground a few feet from us. When I
followed her eyes, I noticed a ten-by-ten-foot engraving in the
brick floor of the Fortress—five lines of words written right in
the middle of the Fortress floor.

"What does it say?" I pondered, and crept closer to the
engraving. The first words I could make out were the big ones
on the top: *The Way of the Fortress.*

It was some kind of poem—or a riddle. And it went like this:
The Way of the Fortress:

A collection of Katrins together must traipse
Through the Fortress where many monsters they shall face
Follow the quarter hall straight, then look to the left
Here a Katrin shall pass to unbearable heft

Luke grunted in frustration.

"What's that supposed to mean?" he grumbled.

"It's giving us some direction," Asher realized. "The four of us have to travel through this monster filled Fortress . . ."

"Well duh," Luke retaliated. I could tell he was trying his best to contain himself, so I didn't say anything when he let out a huff and turned his head toward the wall.

"That part makes pretty good sense, but the second part . . ." I scratched my head. "We're supposed to go down the quarter hall . . . straight? Then look to the left?"

"How are we supposed to know where the quarter hall is?" Ellie queried. Then, her eyes narrowed like she was concentrating. "Oh. Like there are twelve hallways. We've gotta follow the third one—one quarter of twelve."

"First or second floor?" I asked.

"Dunno, we might have to try both of them," Asher suggested. "I say we start at the top—well, because why would they have two floors if they weren't going to use the second?"

"He's got a point," I said. "We've gotta go straight the whole time . . . and then at some point look to the left."

Ellie twisted the corner of her mouth into a half-frown.

"But how do we know when to look to the left?"

I shrugged again. "Dunno, we'll probably know when we get there."

Asher looked back down to the engraving and bit his lip.

"'*There a Katrin shall pass to unbearable heft*,'" he echoed. "Like one of us is going to die?"

"No," I blurted immediately. "None of us are going to die."

"Agreed," Ellie said. "If that's what it means, we'll break through the prophesy. We're all going to make it out . . ." Her voice broke.

"That's right, Ellie."

Luke turned toward us, his expression grim as always, except this time, he looked kind of hurt. I wondered if what I had said earlier was too harsh on him.

"You're all wrong," he said. "Whether you like it or not, we're all going to die—and I think we all know that. But, at least we'll be put out of our misery."

"Luke!" I shouted.

"You can't really disagree. Hundreds of men have died here. I'm just saying. *You* can believe what *you* want to believe, and *I'll* believe what *I know.*"

"If you really think we're all going to die, then why did you come?" Ellie said.

Luke shot her an angry look, but of course it was impossible to be angry at sweet little Ellie, so he let out his frustration in a grunt.

"I already told you," he said.

"Well," Asher said. "Good to know. We've gotta follow the third hallway on top and then when the time comes, look to the left. Case closed. To the Edge."

I wished it could be that easy.

But unfortunately, it wasn't. We found ourselves traipsing across the colosseum and up the stairs to the third hallway—the key to certain death. Fun.

And of course, the very first room we entered was a threat.

It was a square crimson brick room, as all of them were, with a half dozen undead monsters lurking in the shadows. This must've been one of the easiest challenges of the Fortress because we could probably live through it.

The four of us dove into the room. I drew *Falethropis* and

sliced one of the creatures in half. Ellie did the same with her sword. Asher didn't bother using his sword. He ripped the head off a monster with his bare hands and chucked it at another. Ouch.

Luke stood next to a wall, his sword drawn, but he let us do the work, seeming too irritated to do anything useful.

When we finished off the mob, I frowned at Luke. I was going to say, 'What's wrong?' but I probably knew the answer.

The four of us advanced ahead. We traveled straight through the next room, which was pretty much empty, except for a small key that lay in the corner of the room. From there, we followed a branchy hallway straight toward the room ahead.

Now *this* room matched the Fallen Fortress style. It was empty and held no suspicion. It was made of bricks, as usual, and torches holding up blue fire flickered along the walls.

Just as we were about to exit the room, I heard the ground shift.

Everyone jumped at the sound of gears clicking under our feet. Strong metal bars dropped in front of each doorway, trapping us inside the room.

I unsheathed *Falethropis* and a second blade extended out of the hilt. As soon as the weapon was drawn, an intimidating whisper extinguished the flames resting on each of the torches.

The room went completely dark, except for the glow of my sword.

Ellie gasped and took my hand, as she always did when she needed reassurance. I didn't have any to offer.

The whisper continued to whisp around the room. It let off a dim blue light at the far end of the room—only enough to make the spirit visible, nothing else.

Then, a groggy grumble echoed off the walls of the room. It sounded like an angry lawnmower being drowned in jelly, and, at first, I thought it was the noise of a monster grumbling in pain. Then, I realized that it was probably laughing.

"*You will die,*" the gravelly voice cackled from the utter darkness.

Suddenly, a white-outlined silhouette of a monster emerged from the darkness. The first thing that I noticed were its extended claws in our direction.

"Run!" was all I could think to say.

I quickly grabbed Ellie and hauled her with me out of the way. Luke seemed to have gotten away as well. But I heard claws rake against somebody's chest.

Asher wailed in agony and crumbled to the floor. I could only tell because his sword, which radiated a dim light, fell with him. Then, the monster turned toward us, its tongue lolling out of its mouth, and its claws dripping blood—Asher's blood.

"Asher!" I cried as the monster charged us. Then I changed my mind to, "Ellie!"

I didn't have time to run. I didn't have time to scream. The only thing I could think about was apologizing to Mom over and over.

Then I thought, *this would be a stupid way to die.*

Especially after what I said to you in that cavern, Kaila Bear.

Mom's voice returned to me, surging my entire body with uncontainable energy that was already brimming over, much faster than last time.

My limbs became paralyzed and numb. My brain felt like it bounced between dimensions and then off the walls a bunch of times. Then, my bubbling supply of energy exploded.

All I saw from there were pure blue copies of myself shuttering around me, and then I was behind the monster, trailed by a line of blue smoke.

I hadn't run here; hadn't leapt out of the way. I didn't even lose any consciousness, so I couldn't have dashed away and forgotten about it. I simply teleported . . . *glitched*. And Ellie was still with me, sitting on my lap.

Part of me wondered if I was going insane and was seeing things from horror, but the silhouetted monster's back was toward us. I caught a glimpse of him diving at the hard ground, breaking off a few teeth from crushing them against the ground.

The monster screeched in anger, causing the torches on the wall to flicker.

In the brief light provided, I looked down to see Ellie's jaw hanging.

"Kaila, how...?"

"I don't know," I admitted. "Go light the torches on the walls, and I'll help Asher."

"No. I'm okay, Kaila. Go get the monster," Asher croaked from across the room. He was definitely inflamed and needed some help, but he was right about one thing: We had to do something about this monster.

I didn't like it, but I turned to face the monster.

"Luke, now would be the perfect time to help," I called into the darkness.

"You could've asked earlier," Luke said, and swung into action. From the glint of his silver sword, I could only see his frustrated expression.

Ellie had lit the first torch. A dim, but helpful flicker of light illuminated the room, bringing back some color to the walls. Even in the glow, the monster was still a dark silhouette outlined in white. It was a shadow monster—you can't kill it with any weapon. You'd just pass right through it. You'd have to illuminate the room enough for the shadow to shrink down into nothing.

"Luke, keep it distracted. Ellie's gotta torch the room," I called. I could now see Luke's full expression: Grim as always, but still a bit confused about the whole teleporting thing I just did. He began to glare at me, probably a bit irritated from taking orders, but then began to circle the monster.

Ellie lit the next torch. The monster shrieked and lunged at her. I wasn't totally sure how to teleport over again, so I decided to use my legs and run in front of her. I warded its claws away and shoved it back with the side of my sword. It seemed to be startled by the wave of light that reflected off of my sword and backed off. So, maybe you *could* make contact with the shadow monster after all, if your weapon radiated light.

The monster grumbled and turned toward Luke again, now that it realized that it wasn't going to get at Ellie.

As Ellie lit the next torch, Luke dashed toward the monster, his sword held in front of him like a spear. Then at the last second, he dashed a step sideways and rolled to the back of the shadow monster.

I could feel the energy surging through me again—not enough to do anything ridiculously unkatrin, but enough to duck and sidestep about ten attacks from the shadow monster. It felt weird, fighting alongside Luke after everything I'd said to him earlier, but sometimes, you have to do what's necessary to save yourselves.

I hadn't noticed how light the room was getting. Seven torches had been lit—three and a half walls. Now Ellie only had one more to light before the Shadow monster dissolved into the brightly lit room.

I had time to parry one more attack before the last torch was lit and the shadow monster shrieked in pain and turned into a mini tornado of black mist, slowly dissolving into the light.

A grin played across my mouth as I watched the last shadows be swallowed by light. I fought the urge to yell up into the Fortress, *'It was harder to stay awake than it was to fight that thing!'*

I trotted over to Ellie and wrapped her into a hug.

"You were awesome, Ellie!" I crowed, soon shooting Luke a look that read, *'You too'.*

I smiled back at Asher, who had used the wall to rise to his feet. His chest had claw marks running from his heart to the end of his ribs. He winced as he tried to take a step, but when he saw me watching him, he tried to hide his pain.

"I'm okay," he lied.

"Do you have any more of that healing stuff?" I asked.

"Yeah. That's why I'm okay."

Asher grabbed a square of milky white substance, an edible healing snack, and nibbled it down.

It wasn't until after I realized that everyone was okay that I noticed that the bars blocking off the doors hadn't ascended. They still just sat there like they hadn't been designed to move in centuries.

"Hey guys, what's with the doors?" I asked.

Then, as if on cue, every surface in the room rumbled. Gravel crumbled from the ceiling and the floor seemed to detach from the walls.

Ellie stumbled. I caught her arms and tried to hoist her back up, but I began to lose balance, too.

The right side of the floor began to tip upward, the left side dipping down. It took my malfunctioning brain cells a few seconds to figure out that the floor was slanting.

"Grab the right side!" Asher called, but it was a bit too late. The floor was tipping sideways faster than was fair, already too steep to run up the side and grab the ledge.

Ellie's feet slipped out from under her, and I lost her grip. She slid straight into whatever waited at the bottom. Luke stumbled next. Then Asher.

Then my feet slid off of the slant and I found myself freefalling through a hazy, wide brick tube, unwilling to look down at what was about to be splatter-painted with our guts.

CHAPTER 14

The Beans are Spilled

The first thing I was conscious of after my panic attack ended was Ellie's terrified scream. That pretty much woke me up.

Still in midair, I readjusted myself to face my stomach downward so that I could see Ellie twisting and flailing through the air. Suddenly, I didn't care what was down at the bottom—if it would impale both of us, or if Ellie would survive if I wrapped myself under her. I dove headfirst into the brick tube to reach her.

As I passed Asher, he shot me a look of panic and started to dive down with me. Luke did the same. His anger seemed to have vanished. Now he was just plain terrified.

Ellie was at the bottom of the line. When she spotted me, she swam through the air in my direction. Knowing that I was with her seemed to calm her down, even though she was about to die.

I embraced my sister, and she immediately began to sob into my arm.

"What should we do?" Asher cried.

"At this point, I don't think there is anything we can do except hope the landing isn't certain death, which probably isn't happening—" I looked down, hoping to see a pool of bubbles or a thirty-foot deep pile of leaves, but I realized we'd missed our chance. At the top, if we had acted faster, we could've climbed our way around the tilting floor and the gates would've opened up.

We turned to Luke for reassurance that we were dead, but his face was impassive.

I looked down again to see a hard concrete floor rushing toward us at alarming speed. We *had* missed our chance. We had the Void to look forward to.

"Okay everyone," I laughed brokenly. "Group hug."

Nobody argued. Not even Luke. All four of us pulled close together into a big hug. The floor waited eighty feet from us . . . seventy feet . . . sixty feet . . .

At around fifty feet, Luke grabbed all three of us and swung himself under us. He turned his back on the group hug and extended his arms toward the ground.

Luke's back tensed. I could feel it on my thigh where his shoulder blades touched me. At twenty feet away from the ground, a wave of golden debris twisted in from the walls and condensed into a thin layer of golden dust in front of Luke's hands.

Luke twisted around and grabbed us. His fingers dug a little too hard into my arm, but I didn't blame him. His expression looked terrified—not from hitting the floor, but from something else I couldn't discern.

The four of us sank into what felt like a net made of non-stick slime, if that exists. It slowed our fall exponentially.

We stretched the slime net to the point where it broke ten feet before we hit the floor. Luke reached up and grabbed a second layer of golden dust slime like a towel and held onto my arm. With all of us dangling off of each other, we were lowered rather slowly to the concrete floor.

As soon as my feet touched the floor, I gasped and dropped to my knees, squeezing my sister tight.

"Luke, how . . . when . . ." I stammered, feeling unworthy to raise my gaze up to him.

After Luke landed last, he clutched his head and plopped down into a sitting position.

"Guys—half of my identity . . . was just exposed," Luke divulged. "I . . . I am—" his voice broke.

I sat down right across from him. Ellie sat next to me. I tried my hardest to wear a softened expression.

"Luke, that was, hands down, the coolest thing I've ever seen in my entire life! Why have you been hiding that for so long?"

Asher stood a few feet away, twisting his fingers. He probably didn't want to invade this conversation between the three of us, who had been as close as family for two years now.

Luke sighed. "I am the son of the Enchanter," Luke spilled. "And I wasn't allowed to say anything. I figured it out two years ago." He glanced up at Asher.

My eyes stretched as wide as they could go. "Two years ago, . . . when your house burned down?"

Luke bit his lip and looked back down at me. "Yeah."

There were a couple seconds of dead silence. I couldn't believe Luke had been hiding his entire life from me ever since we met him. But the way he'd been darting his eyes back and forth between Asher and me caught my suspicion.

Finally, I looked back at Asher to make sure he still had two eyes, two ears, a nose, and a mouth. The way Luke was looking at him made me want to check. He looked the same, except his face was burning up neon-red.

I had a concerned look on my face.

"Asher, what's wrong?" I looked back at Luke. "Does you being the Enchanter's son have anything to do with Asher?" I felt bad being nosy, but the suspicion was brimming.

"No," Luke blurted.

"Yes," Asher said at the same time.

More silence.

Asher sighed. "I'm the son of another . . . important person," he admitted.

My head spun. "Seriously? Which one?"

"The fire guy?" Ellie guessed, looking down his clothes, which I hadn't realized looked slightly singed until now.

"No, more like . . . I *am* the fire guy." Asher admitted, plopping down in between me and Luke, completing the circle.

"What?" I blurted, trying to picture Asher as one of the most important Katrins in Katroia.

Asher looked like he had just eaten a chili pepper.

"Kaila," Luke described, "There is an elemental lord for everything in Katroia."

Ellie shifted in her seat. "Like . . . gods?"

"No," Luke corrected, "there's only one God. He's mostly involved in the real world though."

"Anyway," Asher continued, "the creator of this game put a bunch of Katrins in charge of certain things, such as Earth, Fire, Water, Magic, etc. . . Anyway, their kids inherit some of their powers. The Enchanter is the magic guy; Luke can perform some magic. I am the son of the Forge and Fire guy; I can summon fire—"

"Wait, you can summon *fire?*" I interrupted, my eyes widening.

"Yeah," he laughed, watching my expression grow hysterical.

Luke picked up Asher's story. "My dad, the Enchanter, and Asher's dad, Fore, have been programmed to be rivals. So, my father ordered me to kill Asher, and he would attack Fore himself, so that the fire element would be wiped out for good."

Asher sighed. "So, Luke ended up burning my house down. But . . . he thought that I was immune to fire—that's why he chose *to* burn it down. He didn't really want to kill me, so he thought he was giving me a chance to run, while making it look like he was trying to follow his dad's orders. But unfortunately, I'm not actually immune to fire, so I almost died trying to escape my burning house . . ."

"Wait—you're *not* immune to fire? Even though you can summon it?" Ellie repeated, stealing the words from my mouth.

"Weird, isn't it?" Asher laughed. "Children of the elemental lords don't inherit *all* of their parent's powers, so I ended up with the power to summon fire, but not immunity to fire. So anyway, I *barely* survived the fire, being the only one, but my family perished and my house was reduced to coal. I was so angry at Luke for burning up my family that I decided to get revenge and burn down *his* house." He shifted in his seat. "It wasn't until later that I realized . . . that Luke thought I was immune to fire and didn't *really* want me dead, so he tried giving me a chance at escape. He didn't know my family was in the house. I felt so *bad* for taking revenge . . ." He lost it at 'bad' and let Luke continue the story.

"When I saw my house burn down, I grew *irate*. I had tried to do something nice—spare somebody's life. I thought Asher was just some cruel kid who tried to kill me for ruining his house even though I had spared his life. And I guess from then on, I didn't feel like wasting my energy on being nice to people," Luke finished, suddenly seeming very interested in the ground.

"I'm *so* sorry, Luke," Asher said.

For the first time since I'd met him, Luke's eyes began to turn glassy.

"I'm sorry too, Asher. When we crossed paths again in the

Fallen Realm, I hadn't yet realized what really happened—until you told me your family died in a fire; *my* fire."

Ellie hugged me, feeling significantly warm inside.

"So," Asher said, "my father ended up being slain by the Enchanter. And I kind of had to take his place as the 'fire lord, In other words, *Asher Lolex.*"

I turned to Luke. "But . . . when I met your dad, I thought he was a pretty nice guy," I recalled, unable to imagine him as a murderer.

"He *is* a nice guy," Luke said, just to make things confusing. "It's just . . . you're nice, right? But when you see a monster, you've gotta kill it, right? It's kind of like that with my dad."

"But why does he hate Fore?"

Luke shrugged. "Magic is a very incarnate subject. Forging is probably one of the most physical elements in Katroia. I guess because they are so opposite, they were programed to resent each other . . . I don't know. How come you suddenly feel the urge to kill a monster when you see one?"

"Because they threaten us," I reasoned.

"And my dad and Fore were programmed to threaten each other, too."

I sighed and tried to take all this in. "Okay, so to sum things up, Asher, you can summon fire and Luke, you can do magical stuff?"

"My power sounds dumb when you put it like that," Luke mumbled.

"Yeah, but it's . . ." I laughed and pointed upward toward the brick tube we'd just fallen through. "But it's not, Luke. It's amazing."

Luke blushed and scratched the back of his head. "Thanks."

"And you, Kaila, can glitch around and turn into Hercules," Asher reminded.

"Hercules?" I echoed.

"Never mind. Just some players telling me about their world—I just meant your insane reflexes and glitching thing is amazing, too."

"So, we're already at a huge advantage on this quest," Luke decided. "We've all got awesome abilities."

"Except for me," Ellie said.

"No, including you," I said. "You're the reason we got past that room with the shadow monster. You lit all of the torches. You may not have a power specifically for fighting, but you're super smart and alert. You noticed the engraving on the ground, didn't you? We wouldn't have known what do without that. Plus, you can charm anyone with your sweetness," I told her, squeezing her tight.

Ellie's cheeks turned into tomatoes. "You really think so?"

Luke smiled at us. The first good, real smile I'd ever seen from him in my entire life. I could never have imagined smile creases at the corner of his eyes or at the edges of his mouth.

And for Katroia sake, Luke had dimples!

"Well," Ellie said, "we fell down here, do we have to get back up?"

"*No,*" boomed the voice of the Fortress. "*Didn't I tell you already? You gotta look left!*"

I blinked. "But didn't we miss the chance up there?"

"*No!*" the Fortress repeated. "*The engraving on the ground is different for everyone—you can't miss a chance!*"

"Soo . . . we were all meant to live?" Ellie guessed. "It only said that one would pass to unbearable heft, but maybe it didn't mean that one of us would die."

"*Incorrect,*" the Fortress boomed. "*One will die soon. And maybe more soon after. But no more help from me! The rest is up to you.*"

I clenched my fists. I had this sick feeling deep down that we were all going to die, but I wasn't ready to admit it. I was never going to admit it.

"Well, on that joyful note, what do you guys say we 'look left', see what happens, and get the heck out of here?"

The Fortress didn't respond after that.

"Sounds good, Kaila," Ellie agreed. "This doesn't make sense, but maybe we should just follow the directions?"

I shrugged. "Everyone, just look left and see if anything happens." It was worth a try. Everyone looked to the left wall.

"Nothing hap . . ." Luke began, but when he looked back to the right wall, he yelped in pain and covered his eyes. "Ow! What in Katroia . . ."

"Are you okay?" I asked. I was thinking of glancing over to see what was with the right wall that had hurt Luke's eyes. Fortunately, common sense won the decision. It was probably not the best idea.

"Ow," Luke repeated. "Do *not* look at the right wall."

"Okay," I said, "We're all looking left . . . Now what?"

Luke gazed back at the left wall. " Now we've gotta walk through the maze behind us and hope we don't step backwards into a bottomless pit."

Asher blinked. "Say *what?*"

"I caught a glimpse of a windy ledge coming up from a *really* deep pit. I've got no idea what's at the bottom, but I don't expect it's survivable." Luke held his hand over his eye again. "There's this searing, bright light on the left wall that . . . Ow."

Ellie arched a frown. "So, we've gotta walk backwards on some narrow ledge that drops off to a bottomless pit, and reach the other side blindly," she summed up.

"I think so," Luke sighed.

Man, this place is so *fun!*

CHAPTER 15

The Fortress' Idea of a Mirror Maze

There have been a whole lot of things I've felt stupid for doing. Fishing in the Pond of Lost Souls, pranking Will, the Forge Master, coming here to the Fallen Realm, etc... But *this*—walking backward onto a narrow, windy ledge that dropped off into death? This probably would top off my list, and that's saying a lot.

I wished I could just glitch over to the other side with everyone, but unfortunately, I couldn't do that on command. I would have to walk backward blindly, hoping my reflexes would stop me before I stepped backward off of an edge.

From the brick tube, I began walking backwards, expecting to hit a wall. Unfortunately, there was an opening and the narrow maze continued, as we followed it hundreds of feet in the air.

The bright side: at least we could look down at where we were stepping, as long as we didn't look too far behind us.

"Sweet!" I whooped, my voice echoing off the walls. "At least we can kind of see where we're going."

"Yeah, but we'll still have to be careful. The closer we get to the right wall, the more risky it gets to look down without catching a bit of that wall with the corner of your eye."

"Good call," Ellie acknowledged.

Luke was right. I ended up looking too far down more times than I'd like to admit, and I'd gotten to see just a bit of the wall, searing whatever part of my eyes caught the glimpse. Then, I would snap my head forward and take a step back, half of my foot off the edge. So far, I could easily step forward again, but every time I got too close to the edge, my adrenaline would kick in, making it even harder to balance. One mistake taken too far, and I'd plummet to my death. And the anxiety forming in my chest didn't help my balance.

The experience was terrifying, but eventually we made it to the end. The four of us backed right into a crimson brick room. I assumed that the wall behind us was safe to look at now that we had backed out of that room.

I checked first. Behind us, an eye-safe brick wall stood, one heavy-looking stone door lodged into it.

"Okay guys, it's safe to look right," I said. Everyone spun around as if looking back was a breath of fresh air.

Immediately, Ellie burst, "It's a trap."

I almost laughed. "Of course it is! Isn't everything here a trap?"

"I guess it's the only way, though," Asher said. "So, we've got two options: spend an hour contemplating the possibilities of the dangers behind that door—or just walk straight through without thinking, hoping for the best."

"I like Option One better," Ellie admitted.

Luke grinned. "I'm for Option Two."

"So am I," I agreed. "The longer you think about it, the worse it will get. I say we just walk in, and hope for the best."

Asher caught Luke's grin. "So, what do we say, Option Two?"

"Fine," Ellie sighed. "I guess we could go waste some bad guys."

***

Asher volunteered to creak open the door.

I saw no light escape the room, so it must be dark inside. Heck, everything in this cursed place was dark. I shouldn't have been surprised. Asher's blue eyes darted around, probably scanning for threats.

"It's just a decagon room with dim lighting around the perimeter of every side. It doesn't appear to be much of a threat right now, but its suspicion level is brimming." He glanced back in our direction. "It *is* the only way, so I guess we don't have a choice."

I didn't like it, but all four of us plunged into the room without objection. It was so obvious this place was a trap, I was starting to imagine words imprinted on the walls: *Omg, everyone's gonna fall for this one!*

When all four of us had entered the room, an unsettling silence hung in the air. None of us were able to keep still. It was just so obvious that something terrible was about to happen.

Jinx.

Suddenly, the dark walls flickered. I saw my reflection shudder through a new addition: mirrors. When I looked through them, I saw a bajilion dim copies of the four of us surrounding me. In every direction I looked, duplicates of us through the mirrors were *so* clear that I felt like I could reach right through each of them and touch our copies.

"Whoa," Ellie marveled in fear next to me. When I glanced down at her, I could almost believe she was fake like the other reflections of us. Just to make sure she really was with me, I patted her head.

"A mirror maze," Luke said. "We've gotta navigate this place somehow."

"Sure, but where to? We're just in a small decagonal room, right? Where's the end?" Asher said. He stepped forward to touch a few mirrors. Somehow, smear marks didn't appear on them. They remained crystal clear.

At one point, where there seemed to be a mirror, Asher's hand fell through behind a wall. "Cool," he grinned. "Stick together, guys. We could lose each other within seconds and never see each other again—other than through mirrors."

"Okay then, maybe you should come back before you lose us," I suggested.

Asher began striding toward us, his eyes locked certainly on our group. Then, he bumped into some kind of invisible wall and stared at it like he was going insane.

"Oh no," he whispered and turned around.

"Maybe this wasn't a good idea," Ellie said, and took a step back.

"Hey, don't let go of my hand. This place could be magical. We could lose each other even if we step a foot away." I reached back and grabbed her hand again, relieved to know she was still there. "Now, how do we get out of here?"

"That's what I asked," Asher said. His voice sounded like it had come from behind us.

"Well, how about we start with finding the real you?" I suggested and turned around to where the voice came from. "Keep talking."

Asher, who seemed to be excited about an excuse to blab off, began to rattle off random facts.

"Have you ever thought about the fact that horses practically run around on their fingernails? Or did you know that the northern leopard frog swallows its prey using its eyes? Or that the total area of Katroia is approximately eleven thousand, six hundred seventy-nine kilometers?" And so, on he rambled.

We bumped into more walls than I'd like to admit. Very rarely did we actually walk through a frame, only to bump into another on the other side. We found ourselves only walking further and further from Asher's voice. It was useless. Was he the one who was supposed to die at this point?

Stop it, I scolded myself. *Nobody's going to die.*

I thought again when I heard a deep grumbling echo off the mirrors. You've got to be kidding me. Trying to keep everyone together *and* figure out a way out of here was enough. You've just *got* to add another monster in here?

The lights dimmed even more. Everything in the mirrors were barely visible and lusterless.

Then, I heard the *clinking* and *clanging* of bones colliding. A tall grey skeleton warrior in Okopik-style armor (an early foreign region in Katroia) emerged from thin air right in front of us and raised a sword that seemed to be made of Falleotite.

I unsheathed *Falethropis* and held it up over Ellie as the skeleton charged. I used my chance and swung at its rib cage, hoping to turn a few of those twenty-four *costae* inside out.

My spirit-gold sword sent sparks flying off of the mirror in front of me. Somehow, a scratch in the reflection never appeared and it remained crystal-clear.

But *gosh,* that noise!

I spun around and held up my sword, closely scanning every copy of the skeleton. They all charged faster than I could keep track of. I tried my luck and swung *Falethropis* widely in front of me . . . But I forgot to cover the back.

I cringed at the sound of a mega rock scraping across metal.

It took my nerves a minute to calm down and realize that Ellie had covered my back. She had made contact with the real grey skeleton!

"There!" She swung again, but her sword crashed against a mirror. "Dang it!"

"This place is definitely magical," I said. "There is no way he backed a foot away from you and disappeared into the mirror maze."

"Agreed."

I spun around and scanned the mirrors. Dozens of reflections of the skeleton marched toward us.

"Ellie, get my back and I'll cover yours," I said. "We can fight this thing. Perhaps then we can get out of here alive."

Ellie swallowed nervously. "Okay."

The grey skeleton dragged toward us, its obsidian blade held upward like it had gotten its arm caught in a rototiller during its childhood and now it was stuck pointing forward.

I noticed at the last millisecond that the skeleton had emerged from a mirror on the right. I deflected its blade and tried for another whack, but more sparks only flew from the glass in front of us.

Ellie and I stood back-to-back, our swords held over our chests and our minds alert. This was all on our reflexes.

That was when I noticed something. Ellie and I stood together in the middle of the mirror maze. Asher was already lost. But, where was *Luke?* How could I forget about him?

I thought I had it the next time the skeleton charged. It was tricky on my reflexes, but I managed to clang my sword against his. Unfortunately, I underestimated the undead-creature. It twisted *Falethropis* right out of the way and jabbed me in the stomach so hard that black spots began to dance around in my vision.

"Wow . . . " I wheezed and dropped my sword. I hunched over so far that I fell on my side. "Ouch."

"Kaila!" Ellie gasped, and slid over to my side.

"Watch out!" I croaked just loud enough to trigger her reflexes. She swung her sword over her head and must've hit something because I heard a clang. Or maybe it was just from crashing into a mirror.

I felt like my insides were spilling out. Black goo oozed out of my stomach where I was stabbed. My nerves tore everything inside me apart without breaking a layer of skin. I could just imagine everything inside of me melting down and my body becoming a waterbed. Never mind. I refused to imagine that.

But *gosh* it hurt. The whole wound in my stomach throbbed like it had been stung by a million bees in one spot. I couldn't help but let out a pained wail.

Ellie began to cry too. "*Please* don't let it be you! Anyone but you! *Please, M*om, *please!* Do something crazy!"

The black skeleton again charged at us on a dozen mirrors, its bottom jaw hanging open and its sword leveled toward Ellie's head.

My brain reduced to mush. Ellie's scream was so muffled out in my head I wasn't motivated to save her. My eyes rolled back in my head.

"KAILA!" Ellie howled.

Sorry Ellie, I mouthed, which took the rest of the energy left in me.

Hannah Jock

CHAPTER 16

I Die

I was sure I was dead.

A black wave of hopelessness settled over me like an extremely uncomfortable blanket squeezing tighter and tighter around me, wringing out the last of my life.

Although, if I was dead, then why did everything *hurt* so much? I wouldn't think I would have a body with nerves that could produce pain. Yet, I felt like I was sinking in a pool of boiling water.

Just a test to make sure I really was in the Void: Did I feel alone? Lost? Hopeless? Depressed?

Check, check, check, and check.

I really was dead.

I wanted to cry, but I didn't have eyes to shed tears. At least I didn't have the throat to have to try and swallow a big bowling ball.

What kind of confused me was the fact that I could think even though I didn't have a brain. Perhaps your soul is what allows you to think, not your brain. Maybe not. My guess is that many of the laws of science don't apply in a video game.

I stopped thinking for a minute and just let my soul float around in the Void. What was I doing, just giving up here and accepting that I was dead? I wasn't supposed to be that girl that just accepts that there is no way out. I am the girl who doesn't care about how impossible something seems, and always finds a way out of it.

When Mom died, I didn't allow myself to accept her death. I'm still not going to accept her death. I'm going to get out of this place one way or another . . .

But has any other Katrin made it out of this abyss before? If it *were* possible to get out of here, I wouldn't be the first one to do it. I probably *was* stuck here forever. Apparently, once a Katrin is deleted from the game, they cannot be restored.

Oh come on, Kaila, whispered Mom's voice out of the darkness, *of course there's a way out!*

I had no body. No brain, no nerves, no substance, no nothing. But suddenly, I could feel uncontainable energy surging up through my spirit, in the form of a Katrin body.

A wave of bright summer colors crashed over me and snapped my soul back to my body. Just barely, I could spot a canopy of trees hanging over me. I was lying on the velvety grass, staring up into the leaves.

It will all make sense in the end, Mom cooed beside me. I turned my head so quickly I experienced whiplash.

Lying next to me was my gorgeous, ever-reassuring Mom. Her caramel brown hair fell over her shoulders; Her smile was brighter than the sun. She turned her head and stared those intense, electric-blue eyes into mine. And when Mom slipped her soft hand into mine, I lost it.

"Mom!" I wailed, and rolled over to hug her. Unfortunately,

her body dissolved just as I wrapped my arms around her, and the scene changed.

I stood in the Void again, except my soul was settled inside my own body. And yes, I literally *stood* in the Void. Not sure how, but my feet were on invisible solid ground.

A golden and white light swam in the darkness. *My spirit rages in here,* purred Mom's affectionate voice. *Even though it was, supposedly, impossible to escape the clutches of the Void, I found a way around eternal depression. I refused to let it take my soul, and with the consciousness I had left, I found a way into the system instead.*

Mom's spirit swirled around me. *In here I have the power to glitch the game. I watch your progress every second in this Void. I've tried my hardest to help you as you get closer to the Void, but Kaila, you must understand the visions I see while spending time here.*

The scene shifted again. I could see myself standing on a huge empty block floating off in the middle of a dark abyss. Ellie lay on the ground, her body seemingly electrocuted and beaten up. An enormous flying figure dove down and completely crushed her.

I tried to scream, but I was without a body again. I saw Luke get flung off the block and into the bottomless chasm yawning beneath him. I saw myself clinging to the edge, my face coated in soot. Then I let go and plummeted down into the nothingness of the Void. I saw Asher limping across the island, looking like a corpse. The veins on his neck had turned black, and they were slowly crawling up the sides of his face. I could tell something else terrible was about to happen to him as well.

"Mom!" I cried, pulling myself out of that future vision and back into the Void.

I'm sorry you had to see that Kaila, but I assure you that this journey leads to the loss of life. I love you for trying to save me, but the future I see isn't reassuring.

"Then, I'll change the future!" I demanded. "I swear, I'm going to get you back, save everyone from the Void, and nobody's going to stop me!"

Kaila, Mom's spirit tried, but her voice began to fade. *I love you,* were the last words I heard before I was sucked into one last vision.

I saw Ellie caterwauling my name and hugging me, and Luke and Asher trying to navigate the mirror maze to find her. The grey skeleton stood over her, making some kind of noise that sounded like a hive of bees in front of a fan. I soon realized that it was laughing.

My chest flooded black ooze. Ellie tried not to touch it, but her shirt was soaking in it as she was leaning over my dead body.

"I hope you like endless, depressing chasms," the skeleton jeered, "because you're about to spend eternity in one." The monster raised its obsidian sword, its laugh getting eerier as Ellie's wail got louder.

The vision slowly became more and more real to me. I could feel pain inside me crumbling away, like I was slowly beginning to wake up from a lucid nightmare. I fought to wake back up. Ellie was doing her best to try to revive me.

I moved a finger. My eyes were still closed, which meant my physical body was still unconscious, but my spirit was working into it. I needed to wake before my sister was killed.

The skeleton whizzed its sword down toward us.

But a blue ripple spread across my body even faster than the sword, and Ellie and I glitched to another place in the maze just before risk of being skewered.

Yeah, we *glitched.* Mom had been hacking glitches in the game during her spare time in the Void.

Ellie didn't seem to realize we were safe until I reached up my hand and stroked her head. It had taken my spirit a while to settle to the point where I could open my eyes.

"Kaila," Ellie sobbed again, as I completely returned to my senses. "How . . ."

"I'll explain later," I promised and wobbled to my feet, my spirit-gold sword firm and well-balanced in my hand as always. Black ooze dripped from my wound still, but the pain had left me. Right as I saw all twelve copies of bonehead trudging toward me, I charged at a random mirror on the left wall and crashed straight through it blindly. Turned out I had managed to skewer the monster clean through with *Falethropis*.

I wish I could read skeleton expressions—because this one would've been *priceless*. The monster's bones fell apart and crumbled to the floor, leaving a pile of dust at my feet.

CHAPTER 17

Welcome to the Edge

It took Ellie a while to stop crying. She hugged me for at least five minutes straight, sobbing into my arm like she'd done while we fell into the brick tube. Asher and Luke stood next to us. The mirrors had finally deactivated, leaving just the bland black walls lined with dim lights along the ceiling and floor. The room was no longer a decagon, but a long winding hallway.

Luke and Asher quickly navigated back to us and found me sitting on the ground with black ooze dripping from my stomach and Ellie exploding into tears. They immediately thought I was dying. They weren't wrong.

After I told them what had happened – all about the Void and the visions (I left out the part about the vision of us dying on the dark stone island), they were thoroughly flabbergasted.

"Who the *heck* is that mother of yours?" Asher marveled.

"She's awesome sauce," I answered with a proud grin.

The conversation went on like that as we bragged about how impressive Mom was.

Finally, we decided we should get back to navigating the rest of the hallway in hopes that something good was at the end.

So, with Ellie's hand in mine and Luke and Asher by our side, we trudged through the halls of the former maze. Nobody was dead—not for good at least. If we could twist the Way of the Fortress, maybe we could change the outcome of the future that I saw in that vision Mom had shown me.

Finally, we came across the end of the winding hallway and spotted a door. Like the last door we entered, we had no idea what was on the other side, but we decided it was the only way to get through the Fortress. Besides, this was where our prophesy ended, so we were probably nearing the end of this horrid place. Asher stopped before the door.

"Ladies," he smirked and swung the door open in the weirdest gentleman gesture possible.

Luke tried to stifle a laugh as he rolled his eyes and walked through the door, curtsying at Asher to tell him that he got the joke.

The four of us plunged into the room, bracing ourselves for an impossible horde of Rechicasts or something.

We found ourselves standing in a room where the walls were *literally* made of tree trunks. A couple dozen trees were growing up against each other so tight that they formed a circular room with a diameter of about twenty feet. Small branches and tropical flowers sprouted from some of the trunks, and ferns sprung up from the mossy floor. A long ray of sunlight beamed into the room from a small crack between two of the trees.

In the middle of the room, sat a two-foot-tall tree stump. All kinds of ferns and flowers grew along the base of the stump . . . in the second darkest realm in Katroia.

"Wow." Ellie made a crooked smile. "Either this is some kind of ploy or there's a glitch in this realm."

I shrugged. "I guess we're about to find out."

I stepped forward toward the tree trunk and looked on top of it. A deep hole dropped down into the middle of the stump. At the bottom of it, a thin green layer of leaves and grass covered my vision of whatever was on the other side.

"Guys, I'm going down," I decided.

"You're *what*?" Ellie shuddered. "No way!"

"Whoa, chill," I laughed. "I'm not just going to jump down, Ellie." I reached into my inventory and pulled out a long, thick rope. "I'm at least smart enough to bring a rope."

Ellie's shoulders relaxed. "Just be careful, Kaila."

I smiled and nodded at her. "Ya'll coming?"

It took us a minute to find a place to secure the rope. Eventually, we found a root that stuck out of the ground that we could wrap the rope around.

I went down first. As I stepped down the knots that were specifically tied to make room for our feet, I silently thanked Freya's sister, Heather, who had taught us survival skills when we were younger. A plain knot won't do for climbing a rope. You've gotta knot it wide enough for your foothold, which required a certain expertise.

When I made it to the layer of leaves, I hesitated. What if this *was* a trap? If it was, whoever made it was really good at making ploys appealing because it was enough to make me want to enter.

I ignored my instincts and let myself fall through the layer of leaves.

The first thing I noticed: Sunlight. Real, warming Overworld sunshine that pressed against my pale skin.

The second: The ground. I could smell the moist dirt under my feet and the oddly satisfying scent of fresh compost wafting through the air. As I looked around, I noticed I was standing smack-dab in the middle of the most gorgeous forest I've ever laid eyes on. The tallest oak trees I have ever seen in my life were scattered along the ground, all kinds of ferns and tendrils growing along their trunks. Roses, tulips, and daisies sprouted naturally from the ground, diffusing their scent throughout the wood. The air was slightly moist, but not muggy. It reminded me of the forest a few hours after rain. The air smelled fresh and clean—washed out.

Sunlight peeked through the leaves and shone beams down to the forest floor, projecting a camouflage pattern on the ground.

Wait, what?

Okay pause, rewind back a minute . . . maybe two. Yeah— right there. Hello? I was kind of *just* standing in the middle of a cold, dark hallway in the Fallen Realm. What was going on?

Ellie slid down next to me. Our rope plunked down from forty feet up, where the canopy hung over us. *That* was the layer of leaves we broke through.

"Wow, this a really appealing hologram," Ellie marveled.

"It's not a hologram," I decided, not knowing where it came from. "The sunlight is real here—I can feel it. And the only light possible in the Fallen Realm is one that is super harmful to your eyes." I scratched my head. "I'd like to say we're in the Overworld . . ." I looked up into the canopy, "But the trees at home aren't this high and these types of flowers don't grow so copiously in the wild. This place feels more . . . natural, in a way."

Ellie scrunched her nose. "You're right. So, where are we?"

"No idea."

Asher and Luke slid down next to us, their eyes immediately stretching wide.

"What . . ." Luke stammered. "Wait . . . where?"

Asher looked perplexed. "Wow, this has got to be . . ." he scratched his head. "Man, I already knew the Edge wasn't as eerie as the Fallen Realm, but this . . ."

"What?" I asked.

"Yeah, this isn't the Fallen Realm, I'm sure of that. And if the Way of the Fortress ends after you die . . . so, this is definitely the Edge."

I bit my lip. "But didn't we have to, like, find the materials to build a portal to the Edge with, then make the portal, *then* jump through it?"

Asher shrugged. "This has to be it, so, I guess not!"

A wave of relief crashed over me like a tidal wave, and suddenly I let out the nervous breath I had been holding the whole way through the Fallen Realm.

"So it's true," I exhaled. "It's over."

"Not exactly," Luke reminded us. "The worst is yet to come."

I decided not to let that change my mind about being content.

"But we can spend a day or two here for refreshment. You know, give your soul a break, chillax a day, eat, drink . . ."

Ellie's eyes began to relax. "That sounds great," she cooed.

"It does—" My voice broke. I wished we could spend these days with Mom. While we relaxed in the sunlight, she fought to stay conscious, to avoid drifting away into pure darkness and depression. "But not for too long, okay?" I was half saying that to Mom, who claimed she was always keeping an eye on me.

Ellie seemed to catch my sadness quickly, so I decided to change the subject.

"So, if we're going to chill here for a day or two, I guess we should find some stuff to make a settlement—or find a village."

"I say we look for a village," Ellie blurted. "I just want to see other people. I want to see something normal for once in, like, a decade."

I couldn't tell if she was being sarcastic or actually thought we were gone for a decade, because it definitely felt like it.

But now, it was over. We were stepping forward into a realm

of sunshine and nature and crisp, after-shower, spring days. The Fallen Realm was behind us—

But the Void was just a few days away.

***

I hadn't noticed how long we'd been walking until I tripped over a stone. Asher grabbed my hand a foot before my face collided with the dirt.

"You good?" he asked.

"Yeah, thanks." I had been daydreaming about the Void—breaking the rules without even knowing it. I had refreshed my memory on our break-in the day before. I hadn't noticed how much Luke looked like his father. I also made the mistake of recalling the five minutes when Mom had been sucked into the Tear. It took everything inside me to switch the subject without tearing up again.

We had probably been walking twenty minutes before I finally broke the silence.

"Why haven't we run into any monsters yet?" I asked out of nowhere.

Asher shrugged. "I guess this is a peaceful realm. Maybe monsters only attack at night like in the Overworld."

As we wandered into a field, I gazed up at the setting sun that painted the sky into infinite shades of red, orange, and magenta. I hadn't seen a magenta sunset in a while.

"Maybe we should settle here for the night," I sighed. "And maybe there aren't villages here in the Edge."

Ellie gazed at the sunset with sad eyes.

"Then where do the elves live?"

"Oh yeah, the elves," I remembered. I had almost forgotten about the race of the Edge. They were supposed to roam these forests all day, but where did they go to sleep every night? And why hadn't we seen any?

At the onset of the clearing, we decided to settle down for the night. Luke sat up against a nearby tree and watched the sunset fade into stars. Asher ripped grass out of the ground in a circle and dug dirt trenches around the circumference to create a fire pit. Ellie and I found some dry leaves and fallen branches from the woods to use as fire feeder.

With a fresh memory of fire-starting from Heather's training, Ellie stacked the sticks and branches over the leaves like a tipi and let Asher do the honors.

Ever since Asher told us he could summon fire, I'd never really seen it in action. Even in the mirror maze, he hadn't even summoned a handful while the lethal skeleton lurked among us. Maybe that was because he wasn't immune to fire ... But then what's the point of having the ability to summon it?

Asher knelt down next to the pile of natural flammables and extended his arm in its direction. He flinched as sparks flew from his hand, and soon erupted into a flame. It was only a handful of fire, but it was enough to light the pile and give us warmth.

When he extinguished his flame, he rubbed his hand against his jeans. "I usually wear special gloves that my dad gave me that protect my hands when I have to summon fire, but I forgot them at home. Stupid me."

"You're not stupid," I said. He didn't exactly respond to that, but just shrugged it off.

Everybody took out something to eat and began devouring it. I hadn't noticed how hungry I was until I took my first sip of beef stew. Suddenly, I was a wild animal gulping down soup like it was my first meal after hibernation.

When we were done, we slipped away our stuff and settled into our sleeping positions. Luke remained with his back against

Hannah Jock

his tree, staring out into the small clearing before us. Asher lay on his back and folded his hands under his head. Ellie curled up into my arms and I spooned her like a protective blanket.

Then out of nowhere, the sky erupted into a lightshow of colorful ribbons dancing across the dark veil of the night. They whisked playfully through the air like living creatures performing the final act of nature's talent show.

"Wow," Ellie gasped. Through her eyes, I could see the purple and electric blue veil of magic swarm across a backdrop of a million stars.

"I wish Mom were here," I whispered in a brittle voice. For some reason, I let myself let go of a few tears. I wasn't particularly sad about anything right now, but for the past few days, I had done an excellent job shoving my emotions down with the hope of getting Mom back.

The Fallen Realm hadn't helped. The whole place was so dark and eerie that it made my soul feel somewhat clogged and muggy. I felt so trapped in fear and anger that it took everything inside of me not to let it show on the outside—except that one time I got mad at Luke.

"Hey Luke," I piped over the crackling fire between us.

"Yeah?"

"I never apologized for what I said back in the Fallen Realm." I shifted my position with holding Ellie. "I take back everything I said."

Luke sighed. "You don't have to take it back, Kaila. It was all true. You don't even have to be sorry. You were right about everything. All I've ever been on this trip was a burden and I've been acting like I hate you."

"You're not a burden, Luke," Asher laughed. "May I remind you that you saved all of us from becoming splotches of guts at the bottom of that big fall?"

Luke gave Asher a perplexed expression. "You forgave me

so fast, man. I wiped out your whole family! And now, you're risking everything to save them because of something that *I* did! And yet, after I threaten to kill you too at the first meet, you manage to keep your cool and try to team up with me to get both of our families back."

Asher shrugged. "I guess I knew you would soften up and let me in."

"Yeah, but I wiped out your family, and then tried to kill you," Luke repeated. "How did you not just decide that I was a ruthless person and take me out for good?"

Asher sat in silence. It was almost like he was just now remembering what Luke had done and was questioning himself *why* he hadn't unleashed his wrath upon Luke.

"I don't know," he admitted, "but my intuition was just *screaming* to spare you and try to work with you."

There was another awkward silence. Nobody spoke after that. At least I had made my point. I *was* sorry for the things I'd said and just needed to make sure Luke knew it. But now, he slumped against his log again, with a look of guilt and embarrassment on his face.

Luke's heart was finally beginning to mend. During every conversation we'd had and every fight we'd conquered, his cold soul had begun to warm up more and more. Luke was definitely changing for the better.

Soon Ellie began to snore. Her body was warm against mine, and I started to use her as a warming pillow. The crackling fire beside me was adding weights to my eyelids. I began to picture Mom's smile and the forest we'd always meandered through.

It will all make sense in the end.

I began to realize how right Mom was. At the beginning, when she died, I was so confused, and lost, and ready to give up on life. And throughout this journey, things have been becoming more clear to me—our chances of rescuing Mom and the rest of the lost souls in the Void; Mom's power in the Void; the mystery behind Luke's past revealed . . . sure, things were getting harder and harder by the hour, but things *were* beginning to make a little more sense.

Sometimes, I would question our ability to succeed when I'd let my mind wander to the fact that so many had tried before and were unsuccessful. I'd have to stop those thoughts in their tracks and remind myself that the men who died on this path didn't have parents like ours. They couldn't *glitch*. Or summon *fire*. Or use *magic*.

We were going to make this trip, and nothing was going to stop us.

And with thoughts like that in my head, somewhere in that night I must've fallen asleep.

Because I woke up to Ellie's frantic gasp and her tight, desperate grip on my hand.

CHAPTER 18

We Are Backed Up

Monsters—a lot of them. Hundreds of dark, deformed shapes circling around us. Through the darkness that closed around us, I noticed green, warty skin and tattered purple clothes. They probably didn't wear shoes either, but I didn't want to get close enough to see.

It was still the middle of the night. More stars than I'd ever seen in my life were wiped across the sky, letting off just enough light for me to see around us. I immediately rolled to grab *Falethropis* and sprung to my feet.

"Asher," I called. "Luke."

Both moaned and rolled over, but when Asher opened an eye and saw the monsters circling us, he sprung off his hands and leapt to his feet. He lost his balance for a moment, probably from jumping up so fast after being dead asleep.

Luke rolled over to reach for his sword, but one of the monsters held it in its hands, examining it like he'd never seen a weapon like it before. Then it threw the opal weapon behind itself and grabbed a gnarly bat from a neighboring monster's hand.

"Hey! Don't throw that!" Luke barked, but then crossed his arms. "Guess I'll have to use something else then."

He placed his hands together, then drew them apart intimidatingly, causing golden dust to slowly accumulate between his hands.

Asher's swords were already on his back, but he didn't draw them.

"These are bohorts. Swords hurt them, but fire disintegrates them."

I grinned. "Good to have you on our side, Asher."

Ellie picked up her golden sword and pointed its edge toward the horde.

"There are so many of them," she wailed. "Too many of them."

"Impossible," Asher smirked. "There are never too many for us to handle."

I patted my sister's back. "It's okay," I lied. There were *definitely* too many of them. "Just stay close to me, okay?"

I could *hear* how hard it was for her to gulp down her fear, but Ellie nodded and shuffled closer to me.

One of the bohorts in the front, who was wearing thick silver armor, made a loud, ear-piercing snort and raised its sword in triumph—even though they hadn't won yet.

"Save it, wart nose," Asher snarled, letting loose tendrils of fire weaving around his fingers and dancing across his thumbs. Surprisingly, only a faint sign of fear was etched into his face— probably because he was being careful not to let the flames touch him.

"You don't know who you're dealing with."

Luke spread his arms out like he was presenting a work

of art. Golden dust gathered from his fingertips and wrapped down his arms.

I could already feel energy surging through my veins. I felt like some little kid who had just eaten five bowls of ice cream and was now longing to bounce around and break something, yet was expected to sit still. Except *I* didn't have to sit still.

I extended *Falethropis's* second edge, and immediately the army of bohorts began to advance toward us. They eyed us so readily that I began to rethink how this would end. But then Mom reminded me it wasn't going to end here, with an extra burst of energy.

***

I was first to lash out. I leapt so fast at the first bohort, my sword had trouble following me.

At the first swing, I disintegrated at least three monsters. I expected to hit more, but their armor was harder to get through than normal. One of the bohorts swung a long, meaty bone at me in a wide arc, which I ducked easily. From a squat, I jumped forward and stabbed the monster in the gut.

If it weren't for my extreme reflexes, I would have been smashed with another stone club, but Mom glitched her energy to me and I rolled out of the way avoiding serious injury.

I didn't know how I did it, but I sensed about three bohorts in a semi-circle behind me. With a split second of planning, I rolled backward onto my hands, sprung up with my feet in the air, and twisted my body around just in time for my feet to hit the ground. I could feel Mom's presence helping me with every move as I stabbed two more bohorts. Noticing the last one, which shook in its boots, I stabbed it clean through the chest— through the armor and all.

That was when I noticed fire—a lot of fire. I heard loud

bursts of flames from behind me, and everything in sight was bathed in an orange tinge. Through the glow of the fire, I could see Asher's shadow spinning around and throwing his arms out in different directions, detonating a frightening burst every time.

Luke was doing awesome, too. He swept his arms around, forming solidified balls of golden dust and hurling them at monsters repeatedly. He looked wicked exhausted, probably from using so much magic at once, but he didn't even stop to take a breather.

I threw myself at a few more monsters and wiped them clean from existence. I then smacked a few more with the side of my sword and stabbed another one. That was when I received my first blow.

I was hit from behind by an enraged ogre. I began to topple forward by the force, but I seemed alright. The tingle it left all over my back kind of felt *good,* as a matter of fact. I didn't know what that was all about.

I swung myself around so hard my sword flung out of my hands and pinned two bohorts to a tree at once.

Now that I had no weapon in my hands, seven bohorts charged at me, holding up their clubs in triumph. I sidestepped one of them, ducked under a swing, and dove forward to avoid a blow that would have crushed a bone or two.

While I was on the ground, two bohorts closed around me. I rolled out of the way of being skewered by some kind of gnarly spear and wrapped my legs around another. I then twisted my body, tripping over the monster I had clung my legs to.

I found a small opening in the direction of *Falethropis* in between two monsters. I took the opportunity and slid straight through the slim crack and out of the horde.

A bohort leapt in my way so fast only my unnatural reflexes

could have saved me. I glitched my whole body through the monster, ending up two feet in front of my spirit-gold sword.

I snatched back my sword from the tree it had pinned two bohorts to, leaving them to slump to the ground and vaporize. Then, I spun around with *Falethropis* back in my hand and gave all seven of the bohorts the stink eye.

"Well?" I prodded, making every single one of them flinch.

That group didn't take long. All I remembered was flying around, slashing and slicing through my adversaries. I may have glitched a few times in the process, but I wasn't sure. My body was in the state it was in back at the mineral cove—my reflexes took over as Mom's strength started to surge through me again.

When I had finished with the group, I took a breather as I scanned the battlefield again. I watched Asher fling fire around like it was a part of him. Luke fought at his backside, hurling golden disks at everything in sight.

If there were a score higher than an A+, I would have given it to them that day.

Ellie, however, wasn't doing so well. She tried her best to swing away at as many monsters as she could, but I could see the terror in her eyes. Her hands shook with every blow, and rarely did she have the strength to annihilate a bohort in one shot.

I rushed over to her side and nodded to her like, 'sup'. When I saw her smile, I rushed forward and single-handedly plowed over a half dozen bohorts.

I always blushed when my little sister looked at me like I was the most skilled fighter in Katroia. I put on my brave smile and gave Ellie a thumbs-up.

"You've got this, girl!" I encouraged.

Ellie's eyes reflected determination as she nodded back at me.

"Yeah," she agreed. "I've got this."

I felt a fraction of Mom's energy leave me as Ellie rushed

toward a nearby group of monsters, swinging her sword like I'd never seen her swing anything before.

I smiled at her. *Thanks for helping Ellie, Mom,* I said to her in my head.

I laughed and turned around to sweep up some more bad guys. I gotta admit, we were doing phenomenaalll. . .

Wow.

Through the huge horde of monsters we'd recently been fighting, I could see a hundred more shoving through. I thought we had wiped a majority of them clean, but I realized with a nauseating feeling that we'd only slaughtered about five percent of all of them.

When a bohort chose to target me with a club blow, I decided that if we were already trapped inside a horde of monsters, we had no choice but to waste every last one of them, no matter how long it took.

Oh well, we've got all day, why not wipe out some bohorts while we're at it?

I continued slashing my way across the battlefield at the edge of the small clearing. The crickets cheered in the background whenever I reduced a bohort to dust.

"Hey Kaila," Asher called from across the battlefield. He held up a fireball for me to see, pointed at my sword, and then redirected his finger towards a squad of bohorts. Hoping I got the message, he threw the fireball in my direction.

I instinctively held up *Falethropis,* and when the fireball hit the edge of my sword, I swung it as hard as I could toward a nearby group of monsters like a baseball bat. Turns out I wasn't so rusty.

The fireball passed through them swiftly, and once the small cloud of smoke it left behind cleared, all I saw in the monsters' place was an ashy pile of green dust.

Awesome! I crowed inside my head. I gave Asher the widest

grin I've ever given anyone and showed him a thumbs-up, which meant, *keep it coming!*

Asher looked satisfied with the new trick and kept pitching fire balls at me every minute or so. He would stop frequently and rub his arms, closing his eyes to regain himself after so much heat. How could he handle encasing himself in so much fire and not burn himself?

With every baseball hit, I felt more and more victorious. Mom was lending me so much strength now, I felt like I could explode and wipe out all five hundred of these losers in one blow. But of course, I had three friends inside of this horde that wouldn't like that so much.

I continued to perform some pretty unnatural fighting techniques, score some perfect fireball shots, and mentally hug Mom for the energy she was lending me. Never in my entire life had I felt so unstoppable—except maybe back at the mineral cove. But this time, I felt more like *myself.* Maybe more victorious, fighting so boldly alongside my four favorite people in Katroia—Asher, Luke, Ellie, and Mom, who was giving me strength from within.

And, somehow, things got a lot better.

"Elves! *Threpos Camillius!*" a new voice shouted from somewhere within the canopy. It sounded like a British-accented teen male shouting orders over an army. Apparently, he was.

Suddenly, a hundred figures in green clothes and golden armor leapt down from forty feet up in the canopy, each rolling to reduce fall damage, and coming up standing. More came sprinting across the clearing in our direction. They appeared to be in their late teens, dressed in woodsy clothes and heavy armor, each holding spears and shields.

Asher put his guard down and gave me a perplexed expression. Then we both shrugged and returned to battle.

Elves mixed in with the battle. I had to admit, they were

pretty good with spears. I've always thought swords to be the best weapons to use when you're in a crowd of zombies, but the incredible technique they used in spear fighting proved me wrong. Same for the shields. They barely used them to protect themselves. All they did with them was smack bohorts in the face and deflect attacks back where they came from.

I continued to slice through monsters with the edges of my sword, relying on Mom's impossible skill as I bulldozed over dozens at a time. Every once in a while, a few elves would stop and look at me like I was the Elemental Lady of Battle, which would always make me shrink back behind another crowd of bohorts.

I saw the way the elves looked at Luke, too. With the thick cloud of golden dust constantly swirling around him, he looked invincible in the way he bent the dust into solid golden spheres and chucked them everywhere.

But many of them tried to advance on Asher with their weapons ready. Clearly, he was a threat to them, but the immense explosion of fire all around him was making it impossible to get to him.

I hadn't noticed it before, but the way Asher fought actually *made* him look like a threat after all. Every time he spun around, I could see an unreadable expression in his face—pain, maybe anger, maybe concentration, or maybe just pride—I had no idea. Fire crept along the edges of his T-shirt, his jeans were singed black, and his brown boots looked neon-orange in the firelight.

Before I could tell the elves that he was a good guy, one of them found an entrance and sprung through the wall of flames.

"Asher, look out!" I cried, but he didn't have sharp enough reflexes to turn around in time. The swift female elf had already made it to the core of the firestorm and had stabbed him right in the ribs with her spear.

Asher wailed in agony and dropped to the ground, holding

his side where the girl had stabbed him. I forgot about the horde and sprinted toward him.

"What did you do?" I wailed and stared a hole through the elf's head. She gave me a confused look and glanced down at Asher, as if expecting him to turn into a pile of ashes.

"He's not a monster?" she asked, in a slightly British accent mixed with another accent I'd never heard before.

"*No,* he's not a monster! Does he look like one?" I snapped.

The girl gave me a twisted expression of embarrassment and pity. "I'm sorry."

Asher groaned and hugged his ribs. Fire was still dancing along the edges of his T-shirt. His face was smeared with soot and his hair looked like it had just come out of a clothes dryer. "That was my fireproof shirt," he moaned, covering his hand over the new puncture in his side like the shirt was the only thing that mattered.

I slid next to him. "Are you okay? Can I see?"

Asher moaned again, but he let me remove his hands from the stab and take a look.

When the elf who had skewered Asher saw the wound, she apologized again and jumped back into the fight, while I tried my best to examine it.

"How much does it hurt?"

"A lot," Asher said.

"Can you sit up?"

Asher rubbed a hand across his forehead, clearly in stress.

"I don't think so, but this fight has to end soon if I'm going to live."

I scanned the battlefield as quickly as I could.

"I think this can be over in a minute or two," I said. We had the bohorts completely outmatched. Now we just had to finish them off.

"Hey you," called the same male voice that had ordered

the elves to join the battle. He jogged into view in front of us. Unlike all the other elves, he wore a really large golden leaf tightly stitched together. He had a mop of course blond hair on his head, and a glistening golden circlet crowned his head. Just one glance at the intense look in his eyes and I knew he was some kind of leader.

"I know this looks like a rescue, but we need to get you guys back to our kingdom," the boy said. "My name is Zyler, and I am the lead elf of the Wikasai army."

I hadn't noticed that I was scowling.

"You didn't rescue us," was the first thing that left my mouth, and I already regretted it.

Zyler frowned at Asher.

"Sorry about him, but fire is a really big threat in this realm. We haven't seen fire in decades and when we spotted smoke, I was immediately commanded to send out my crew and annihilate whatever was causing it. He pointed his golden spear at Asher's chest. "Which is why we have to keep a *very* close eye on you, buddy."

"You have to heal him," I demanded. The guy was much older than me, and had way more power than me, but I totally forgot to be afraid when my friend needed help. "Please," I added.

I could tell Zyler didn't like it, but he grunted, "Fine, but we have to discuss what to do with him afterwards."

"What we *have* to do afterwards is find the portal to the Void," I told him. "That's why we even came here in the first place."

"Came here?" Zyler repeated, perplexed.

"Do we look like we live here? We just came from the Fallen Realm!" I retorted, immediately feeling guilt for how harsh I was being on this guy.

Zyler's brow furrowed. "You just came from the *Fallen Realm?*" he gasped, his voice now sounding angry. "And you plan to break into our sacred chamber, or the *Void?* Who do you think you are?"

"A daughter of Maya Kinsworth," I answered proudly.

Zyler's expression immediately softened. "Oh, I see," he whispered. "Who told you about the Void?"

"The Enchanted Library."

Zyler's expression twisted drastically. "How . . . hang on. We *must* pick up this conversation in the palace. Come."

Zyler reached down his hand, and I immediately felt bad for using the tone that I'd just used with him. The look in his eyes told me that he wasn't putting us in danger, so I took his hand and let him help me up. My heart fluttered for a second at first, until I mentally slapped myself in the face and told myself to cut it out.

Asher hugged his ribs with one hand and accepted Zyler's help with the other. As soon as he was on two feet, however, he leaned forward against Zyler's chest to keep his balance.

"Sorry," he wheezed. "I can't stand up alone."

"It's cool." Zyler reached into his inventory and grabbed a blue bubbling vial. "Drink this. It will get rid of the wound."

Asher took the vial and poured it down his throat. Almost immediately, his posture straightened and the wound in his ribs closed up. But he was still left with a slight hunch that he looked like he was trying to hide.

"Thanks," he said gratefully.

Zyler nodded at him, and then redirected his attention toward me.

"You ready to go?" he asked, and I realized the offer wasn't optional.

CHAPTER 19

We Are Offered a
Trust Exercise

The first thing I noticed after fifteen minutes of
trudging through the woods—tropical flowers. Dozens and
dozens of different shades and designs of tropical flowers that
were next to impossible to find in the Overworld. The next
thing I noticed—braided vines and trees, bamboo, birch logs,
and water—crystal clear, turquoise water that made me want to
jump in and float away forever.

As we emerged into a thinned-out section of the woods,
I noticed that the braided trees I thought I'd been seeing were
actually treehouses—*real* tree houses. I'm talking about braided
bark sprouting from the ground and growing so close together they
formed walls. The branches twined together tighter and tighter
until they reached a point at the top, where a massive bouquet of
mythical flowers and green vines hung over the house.

The other half of the houses were made of glazed birch logs
and stones. Each one was so well luminated, that every white

home seemed to be bioluminescent, giving off rays of golden light. Mixed with the sunrise fireflies, the place looked magical.

A packed dirt trail snaked between the houses and rode over hills like a roller coaster. Each house was surrounded with stunning gardens. And gosh, talk about the gardens! Who in Katroia even designed them? Turquoise glistening waterfalls flowed down the center of each one, pots of extraordinary plants hanging from shelves that surrounded them. Alluring, flowering willow trees bent over their rivers, leaving their vines to dip into the relaxing, trickling water. The rest of the garden was a complex cluster of colorful plants, only half of them even existing in the Overworld. The other half were simply too unbelievably striking to be found back where we lived.

Six crystal-clear rivers flowed through the village, each equally ataractic. Whoever fashioned the flow of these rivers showed off their creativity in making them. I admired how many different kinds of waterfalls rolled down the stream, each one somehow matching the gorgeous style of the whole village. Fruit trees sprung from the ground everywhere I looked, berry bushes freckled among them . . .

"Pretty cool, huh?" Zyler grinned beside me. I was speechless.

"Yeah, it's . . . absolutely incredible," I marveled. "The Overworld is nothing like this."

Zyler grinned. "We're proud of it." He kept leading us along a bit further. I squeezed Ellie's hand as she stared dumbfounded at the majestic elvin village. Luke and Asher seemed just as awestruck.

I have to admit, this is *nothing* like how I imagined elves to be. I thought they'd be short, stubby little creatures that spoke in Old English and had strict laws where they readily threw out the death penalty, and all.

"Hey, can I have your guys' names?" Zyler asked.

"Yeah. I'm Kaila and this is my little sister, Ellie." I pointed to my sister, and she blinked the glossiness out of her eyes.

"This is Luke, my . . . uh . . ."

"Brother," Luke finished, with a smile and a nudge at my ribs.

"And I'm Asher." Asher stuck his thumbs at his chest. "You can remember my name because it's related to fire."

Zyler's friendly smile vanished. "Sure."

The sun began to peek over the horizon, painting the scenery into an ombre of infinite colors—different colors from last night, but just as impressive. A thin mist rose from the ground all around us, making the whole elvin village look even more magical, which seemed impossible. Birds began to flutter in the air above us—vibrantly colored birds I'd never seen in my whole life. Not one of them was familiar. But they were beautiful.

When the birds began to tweet their morning songs, it took everything inside me not to begin sobbing. The tweets and whistles were so foreign to me, but they were the most beautiful sounds I've ever heard. I listened as the noises in the air came together to form a wild orchestra.

The melody was so beautiful this morning I felt like collapsing right here, right then, to fall back asleep to the lulling purr of the symphony. It reminded me so much of Mom I was tempted to cover my ears so I wouldn't cry in front of everyone.

I tried not to focus on the delightful band of tweets and chirps as we walked along the packed dirt road that wound through the village. All the gorgeous radiant homes that dotted the elvin village seemed to grow out from one huge main building in the center. Twelve main roads branched out from the center building, each branching off into smaller roads that led to each lustered home—kind of like our village, except a *lot* bigger and *way* more beautiful.

The middle building looked like a huge oakwood lodge

coated with log glaze an inch thick. The building was the size of a football field, containing so many complex dimensions, I couldn't imagine memorizing the way through all of the rooms.

It took me a minute to realize that we were headed straight for the immense lodge in the middle of the village—the one that was probably the most supreme.

I hated myself for being brave, but I forced my legs to keep walking forward.

"So, Sir Zyler, where are you taking us?" I asked.

"Please, just call me Zyler, and we're taking you to the Central Building of The Evelade County," Zyler informed us.

I gulped. "And what do you plan to do with us?"

"Hand you over to the Senators, and they'll decide that."

"What do you think they'll do?"

"Stop asking questions."

I tried to swallow down my fear, squeeze Ellie's hand again, and keep trudging down the glassy roads. But with every step closer to that central building, the more I wanted to run away like a gutless coward. Unfortunately, I was able to force myself to keep walking.

Finally, Zyler stopped before the huge oak log double doors that led inside. He wished us luck and pulled the doors wide open.

The place was five times more gorgeous than the alluring outside. The entire chamber we stood in was lined with braided branches with hundreds of vividly colored flowers sprouting from the cracks. The floor was so vast and empty, I wanted to belly slide across it all—and I would have, if it weren't for Zyler and the band of elves following us.

Ten yards ahead of us, a ring of six fire opal thrones loomed arrogantly before us, probably belonging to the leaders. Each throne radiated a dim light, which together provided the entire light source for the room. Except for the chandelier that hung over our heads . . . Gosh, that chandelier!

The most massive chandelier known to Katroia grinned pompously down at us. It held up a combination of uncountable precious stones that didn't even exist in the Overworld. The thing was ten times as tall as me and five times as wide. Even more jewels hung in the air thirty feet up—that's right, the jewels literally floated in the air on their own. This place was just so full of surprises.

Enthralling flower gardens lined the walls, each presenting a grand waterfall and dozens of different plant species I'd never known existed. For a video game, there was a remarkably wide variety of plants and animals.

From somewhere behind a wall came a gasp. A crystal door flung open, and an older-looking version of Zyler stepped into the immense room.

"Are these . . ." he began.

One of the elves behind us patted Asher's shoulder.

"This is the one who was causing all of the fire."

Zyler's look-alike frowned.

"A kid? How did he cause the fire?"

The elf behind us shrugged.

"It doesn't make much sense, but it seemed to be radiating off of him, Lord Randor."

The so called Randor's expression twisted into one I couldn't read.

"He was summoning it?"

"I guess so."

Randor narrowed his eyes toward Asher.

"Do you have any idea what a law breaker you are? We haven't seen fire in decades!"

Asher clenched his jaw, like he wanted to spit back a retort, but decided it wouldn't be helpful.

"And how in Katroia are you able to summon fire? That's impossible!" Randor shouted.

"He's more hospitable than most creatures we've seen on this trip," I muttered under my breath.

"I know," Asher agreed. Luke bumped his shoulder and raised his eyebrows, like, *not now, guys.*

Randor grunted. "So, what should we do with a fire summoner and his sidekicks?"

Asher stifled a laugh.

"They're not my sidekicks, trust me." He nudged my arm. "This one has superhuman reflexes and can teleport." He patted Luke on the shoulder. "This one's the son of The Enchanter."

A collective gasp echoed through the room. I had almost forgotten about the dozen elves that stood behind us.

"And I'm a son of Fore."

Another volley of stunned gasps.

"And, I've got nothing," Ellie muttered.

I nudged her arm. "Don't you *dare* say that."

"So, listen up, peeps. Either you let us through so we can find the portal to the Void, or you can try to execute us or something of the sort and we'll escape anyway and find the portal ourselves, probably breaking a few beautiful things in the process. Your call," Asher offered.

Randor's eyes darted between the four of us, his worry lines creasing deeper at every second. I could practically see inside his head that he was considering a whole lot of ways that we could be painfully executed. He knew it would be hard to contain us, but he was plotting how he'd do so.

And suddenly, the door swung open again, and five more elves filed into the room. Without a word, they each wandered to their specified thrones and took their seat.

Randor's train of thought was cut off when he noticed the rest of the senators. He grunted and strode back to his seat to settle down.

"You guys are dead," he noted before the official trial began.

One of the Senators on the right frowned.

"Is this the big threat?" She didn't sound disappointed or impressed, but completely focused and oriented.

"It sure is," Randor affirmed. His white cloak and pale skin stood out among all of the Senators. The rest of them wore blue togas with golden threads embroidered along the edges and hanging over their shoulders. He was obviously their leader— the King of the Evelade County perhaps.

"This kid is the son of Fore," Randor denounced, and pointed to Asher. Then he redirected his finger toward Luke, "And this one is the son of the Enchanter. The older girl has super-human reflexes and can 'teleport', as our friend, Asher, has described."

Another wave of angry gasps echoed the room.

"If he really is the son of *Fore,* then he is most definitely *not* our friend," one of the senators insisted, his cold stare beginning to singe off Asher's hairs.

"This is true," Another agreed. "He should definitely be exiled, or something."

Ellie frowned. "Who even *are* you guys?" she demanded. "We've just come out of the Fallen Realm, almost dying on every step—In fact, my sister *literally* died at one point . . ." Her voice broke. "But she was resurrected . . . and when we finally collapsed into the Edge, we walked for miles, attempting to find an elvin village to stay at. We fell asleep in the middle of nowhere, and woke up to a few hundred monsters threatening us in the middle of the night. And now, you guys drag us back here, tell us our existence is illegal, and order us to be exiled. Sorry, Mr. I-love-exiling-travelers-because-I-can, but we've got some families to save from an eerie afterlife. Now if you'll excuse us . . ."

"Ellie!" I shouted and shot her a look so murderous she went pale. "What the *heck* are you thinking?!"

All six senators froze so still I had to clear my throat just to make sure they weren't under some kind of spell or something.

Randor opened his mouth and lisped some gibberish. Then he went back to his frozen state and his eyes looked more focused than ever.

"Sorry," grunted one of the senators on the right end of the semi-circle. "I guess we were being a bit harsh."

My mouth fell open. Every second the senators were frozen, I was totally on alert for an abrupt attack. I'd never heard my little sister talk like that before.

"My name is Droik," said the same senator on the right. "The man seated next to me is named Telix."

What kinds of names are those?

"Down the line are Ritu, Mendrik, Urluis, Quantiz, and Pofris."

I was never good at memorizing names.

Senator Droik sighed.

"So, what do you guys think? The one called Ellie has made a good point. It is extremely unjust to find a bunch of teens who've just been through some pretty tough things and exile them just for using their abilities."

Randor grunted. "Well, we can't trust them! They've got a fire summoner on their side! Do you have any idea how incredibly perilous it would be to let them go?"

"This is also true," Droik considered. "But we can't punish them for using their abilities to defend themselves during battle."

"Yes, we can!" Randor blustered.

"Look, Mr. I-love-exiling-travelers-because-I-can, but there has to be another way. We all know we can't exile a bunch of teens for this," Droik reasoned.

All of the Senators except for Randor nodded slowly.

Senator Urluis stroked her chin. "I have an idea," she offered.

All of the Senators turned toward her, prodding her for continuance. Urluis hesitated a second before sharing her suggestion.

"The raids," was all she had to say.

There was a hum of agreement among the senate.

"Very considerable," Pofris whispered.

Telix straightened his posture. "This is indeed a very considerable suggestion. It offers a chance for trust and will benefit Evelade greatly." He nodded again.

"What?" Asher queried.

Telix turned toward him. "How do you guys feel about doing an investigation that involves a pinch of combat?"

***

"Listen up kids, and listen well," Randor announced after a lot of convincing that counting on us to 'save' the village was a good idea. "Our village has been under attack for the past two months. Every night, a horde of thousands of zombies shows up and threatens our poor citizens. As fast as we could, we whipped together an elvin army of two hundred hunters to defend the village every night . . ."

Asher whistled. "Did they sleep at all?"

Senator Ritu sighed. "It's been really tough the past few months, Asher. Nobody slept – not even the citizens, in their fear of being attacked while they were asleep. A lot of our elves sleep during the day twice a week or so."

Asher frowned. "Wow, man, that's really tough. Imagine not getting as much beauty sleep as you need—am I right, Luke?"

I gave Asher a *not now* glare, but Luke shrugged it off.

Senator Randor cleared his throat. "Anyway . . . All of us know that these hordes come from a specific source. The Edge is known for being generally peaceful; nightly attacks of thousands of zombies is *definitely* not normal here."

"So, I've heard a lot about your incredible combat. Not only from your mouth, but from plenty of other elves. Apparently, the four of you together are seriously unstoppable." Randor puffed up his chest. "So I, Randor Wrendol, offer to you a bargain. Tonight, you fight your way across Evelade and investigate the invasion to the core. The source of the nightly hordes must be terminated."

"And in return, we lead you to the entrance to the Void."

One...two...three seconds of silence.

"*SOLD!*" Asher crowed, pumping his fist. "Sure, why not kick some butt and rescue an elvin village? Why not take a free cruise to the *Void* and kick some more butt while we're at it?"

I let out the nervous breath I'd been holding the whole time we'd been inside this building.

"*Thank* you," I beamed, with a genuinely grateful smile. Ellie took the opportunity to wrap her arms around me.

"Ellie," I sighed, "I still can't believe you said what you did back there . . . but it got us here, so . . . thanks, I guess."

"Do I get to use my fire in combat?" Asher suggested with a smirk.

"No," all six senators blurted at once.

"All right, fine."

Walking in, I didn't think this moment would come, but with Ellie's hand in mine and Luke and Asher beside us in one piece, the four of us marched back outside with grins on our faces in the hope of seeing the Void tomorrow.

I almost laughed out loud when I let the sentence I'd just said in my head sink in:

Hooray! Looks like we've just earned ourselves a few free passes into guaranteed death!

CHAPTER 20

The Final Raid Begins

The elves' armory was *way* more upgraded than ours. Pretty much every weapon was made of pure crystal blades and golden hilts—and there were a *lot* of them. I'm talking about four, ten-yard-long walls liberally stocked with dangerous crystal weapons. Most of the elves grabbed a spear and trudged back to sit on a bench and talk to their friends.

The armory was *massive*. There was a large, square room packed with lethal weapons. On the right wall, a rather large doorway led into the lounge room where hunters—or elves—sat around and chatted before they were released into combat. The lounge was three times as massive as the weaponry. In this room, a ton of benches lined the walls and a small stage sat on the far end of the room, probably for when the huntmaster stepped out to release everyone into combat.

Ellie's spirits were the highest I'd seen them on this entire trip. The smile on her face lit up the entire room.

"You look in good spirits," I laughed, and nudged her with my elbow.

"Yeah, well, I've been waiting quite a while to legally join the hunt so . . ." Her cheeks turned rosy when another wide smile slipped across her lips. Cutest. Girl. Ever.

I couldn't resist smiling back at her.

"Well, welcome to the hunt!" I announced, spreading my arms with a grin.

Asher and Luke sat on a bench in the corner of the room, awkwardly chatting as if they'd never met. I was thinking about joining them to end the awkward mist that settled in that entire corner, but I figured they were getting to know each other. Their parents were mortal enemies, after all.

"Elves!" boomed a skin-crawling, gravelly voice from behind the stage of the lounge room. The burliest man I've ever laid eyes on stalked out of a wooden door beside the stage. His incredible set of muscles upon muscles almost looked unreal— but so was literally everything in this realm, so I wasn't so awestruck this time.

The guy wore black leather clothes and boots that looked so heavy, I doubt that I could walk two yards in them without doubling over in exhaustion. The beast was seven feet tall. Did elves even get that tall?

"Tonight, we have some special guests," the guy thundered. "In this room we've got four Katrins."

The room echoed with snickers.

"One of which is the son of The Enchanter."

A mood swing to a volley of gasps.

"Another has superhuman reflexes and can teleport."

More gasps.

"And one is the son of *Fore,* the source of *fire* in Katroia."

A few fainted.

All eyes turned toward the four of us. Everyone seemed

to realize that we stood out among the rest of the elves. Asher wriggled his eyebrows.

"Sup."

"So," the huntmaster continued, "these four kids have agreed to hunt down the source of these nightly raids and put a stop to it once and for all . . . and don't worry, Fore's son won't be producing a spark tonight . . ." He gave Asher the hairy eyeball.

"Kapeesh?"

"Kapeesh," Asher confirmed with a grin.

"Then that's it. Tonight, the raids end!"

I swear this crowd of two hundred hunters cheering could have been louder than a thousand. All of a sudden, I felt so appreciated as everyone around me showed me smiles wider than Evelade. I joined in the new mood swing as the huntmaster released us into the street-lit village for the final hunt of the Evelade Raids.

CHAPTER 21

We Kick Some Serious Butt

I **had almost forgotten about the lights.** The second I stepped out into the cool, crisp night of the Edge, I felt the presence of a sublime magnetic force overhead. The colors swirled across the dark veil shadowing the daylight, circling Evelade Village as if it were its own child.

Ellie seemed just as charmed, standing beside me with glazy eyes and an awestruck expression on her face. The grand natural lightshow of tonight selected different colors than last night— orange, green, magenta, and sky blue, mixed with other colors for ancillary effect.

"You guys ready to unleash our true butt-kickery skills?" I asked everyone, unsheathing *Falethropis*.

"Are you kidding?" Asher snorted. "I was born ready!"

"So was I!" Ellie cheered, as she drew her topaz sword.

And that was all the pep talk I needed. As soon as I realized that everyone was ready to wipe this village clean from zombies, I felt Mom's presence return. With Mom's ability to glitch her spirit to me at critical times, I felt fortified knowing she'd be with me in battle.

And after just a few more moments of grinning at each other, the four of us dispatched into the aroura-overhung night, daring any monster out there to step in our path and see what happens.

**

Green boiled-skinned, rotten-fleshed monsters dragged their limp bodies across the village's roads. Thin, purple torn clothes hung off of their chests and legs. Each one had one black eye and one red eye and green drool was constantly dribbling out of their mouths.

The two hundred elves selected for the hunt flung themselves around, desperately slicing zombies in half and rushing to find another. Through the windows of the homes, I could see families peeking downstairs at all the hunters working their butts off to keep them safe from the monsters—though they still seemed terrified that one of them would sneak past the hunters and drag into their homes.

"Over there!" Ellie called over the sound of our clattering feet on the Evelade dirt road. To our right, a squad of seven zombies lurked in the shadows of a birch log building.

The four of us flung ourselves at the group, our swords leveled at their heads. I skewered two zombies on my sword like a shish kabob. Asher, Ellie, and Luke had already taken care of the rest before the monsters on my sword even melted away.

"I'll get those," Luke offered, and began to charge at a group of four zombies, who were trying to hack open a door and attack the family inside. The father of the household was sneaking across the first floor to grab a frying pan.

"And I'll get those," Asher told me, and dashed off to pulverize six zombies that trudged through a garden.

"And I'll get these over here." Ellie plowed over a five-zombie patch that lingered through the streets.

I decided to begin investigating the horde. The zombies were all scattered around the village in groups, but they didn't seem to all be facing a certain way, which means it would be almost impossible to find their source.

Almost.

Maybe if we jogged around the village to find out where the hordes were most crowded, we could figure out where the zombies were coming from by following the thickness of the horde.

I hadn't noticed a group of eleven zombies crawling up behind me until Mom started to glitch in and I could feel her reflexes taking control as I swung blindly around, disintegrating five of them in the process. I silently thanked Mom and wasted the last six.

Luke and Asher jogged up from my right.

"Hey Kaila, got any ideas?" Asher asked.

"Yeah, actually, I think I've come up with a good method," I told them. "Where's Ellie?"

"Here," Ellie chirped from behind me as she bounced to my side, her sword sheathed. "So, what's up?"

I explained my theory as quickly as I could before more zombies interrupted me. I told them that if we followed the horde by the thickness, maybe we'd come across the source.

Asher, Ellie, and Luke quickly agreed.

So, the next ten minutes we spent jogging down streets and canals, bulldozing through batches of rotten flesh, and receiving looks of awe from other hunters.

So far, my theory was proving right. Every time we saw a bigger band of zombies, we mowed over them and found an even bigger group to chase after. We got so deep into the horde that everywhere we looked, zombies were dragging toward us, just yards away.

I sliced through three zombies at once and flipped over another two. It wasn't long before I found myself glitching through the hordes, melting away dozens every five seconds.

But there were just *so* many more to get rid of.

Finally, after I'd disintegrated a hundred zombies, I was struck in the back by a rotten fist. When I spun around to backfire, I noticed the zombie was wearing iron armor. That one took three hits to recede to green slime.

Again, if it weren't for Mom's reflexes, I would have been struck once more. Not knowing what was behind me, or when it would strike, I hit the deck and swept my sword on the ground behind me. Turns out I had knocked three armored zombies off their feet. I didn't even *know* zombies wore armor!

I sprang off my hands into a standing position and kept fighting.

As we slowly crept deeper into the horde, I noticed we were nearing the onset of Evelade. The forest loomed in front of us, where a ridiculous number of zombies fled into the village. I'm talking about *thousands* of zombies in one section of forest—almost too many for us to handle.

Almost.

"Come on!" I called to my friends and sister. "They're coming from the woods!"

Ellie froze. "No *way* I'm going in there," she muttered.

"We *have* to! It's where the zombies are coming from!"

Ellie shook her head. "Are you crazy? There are like five thousand of those things in there!" A zombie came up from behind her and raised its arms to attack her, but my sister blindly backflipped over it, stabbing it in the back when she landed.

I grinned. "Mom's in you too?"

Ellie's eyes turned intense. Zombies still swarmed around us. I could tell how much Ellie dreaded going inside of those woods.

Luke and Asher seemed hesitant as well, but the look in their eyes told me that they were willing to do anything to get to the Void.

I sighed. "Maybe I should just go in alone."

Asher erupted into flames. "WHAT!?"

I gasped. "Asher, watch it!"

Asher's ears went red, and he patted the flames off of the edges of his shirt.

"Sorry Kaila, but that's not going to happen."

"I'll glitch through."

"No."

I bit my lip. It *was* a pretty dumb idea. But for once, I doubted that even the four of us could plow through thousands of zombies. Back when we'd woken up with all of the ogres, there were only a few hundred of them and we'd had Asher's fire. I'm not sure we could have done that so easily without him. *This* was asking a lot.

"I won't be able to live with myself if I led you into something you ended up dying in . . ." I choked on those last words as I remembered that was something I'd actually done before.

"Not again," I added, reaching my limit of words before I started crying.

"Kaila . . ." Ellie whimpered.

"Please let me go. I can glitch through the whole thing and find the source," I pleaded like I actually wanted to do this. "It's the only way."

"Kaila, that's the stupidest thing I've ever heard anybody offer to do," Luke said. "You're gonna die, Kaila . . ." Those four words came out in a whimper. It wasn't until he lifted his eyes toward me when I noticed the new emotions in his voice:

Love.

Care.

Empathy.

All of which I never thought I'd see in Luke's eyes—especially toward me.

I rushed forward and wrapped Luke into a tight hug.

"I'll be okay," I promised, as I felt Ellie join the hug.

And then, without further confirmation, I called on Mom's power to take me away into a glitch.

'Okay my Kaila Bear,' I could hear Mom say, *'Now let's kick some serious butt, shall we?'*

***

As soon as my body materialized, I felt the glare of a hundred zombies upon me. Again, if it weren't for Mom's reflexes, I would have already been a shish kabob by now.

I slid across the rocky ground, slicing multiple monsters in the process, just to give them my signature before springing into the air and glitching further into the horde mid-jump.

As soon as I materialized again, I only saw a blur of green and purple before I glitched away again.

The next time I landed, a sudden wave of exhaustion settled over me like darkness over a plain. The zombies took their chance to take a swing at my head. For the moment Mom's reflexes left me, I was too exhausted to fend off the attack. I openly received a blow to the temple, inflaming my entire nervous system.

Be right back, sorry Kaila, Mom wheezed in my mind. Glitching seemed to take a lot out of her.

I unsheathed *Falethropis* and raised up on wobbly feet. The first zombie I swung at was the one who'd struck me. That only made my new headache worse.

I twirled myself around as fast as I could, my sword colliding with half a dozen zombies in the process. When another zombie swung its arm in my direction, I held up my sword to block the attack instead of attacking. This cost me greatly.

A zombie from behind shoved me so hard I contemplated whether or not it was really a zombie, or something else. Then I hit the ground. The same temple that had taken a hit from another zombie collided with a stone on the earth. I fought the urge to wail in pain as everything went black.

I would have passed out if I hadn't been kicked in the gut by another undead limb. It took almost everything inside me to roll over to my feet instead of curling up into a ball and crying. Black spots danced around in my vision at first, but I tried to shake it off and keep defending myself while Mom was on vacation.

Okay Mom! I urged. *Last jump!*

My body erupted into blue and purple shadows, and Mom's glitch took me away on one last trip.

This time, I ended up sitting among broad branches in an oak tree twenty feet above the ground. As soon as I got the chance, I closed my eyes and let my head rest against a branch behind me.

"I'm nothing without you, Mom," I whispered. "You saw what happened when you left me."

Don't even start, Kaila. Sure, you have superhuman *abilities when I'm with you, but you were still a legend on your own.*

I sighed. "Yeah sure. Thanks, Mom." When I noticed the sarcasm in my voice, I added, "Love you."

Love you too, Kaila Bear. Now I might need a few minutes before we jump down there and finish this off, Mom panted inside my head. *You need to be at max energy for this part.*

My face stretched into a wide grin. "Okay. I guess I need a break as well," I admitted. "I miss you."

Mom didn't seem to have the energy to reply to that, but I knew if she did, she would tell me, *"I miss you too, Kaila Bear."*

It was still the middle of the night. The arouras swirled in the sky overhead, attempting to lull me to sleep. I wanted to listen to them so badly.

I wondered what Ellie, Asher, and Luke were doing right now. Maybe they had abandoned the thick horde of zombies and were waiting on top of a building for me or something. Maybe they were fighting for their lives, clinging to the hope that I would end the raid so that they could just get the night over with and accept the free pass to the Void.

Okay, Kaila. You ready, girl? Mom urged.

Already? I transmitted back.

Why wait?

A smile tugged at the corner of my mouth as I unsheathed *Falethropis* and rose to my feet. When I glanced over the edge of the branch I stood on, I saw thousands of zombies shoving past each other to get into Evelade. But for some reason, I didn't feel even a speck of fear. And I wasn't surprised. I had Maya Kinsworth on my side.

In the center of the thickest part of the horde, a tall golden structure sprung from the ground. I watched as it mesmerizingly pulsed over and over again, radiating a green light every time, and spawning a dozen zombies with each flash. That's a *lot* of zombies.

I held up *Falethropis* and straightened my spine. My plan was not at all well thought out, but this isn't where the vision that Mom had shown me predicted I would die, so I decided it couldn't be so bad.

I held my breath and told Mom I loved her, over and over again. Then, I apologized to Ellie and Asher and Luke in advance, in case I got really hurt. Everything inside of me screamed *ARE YOU INSANE!?* But I ignored my brain and jumped off the oak branch, my sword facing down at the golden monster-spawner.

As soon as the tip of my sword touched the golden spawner, I felt a gravitational shift. An immense globe of light expanded a hundred feet in every direction, swallowing me in blinding light. Then, the impact of a bajillion volcanoes erupting at once bathed everything in bright orange and incinerated every atom within those hundred feet . . .

Including me.

The last thing I remembered was my ragdoll body shooting up . . . up . . . up . . . then, floating a second in the air, then, down . . . down . . . down . . .

At the sound of my violent screaming, my vision went black, and everything shut down.

CHAPTER 22

I Find My Way Home

*C*lean running water. Cool, crystal clear H2O trickling down a stream along with small pebbles clattering down with it.

Suddenly, nothing in the world mattered more. I needed to get to that stream.

Without knowing how badly I was hurt or how long I'd been out, I dragged myself along the ground toward the sound of water. My eyes refused to open; I had no idea where I was. I knew I had a mission and friends waiting for me, but I had no idea what and who. All I knew was that I needed *water*.

Then I found it. After a few yards of crawling, my hand dipped into a running stream—not a deep stream, but a stream with enough water to quench my thirst.

I didn't mind being unceremonious as I dipped my face in the water. I couldn't waste the time of using my hands to sip from. I dipped my whole face in the stream and filled my mouth with so much cold, refreshing water I almost couldn't swallow it without choking. I kept consuming mouthfuls.

The water brought me enough consciousness to clear the thick haze in my head. I remembered a smiling, blonde, eleven-year old girl . . . my sister. And a boy my age with small dimples when he smiled . . . my . . .brother? Best friend? I didn't know at this point. There was another boy my age. He liked fire . . .

That was when it hit me.

"Mother!" I cried, my voice seeming to work again. "How long have I been out? How far am I from Evelade? Where's my sister?"

My mother didn't respond.

I suddenly remembered everything—my mother's death, the quest, the Fallen Realm...

I cringed at every thought I replayed in my head. This journey had been dreadful and dark . . .

I remembered myself being blown up by some kind of spawner . . .

Gosh, Evelade was lucky the spawner wasn't within a hundred feet of their village. It was close, but they were out of range.

My stomach rumbled. Now I was *famished.*

I moaned at the struggle of rolling to my feet. Just one look at the woods around me, and I suspected it was probably one in the morning. The sun wasn't high in the sky and morning mist hung in the air throughout the forest.

I asked myself the question again. "Have I been out the whole rest of the night *and* an hour into the morning?"

I suspected that Mom had used everything inside her to shield me from the explosion and keep me alive, breaking our communication for a while in the process. *It's okay, Mom,* I told her in case she was still able to watch me. *Thanks for saving my life.*

I set aside my hunger for a minute and searched for a good

tree to climb. Maybe I would be able to see Evelade from here, thanks to how tall the buildings were.

Finally, I spotted a tall oak—not the one I'd climbed during the raid, but a taller, more branchy one. I immediately jogged toward it and leapt up the branches as fast as I could.

Hallelujah! I could *see* Evelade Village from here! It was probably going to be a fifteen-minute walk to get there, but my friends were waiting for my return, probably scared out of their minds. They had seen the explosion the night before, no doubt about it. They probably thought I was dying out here.

I leapt out of the tree and began jogging on my way. I hated every second I spent out there while my friends were probably freaking out over whether or not I was dead.

"Too much water," I muttered. "Too much running." I hugged the cramp in my stomach and continued to limp back to Evelade.

It felt like seven hours before I finally managed to drag myself back to the village. I wasn't sure exactly which side I had popped up on, but all I knew was that I had to find the central building, which was easily in the middle of the village.

The cramp had left me a few minutes after I began walking down the roads. I had obviously popped up on the opposite side of Evelade than I'd explored, because I didn't recognize anything. Even after ten minutes straight of walking, the central building never came into sight.

I spotted an elf on my way. He wore a blue toga over a long-sleeved black shirt. He looked at me like I had eleven eyes and tried to act natural as he scurried back along.

"Hey," I called to the elf, who flinched at my voice. "Excuse me?"

The elf turned around.

"Yeah?"

"Can you help me real quick? I need to find the central building."

The elf's expression turned perplexed. "I'm sorry?"

"The central building. Where all of the senators are?"

The elf was confused.

"Uhh, what do you mean?"

My heart skipped a beat.

"There isn't . . . a central building?" I asked nervously. "No senators?"

"I have no idea what you're talking about."

"Are we in Evelade?"

"No."

My heart did a triple backflip and landed on its face. My vision pulsed black for a moment and I almost lost my balance.

"You okay?" Another elf with a gruff voice asked behind me when I noticed I'd used his chest to stabilize myself.

"I'm sorry . . . I just . . . thought I was in Evelade." I blushed and walked away, chanting in my head, *I'm lost; I'm lost; I'm lost.*

"Do you need help?" The gruff elf asked. "Are you lost?"

I rubbed my temples. "Yes. Sorry, I was blown up in some kind of explosion trying to stop some raids and ended up in a whole other village."

"Raids?" the elf asked.

"Never mind. Is there a way you can get me into Evelade? Do you know where it is?"

The elf remained speechless. "Yeah, I think Evelade is on the other side of the forest. I can get you there if you'd like . . . I'm Jasper by the way. You?"

"Kaila."

"Cool—is this what elves from Evelade wear?" Jasper asked, examining my Overworld clothes.

"Oh—no. I'm from the Overworld."

Jasper looked surprised. "Really? Isn't that impossible?"

"I came through the Fallen Realm to get here."

Jasper's eyebrows shot up. Then he reexamined me like he was second thinking helping me home.

"O—okay then. If you go straight that way into the woods, you should pop out on the other side in Evelade," he directed abruptly.

"Huh," I snorted. "Okay, thanks, Jasper."

I spun around and took off into the woods. When I looked over my shoulder, he was blushing and running his hands through his hair nervously, as if he was thinking, *dang it, I blew it.*

Another half an hour of jogging through the woods. The whole time, I kept my fingers crossed, hoping Jasper gave me the correct directions as I ran. I couldn't stand the thought of Ellie crying over me again. No water cramps this time. It was probably two by now, and I'd fully recovered from my *hours* of being unconscious.

Still, my stomach screamed for food as I ran through the woods, promising myself that I'd fill up as soon as I got to Ellie, Asher, and Luke.

I'm not sure how I did it, but I eventually managed to pop out on the other side to the woods and into Evelade. The *real* one this time, because I immediately spotted the central building.

I didn't stop running until I met the double doors of the building. I couldn't resist leaning against the doors and stopping for a breath before taking the handles and swinging open the door.

I saw a crowd of elves inside the building—the six senators, a large group of elves, Ellie, Luke, and Asher. The senators all sat in their seats while my two friends and sister stood at the edge of the stage. Ellie's eyes were red and puffy. Luke and Asher looked completely drained and miserable.

Senator Droik apparently had been speaking because he stood in front of his throne with his head dipped low.

"But sadly, it cost the life of Kaila Kinsworth."

The crowd of elves murmured sadly.

That's when it hit me—I stood in the doorway of some kind of ceremony declaring the end of the raids—the morning after what they thought was my death? Seriously?

Well, I guess that explosion was pretty convincing of the end of the raids, and the senators realized that Ellie, Asher, and Luke needed to leave for the Void *now*.

"She died a hero, that's for sure. She aimed to rescue the Void with her companions . . ." he sighed, "but because of our lack of trust, she died to save our village instead. And for that, we are thankful."

Ellie lifted her head and caught a glimpse of me. She let out a shriek that cut through the room and caused everyone to pause to see what the clamor was about. My sister flew from her seat and sprinted across the room faster than I'd ever seen her run before. Her footsteps echoed the central building with every step, and when she was a yard away, she dove to strangle me with a hug so tight I couldn't breathe—but I was okay with it in this circumstance, because I felt like doing the same.

I'd felt plenty of insecurity as I ran back and forth through the woods and along the roads of another village. Now, with Ellie in my arms, every trace of pressure left me. I was safe now. Then, Luke clobbered me so hard I almost fell over.

"Kaila, what were you *thinking?*" His voice was so raspy I was worried for his health.

"I'm so sorry, guys. When I woke up in the woods after being exploded, I walked into another village on the other side of the forest from Evelade, then met some guy who said I was miles away from Evelade, then I started to run back across the forest . . ." I effused.

"We all thought you were *dead!*" Ellie cried.

"That explains the funeral . . ."

"It's not a funeral," Droik noted from his throne.

Kaila, you've been gone for *four* days!" Ellie bewailed. "FOUR DAYS! Do you have any idea what that put me through?"

My vision struggled to stay vivid.

"Wait, what? I thought I had just been out the rest of the night . . ."

"No, you weren't!" Ellie said.

Asher joined the hug.

"I'm . . . so sorry, guys . . ."

"And Mom . . . She's been *waiting* in the Void for so long now . . ."

"I'm sorry!"

"Kaila, you keep brushing *way* too close to death! I'm losing too much of my mind before we even see the Void!"

I could tell Ellie had more on her tongue, but she just totally lost it and collapsed into tears at my feet.

"Oh Ellie, I don't know how to apologize about this." I dropped next to my sister and hugged her almost as tight as she'd hugged me when she first saw me.

Poor girl just lost her mom, which was bad enough, and was clinging to her older sister to hold on to her sanity. Then her sister dies, leaving her alone in the middle of the Edge, to attempt saving them both by fighting a crazy powerful dragon in the Void.

I let out all the tears that were stored inside my eyes as I embraced my sister.

Senator Droik blinked.

"Okay then, scratch the last few sentences I just said. So, hooray! Evelade has been rescued from the raids, and all four warriors survived!"

The crowd of elves clapped cheerfully and eventually began

to file out. That was when I noticed how much of a scene we'd just caused. Half of me was fine with it, though. Half of me didn't care, as long as Ellie and my friends knew I was alive.

After everyone left and the central building was empty, Ellie and I still sat together, sharing tears while Luke and Asher tried to comfort us. Luke seemed really worked up about this, but not as bad as Ellie.

"Kaila, I can't believe what you've been through," Luke said. "You glitched away into the forest full of thousands of zombies without our full permission. Then you get exploded by a monster spawner, decide to pass out for four days, wake up next to another village, find your way back to Evelade, and now here you are, looking like a corpse yourself. Do you, like, want some food or something? How did you survive four days without water?"

"I barely did," I muttered. "And, yes, I would definitely appreciate some food."

"On it." Asher rushed away and flew behind a door in the back of the central room.

"The senators showed him around, if you're wondering how he knows where the food is," Luke noted.

"Hey kids," Senator Ritu chirped as she slid through the double doors. "How are you guys doing?"

I hoped my face wasn't as red as it felt when I muttered, "Uh, we're doing fine. Thanks."

Ritu smiled. "Okay, you guys still in for the Void? We've got the portal right underground. Do you want to stay another night, or would you like to leave straight away?"

Ellie looked up at me. "Mom," she whispered.

"Mom used a lot of her energy saving my life during the explosion. Our communication is broken up for now, which means I probably won't have enough of Mom's power to use her reflexes and glitch," I told Ellie.

"But she's been in the Void for so long . . ."

"Yes, but she's not in the same state that most people are in during their time in the Void. She's watching us the whole time. She told me herself."

Ellie bit her lip. "Oh, yeah. That vision."

"And plus, I know she wants to be able to help me in the final battle of the Void," I added.

Ellie suddenly became very interested in the ground.

"Yeah, okay." Then she remained silent for the next few seconds.

"So would you guys like to stay here overnight?" Ritu asked cordially.

I nodded. "Thank you so much."

***

As Senator Ritu led us down the roads of Evelade, I decided it was the right time to ask the question I'd been waiting to ask for a while.

"So, what was the meeting about?" I asked, remembering the feeling when I'd walked in that I was watching my own funeral filled with a hundred elves I didn't know.

"It was a ceremony declaring that the nightly raids were officially over. It's kind of a big deal, you know, to experience lethal raids every night for months—in a rather peaceful realm," Ellie explained. "You just happened to walk in right when they informed everyone what it cost . . ." She choked on her own words.

I draped my arm around my sister's shoulders. "It's okay. I'm here now."

Ellie shuddered, probably from replaying the past four days as she'd waited for my return.

"I know, but . . . It was just really scary for me, that's all."

"I know," I consoled. "I'm so sorry, Ellie."

"And us," Luke chimed in, walking up next to me with Asher at his side. Those boys were getting along way better than I'd thought they would. They were like, best buddies now.

"Yeah, and you. I'm sorry."

"Hey kids," Senator Ritu tweeted over her shoulder. "We're here." She extended her arm towards an Overworld-sized house made of twisted branches, like every other house in this realm. Vines sprouted from the ceiling and covered the view of the entire second floor, but the first was completely exposed.

"This is your hotel house for the night. Make yourselves at home," Ritu said before squeezing our shoulders to signal us it was okay to enter.

We thanked the hospitable senator and meandered inside our new overnight 'hotel house.'

CHAPTER 23

We Prepare for the Void

The house was, hands down, the most beautiful building I'd ever seen—and that's saying a lot, considering being in the 'realm of beautiful buildings'.

The floor was made of soft, beachy birch tiles that were slippery under my feet. The walls were lined with gardens that were covered with unidentifiable species of plants, each plant was unique from ones that I'd ever seen—even the ones in the central building. Complex waterfalls were stacked at the ends of the gardens, a thin layer of water tracing down the crystal structure.

An amber chandelier hung from the ceiling, filtering the light that shone through the glass windows, and projecting tiny rainbows around the room.

A marble counter carved the corner of the room, stacked with rare fruits and soup bowls. Ingredients upon ingredients were neatly organized in the corner. There were exactly two hundred different kinds of foods and ingredients in

Elvelade—and I think this counter showed at least one-eighth of them.

Three velvet-lined fabric couches formed a semi-circle in the center of the room, a plain, milky-white carpet filling the gap in between them. An opal round table with three crisscrossed golden legs stood in the middle of the carpet. Even more plant pots sprouting bamboo and mini tropical trees were set up around the couch area. In the Overworld, exactly thirty-five plant species existed. I'm pretty sure the Edge has fifteen times more. Whoever created this game must've spent eighteen hours of their day working on it and updating it. 'Cause they went overboard.

"Wow," Ellie marveled. "This is . . ."

"This is where we're supposed to stay overnight?" I gawked. "We're unworthy."

The next ten minutes went on like that.

Finally, we got used to our good fortune and took a look upstairs, which was even better. Two huge velvety beds with white and tan covers sat in the corners next to marble nightstands with soft orange lamps. The whole floor was blanketed with a silky light tan carpet. The air was diffused with a sweet flowery scent that made me want to collapse right on the floor and fall asleep.

Ellie sprawled onto one of the beds, practically hugging it. "I'm going to fall asleep so fast tonight . . ." she began, but immediately curled up into a ball and passed out.

I found a window split in the braided vines and meandered over to it, spotting a painting of sunset colors.

"I guess we can get some sleep early," I said, yawning. "Big day tomorrow."

Asher caught my yawn and strode to the other bed, but before settling down on it, he froze, doing the math in his head.

"Yeah, you might have to sleep in the same bed as the son of The Enchanter," I laughed. "Sweet dreams."

Luke frowned. "As long as I get to sleep . . ." He face-planted on the mattress and barely managed to drag the rest of his body on top of it and tuck himself in before he was out cold. Asher shrugged and did the same.

I couldn't believe my eyes. Fore and The Enchanter were *programmed* to be enemies—but their sons had sleepovers.

My eyelids suddenly felt like concrete, and the bed like a magnet.

I slid under the velvety covers of the memory-foam mattress, tucked Ellie in, who had fallen asleep on top of the covers, and closed my eyes. With all that was on my mind, I didn't think I'd ever be able to sleep. Heck, I'd been sleeping for the past *four* days. But with all the running through the woods and walking down roads I'd done in the few hours I'd been awake, mixed with the lulling scent of the sweet flowers in the air, I found myself snoring within seconds.

***

The one downside of sleeping in the Edge: you can't sleep in until one in the morning. The light seeping through the windows was so *bright* that I woke up right at the crack of dawn. Ellie, Luke, and Asher, however, probably hadn't slept in days, so they remained sound asleep.

I stared at the ceiling, my mind blank for two or three minutes before I decided I was boring myself to death and eating would be more enjoyable. As carefully as I could, I picked off my covers and slid off of the bed. I made a few errors and rocked Ellie a few times, but she didn't budge.

As I was tiptoeing toward the stairs to the first floor, I caught a glimpse of Luke and Asher—snuggling. I had to hold my hand over my lips to prevent a giggle from slipping out. They were so stinking cute, the way they cuddled up against each other like they were little twins. *Aww . . .*

I crept downstairs to inspect the huge pantry provided for us on the marble counter. A huge opportunity to throw together a delicious breakfast for everyone sat right in front of me.

I used flint and steel that I found tucked somewhere deep into my inventory to set a fire under a granite cooking bowl that stood at the edge of the kitchen. It was the most fun I'd had in days, pouring water into the bowl and throwing in a bunch of veggies and spices that you'd never find in the Overworld. I had no idea what I was doing, tasting everything, deciding whether it would taste good with everything else and throwing it in, hoping for the best. Every once in a while, I would taste my soup and make sure it tasted breakfasty. So far, it was okay.

"Kaila?" A sweet, lethargic voice yawned from upstairs. My sister, her hair a nest, yet still looking beautiful, strode down the stairs, a white sheet still draped around her shoulders.

"Good morning, Ellie," I smiled up from my soup, earning a small twist at the corner of Ellie's mouth.

"Good morning." Ellie rubbed her eyes. "What's cooking?"

I shrugged. "No idea, but it tastes breakfasty. Want to try some?"

Ellie smiled and slid next to me. "Sure!"

I handed my sister a wooden ladle and she gladly scooped up some soup and held it up to her mouth. Even before she got a taste, she hummed in delight.

"It smells like heaven."

She tilted the ladle to her lips and took a sip of the breakfast soup. Ellie gasped as she withdrew the ladle and wiped her mouth.

"Wow Kaila," she beamed. "That's *great.*"

"Thanks!"

Luke walked down the stairs next.

"Morning," he greeted.

Asher came down right after him. For some reason, his face was a bit pale, and he hunched slightly as he walked down the stairs. Maybe that was just his morning state.

"Hey guys, get your breakfast while it's hot!" I sang, cracking some salt into the soup.

"Ooh, Chef Kaila's on a roll," Asher noted as he leaned over the cooking pot, which was filled with soft veggies, broth, corned beef, cabbage, and a bunch of other spices.

"It's super good," Ellie assured him and grabbed him a bowl. "Here, try some."

Asher, Luke, Ellie and I took turns ladling food into our bowls. If it were a normal day, I probably would've whipped together some pancakes for everyone, but today, we needed to be filled up with good protein. In maybe an hour from now, we were going to stand in front of the portal to the Void. We were going to fight with everything inside us, slay the dragon, and save our families—and all the other million souls drifting inside the Void.

We were going to perform a major update and open up a whole new realm.

After breakfast, the four of us did a sweep of the house to make sure we didn't leave anything around. Then we made the beds, leaving the place looking good as new, and set off to the central building.

The whole way there, my stomach fought to crawl into my throat. During this whole trip, we'd encountered impossible trials I'm still not sure how we'd gotten out of. Now that we were at the Edge, I had been feeling so relieved that it was all *over*.

But I kept trying to convince myself that things weren't about to get so much harder. And now we were preparing ourselves to face a battle that a thousand men couldn't win.

Ellie kept tugging at my shirt and gaping up into my eyes,

her face pale. I tried my best to reassure her, but it was hard to as I was trying to give even myself reassurance. The truth was, the odds were stacked against us. Sure, we had amazing talents that could give us a great advantage, unlike all the other men that had tried to save their loved ones . . . But still . . .

"Children," a familiar voice chirped from the door of the Central Building. Senator Ritu peeked her head around the corner and motioned us inside.

CHAPTER 24

The Cavern of The Void

"**A**re you sure you want to do this?**"** Randor asked, a hint of empathy in his voice. Zyler stood at his side, seeming suddenly interested in the ground.

"We're sure," I confirmed, refusing to let fear mix into my tone. Just to make sure I wasn't lying I checked my friends' faces. Ellie gave me a reassuring nod, and the boys shrugged.

"Okay then, we must keep our promise." He cleared his throat and his eyes drifted into space. "It just doesn't feel right letting four children go into certain death . . ."

Ellie gulped beside me, and I took her hand.

"But I guess we don't have another choice, so if you truly do wish to see the Void, follow my son, Zyler." Randor instructed, motioning his hand over his son's head. "He'll take you to the Cavern of the Void."

"Great," Asher said, pumping his fist sarcastically as Zyler strode toward them. He didn't look happy about it, but he signaled us to follow. I ignored my thoughts and forced my legs to cooperate.

Zyler led us to the back of the Central Room, through a few doors, and to the back of a concrete room that reeked like dank flannel. He sighed enough times for me to almost feel bad for him before he stood before the back wall of the room and pressed his hands against it, breathing heavily.

What happened next was puzzling. It seemed as though Zyler's hands had sunk through the wall, and he was parting the concrete like it was putty. Then, smoke began to curl out from the crack he'd formed, turning the concrete around it black and hard.

Zyler jumped back from the entrance he'd made and stared at it sadly.

"Well, good luck out there kids," he smiled, totally not reassuringly, but at least friendlily. Everything we were about so see from this point on was *definitely* no longer going to be friendly.

The pit in my stomach stretched wider as I fought not to hunch over and hug myself, shivering before the entrance of certain death. Instead, I grabbed Ellie's hand and squeezed it. This was it. The entrance was open and directly in front of us:

The entrance of *hope* and *opportunity* to save Mom . . . *and* the following millions of lost souls in the Void.

"Well, what are we waiting for?" I urged, silently praying that everyone would walk in within ten seconds while I could hold my brave face and not drop the whole deal and get the heck out of here.

Whether it was a good thing or not, I didn't know, but my sister, my *brother,* and my *best friend* held their heads high and took the first step toward the Void. Then another. Then another . . .

And before we knew it, we had stepped through the gap that Zyler had created for us that led into the Cavern of the Void.

***

As soon as all four of us had stepped through the crease in the concrete wall, I dropped everyone's hands and grabbed my forehead, brainstorming the possibility of some kind of strategy, but I had nothing.

Now that we were on the other side of that wall, there was *no* turning back—literally this time. We were trapped in the perilous Cavern of the Void. And now we had to keep clear thoughts as we tried to search for the actual portal to the Void.

So far, we stood in a pitch-black room with seemingly no walls, ceiling, or floor, but we were standing on something, so obviously there was some substance in this place.

A few yards ahead of us, there must've been some kind of pit because I noticed white and golden flecks drifting up from the ground.

"Everyone alive?" I squeaked, not even recognizing my voice.

I meant it as a joke, but nobody found it funny. Probably because they knew that in five minutes, I could ask that question again and the answer could be no.

I gulped as I tried not to remember the visions Mom had given me. She was literally sharing the future with me. I was thinking we were all going to die. I was clearly warned—yet, I decided anyway to keep trudging along toward the Void, telling myself I could somehow change the future—which isn't even possible.

Though here I was, trapped in the Cavern of the Void, with no direction to go except *forward,* deeper into the assurance of our death and towards the lethal future I'd already seen was going to happen.

But I found myself pressing forward towards the pit, anyway.

When I reached the edge of the pit, I peered down into it to find a two-yard drop down to a floor of purple and black slime mixed together. I didn't know whether or not it was too sticky or sinky to walk in, but then again, I decided it was the only way.

White and golden specks of light swarmed around down there. I remembered that the more dense the red flakes were in the Fallen Realm, the closer we apparently were to the portal. I guessed this was the same situation.

"Looks like we're jumping down there," I said. "It only looks like a six-foot drop."

"Yeah, it may *look* like it," Luke mumbled.

"Well, there's only one way to find out," I told him as I slid toward the pit and dropped through. Asher and Ellie flinched, as if expecting something terrible to happen, but I already knew where our deaths would occur.

Turns out, the drop *was* just about six feet because I landed on my feet a second after I dropped.

"Yep, it's all clear own here!"

Ellie was the first to peek down at me.

"Okay, if you say so . . ."

She slid into the pit after me and I caught her body effortlessly. Asher came down next. He landed clean on his feet as well—except, I could have sworn, he flinched when he stood back up from a squat. When Luke attempted to make his way down, however, his feet slid out from under him, and he landed in a sprawled mess.

The three of us laughed as he got back up.

Everything seemed to pause. We were standing in a huge school of golden flecks that floated through the air. And, they didn't seem like the little, lifeless, red flakes we'd seen in the

Fallen Realm. After a few seconds of watching them swarm around me, the realization hit me like ice water on a scorching hundred-degree day.

"They're lost souls," I whispered, my voice echoing the walls, helping me realize where we were.

Okay, maybe the drop *did* just feel like six feet—because this place was *massive!* The four of us stood in a gooey cavern with nonsolid walls made purely of slime. The ceiling dripped with the same purplish-blackish ooze. Though the floor was also made of this material, it was completely solid to stand on. It was kind of like when you mix together starch and water—when you bang on it, it feels solid, but when you pick it up, it liquefies and drips off your hands.

Obviously, this place hadn't been put together with much care, because it was merely a huge, slimy cavern with a few lost souls trying to claw their way out of eternal devastation. And I could hear them crying. Every time a golden fleck drifted by piteous, sobbing whispers followed it.

Ellie gave me a reassuring hug, being the only thing that could cheer one up in this place.

Then, I heard a louder groan from behind a waterfall of slime—a real, gurgling one that didn't come from a lost soul . . . but, from a monster. The next series of groans told me that there were *multiple* monsters, in fact. I'd never heard a monster that sounded like these did, but when six, inky-black figures lurked out from behind a purple-black waterfall, I decided that these guys probably weren't friends. In fact, they were probably what caused the black streaks in the purple slime—I could tell by the trail they left behind.

The pit in my stomach stretched wider as I realized that these six bad guys weren't going to be an easy match.

CHAPTER 25

Ellie is Kidnapped by Slime

I unsheathed Falethropis, which suddenly was difficult to hold with the uncontrollable shaking in my hands. The inky monsters slid toward us, riding on the too-disgusting-to-look-at-current that the Cavern offered them.

Asher tried blasting them with fire, but when the flames hit the monsters, they only spread in different directions, extinguishing in milliseconds. After realizing fire wasn't going to work on these guys, Asher grunted and patted out the small fires licking up his shirt, unsheathing his wide dual swords.

Luke hurled a golden ball at the nearest monster. The pure light must've been the inky monster's weak point, because the golden rays seeped into the slime, stunning them in pain as they tried to filter out the light. After a few seconds, however, they made some awful gurgling noise and kept creeping closer.

"I wonder how swords work on these guys," I told everyone, as I began to charge at the monsters with *Falethropis*. Ellie yelled my name as I stabbed through one of the monsters. It groaned and doubled over in pain, only to reform a few seconds later.

"Kaila, you can't just blindly charge into a strange monster when we don't know what it can do!" Ellie bleated, but she bounded towards me to fight by my side, anyway.

"It's not like we're going to die here, anyway," recalling the vision I had seen, giving out a nervous laugh, whishing I could take back the words I had just said.

"And what makes you think that?"

I bit my lip and tried not to look suspicious.

"I don't know, we've just come so far . . . This would just be a dumb time to die, I guess," I fibbed, hating how bad I was at lying. "I don't know, sorry I worried you. That was stupid of me."

Ellie shrugged. "Well at least you're okay." She added a cute smile to let me know that I was forgiven.

We'd sliced down two monsters before the rest of them decided that this wasn't worth it and disappeared into the ground, leaving behind four pools of black slime.

"Phew! I didn't think a monster had the brains to not mess with us . . ." I shrugged. "But I guess even a monster can learn its lesson."

I slid *Falethropis* back into its sheath and the second blade disappeared, as always.

"Oookay . . . so, I guess now we've gotta walk around and find . . ." Ellie's last few words were drowned out by the echoing *sluuurp* of the black and purple slime emerging from the ground into an enormous blob. Ellie stopped talking to spin around just in time to see the blob expand drippy arms toward her and collapse onto her. She had just enough time to scream before she was swallowed up by the gloopy mass.

"*Ellie!*" I wailed, unsheathing *Falethropis* again to charge at the huge mass of jelly that contained my sister. It was surprisingly fast for a whale-sized-blob of slime.

Through the massive glop rolling ahead of me, I could hear Ellie's muffled screams. "*Kaaiii . . .laa!!!*" was all I could make out through the thick slime containing her.

"I'm coming!" I yelled back, sprinting faster than I'd ever sprinted before in my life. "I'm going to get you out of there, Ellie! Can you breathe?"

"*Nnnnn . . .ooo . . .*" Then I heard coughing.

I almost screamed at the thought of my little sister suffocating inside a huge black and purple blob of slime and let myself glitch on top of it. I yelled again as I shoved my way into the slime ball after I noticed that I couldn't glitch inside. All I needed was to touch my sister and glitch, and we'd be safe.

When I noticed that Ellie had stopped screaming, my movements grew more frantic. "LET MY SISTER GO!!!" I roared, as I let my arms burn trying to wrench open this monster and rescue her.

What if this was the huge mass that crushed Ellie in Mom's vision? What if I couldn't keep it from happening?

As soon as I felt solid skin, I closed my eyes and glitched myself—and, hopefully, my sister—to the safest place I could find.

Turns out I *had* extracted my sister from the slime—but her skin was so pale I began to feel nauseous myself. She wasn't breathing. Her body was limp.

"NO!!!" I howled at the ceiling and desperately tried to perform CPR. "Mom, please, you can heal me, you can heal my sister . . ."

Ellie still refused to breathe.

Luke and Asher scrambled up behind me.

"*Whathappened?*" Asher slurred too fast for me to understand.

"Oh no," Luke said. "No, gosh, no. . ."

Ellie coughed.

"SHE'S ALIVE!" I shouted and continued to perform CPR on my sister, silently praying for another cough. "Ellie, cough it out."

Ellie responded with another set of coughs and her eyes flew open when she began to double over and violently choke out black slime. It seemed she was trying to say something between coughs, but I patted her back.

"You're okay. Just breathe."

Ellie obeyed gladly. She continued to cough it out, but I began to hear her sucking in tricky breaths.

I flung my body backward onto the ground. "THANK THE GOOD LORD," I exhaled with every ounce of carbon dioxide inside of me. "Ellie's okay!"

Luke and Asher plopped down beside me.

"What the *heck* even was that thing?" Luke said. "It looked like an overweight jellyfish. . ."

"Something that's going to regret messing with my sister if it shows itself again," I hissed.

"Kai . . . la," Ellie coughed.

"Yeah, you're okay, Ellie. It's gone," I said. "I'm sorry."

Still breathing heavily as ever, Ellie used my shoulder to sit herself up and hug me with trembling arms. "You saved me."

"Of course I did – I'm your sister."

"I thought I was going to die . . . I thought the slime was too fast and suffocating . . ." She coughed again.

I gave Ellie a gentle hug—one that wasn't going to squeeze the air out of her.

"You're okay, Ellie."

A rather large golden fleck drifted between us and the boys. It glittered brighter than the rest and zipped around faster.

"What's it doing?" I asked, as I watched it circle Luke's head several times, zip away, and then come back to circle my head and fly in that same direction.

"Maybe it wants us to follow," Asher suggested, as the spirit flew back to circle his head.

"Maybe."

Once the golden orb came back to circle my head a second time, I let go of Ellie.

"Okay, maybe we should actually follow it."

I let Ellie ride on my back as the four of us followed the spirit into the Cavern of the Void. It wasn't much different from the canals of the Fallen Realm, except it was half the size.

The further the spirit led us, the more lost souls swam through the air. We hadn't encountered any more monsters, thank goodness, but I was starting to get suspicious of where this thing was taking us. I was about to tell everyone that trusting the wrong thing could prove lethal, until I noticed something abnormal ahead of us.

The golden fleck led us to a dead end of the gloppy cavern canals. But this wasn't just any dead end. The walls were pitch-black, and every surface was lined with white—like the creator of this game had forgotten to add color . . . or just hadn't filled in this place yet . . .

Or, maybe this was the end of the creation . . . the *edge* of the Edge—where the entire world of Katroia officially came to an end.

And in the middle of the half-created room was a circular obsidian opening in the ground that was filled with the darkest, inkiest substance I'd ever seen swallowing any trace of light that threatened to disturb its terrible darkness . . .

It was the entrance to the Void.

***

"I can't," Ellie gasped over my ear. "Oh goodness, no way..."
Ellie hugged around my neck harder. "Gosh, Kaila, that's the
scariest thing I've ever seen."

I held onto her wrists tight.

"We've come this far," I reminded her. "We can't go back...
literally."

Ellie dropped from my back and took a few steps back.

"No, Kaila, please make a way. You *always* make a way." Ellie
wiped her eyes. "Kaila, I want to go home! I want to be in the
woods under the sunshine again!"

"With or without Mom?" I challenged.

Ellie dropped to her knees and stuffed her hands into her
face.

"I want to go home, Kaila!"

Luke's expression dropped as well, as if just noticing that
this was completely and utterly hopeless. Even Asher looked
discouraged.

"Come on guys! Forget about what happened to those men
in the past! They didn't have *superpowers!*" I cajoled. "Look, I
know this is . . . incredibly terrifying, but the more you think
about it, the more you don't want to do it, so I suggest we go
in *now*."

"I guess you're right," Asher sighed and took a step closer to
me. "Forget the fear--just ignore the emotion for now. Come on!
Let's kick some more butt! It's our specialty, after all!"

Luke grunted and took his spot next to Asher. "Okay, I'm
ready."

All three of us looked down at Ellie, who remained crouched
on the ground, staring at her knees. At first I thought she was
going to take a while, but, to my surprise, she wiped tears out of
her eyes and stood on two unstable legs.

"Okay then . . . I guess we have to . . ." Her voice broke and
she covered her mouth, taking my side and grabbing my hand.

"So," I prompted, taking Asher's suggestion, and trying my best to shove down my fear. "I guess this is the part when we get to storm into the Void, put an end to whatever shenanigans go on beyond that portal, and in no time, we'll be in our families' arms, soaking up their love for the rest of eternity. Kapeesh?"

"Kapeesh," Luke, Asher and Ellie agreed at the same time.

The four of us grabbed hands and stepped closer to the portal, our legs shaking, but with our brave faces on. Right before we stepped into the endless darkness, each of us seemed to hesitate just a sliver.

"Don't look at it—just go!" I yelled, giving everyone the last bit of energy to take one more step . . .

And we found ourselves freefalling into an endless pit of darkness, the sanity we'd been able to keep for so long being torn away so fast, I hadn't realized I was screaming violently.

CHAPTER 26

Welcome to The Void

"ELLIE!" was the first thing I was able to scream in the form of words. Then it was, "LUKE!" Then it was, "ASHER!"

It took me longer than it should have to realize I was on my own. I looked down at my fingers and noticed I wasn't holding anyone's hands.

The darkness that yawned below me stretched deeper and thicker the further I fell. I felt like my whole body was going numb as I spiraled deeper into the eternally black abyss. The more I screamed, the more muffled my voice got—until all I heard of myself was a fuzzy, frantic hum.

I couldn't move anything. I couldn't feel anything. I couldn't see anything. Even my thoughts were blurring out.

All I could hear was a faint buzzing sound in the distance— one that sounded like electricity running through copper wires—

The system.

Suddenly, an unbearable blanket of darkness and silence swallowed me and ripped away my thoughts like they were unnecessary objects in the presence of the Void. The darkness seeped into my soul and suffocated my consciousness to the point where I felt my soul leave my body and drift away into the eternal darkness.

No, I thought—the first clear thought I'd been able to think since the dark veil settled over me. *It's not over…*

But what wasn't over? Why was I even here?

Think! I screamed inside my head. *Thinnnn…*

STOP! I tried to shake my body . . . or my soul . . . or do anything that could possibly snap me awake. I knew that I was here for a reason, and no matter what happened, I had no room to give up.

But I was completely losing my thoughts. Everything I tried to think seemed to evaporate before I could make sense of it. I was looo . . . losss . . . ttt

Lost.

***

Buzzzzz…
Buzzzzz…
Thump… Thump… Thump…

At this point, I didn't recognize these sounds, but at least I was lucid enough to hear them now.

Thump…Thump… Thump…
Screech!
POP!

And, all of a sudden, out of the pure darkness and unconsciousness, an enormous tidal wave of an overload of all five senses shot into me so hard, I felt like I'd never seen, heard, felt, or smelled before in my life. At first, I didn't even recognize the sense of sight as I opened my eyes to see blurry, thin white lines that I couldn't make into a shape yet. I heard sharp breaths echoing through my ears, yet I didn't know whose they were. When I realized how my chest was moving and how much I needed to breathe, however, I noticed that the labored breaths were mine.

When my skin touched the ground, an ice-cold feeling shot up my nerves like I was lying on the tiled floor of a meat locker—though I didn't squirm to my feet to get away from it. Instead, I embraced it and let the cold seep into my skin, taking in what little time I had to live before spending the rest of eternity lost in a depressing chasm.

And just before I got ready to drift asleep, I heard my sister's sharp voice shred through my drowsy thoughts.

"Kaila!" she wailed, no further than ten yards from me.

I let my eyes fly open and search my surroundings for Ellie. When I spotted her, lying on the ground in a tight ball, her skin pale and shivering, all energy lost in the Void came flooding back to me. I channeled the new strength to my legs, and I scrambled to my hands and knees to crawl toward my helpless sister.

I heard a new set of deep, labored breaths somewhere nearby and turned my head to spot Luke on his hands and knees in a trance. When I looked right, I found Asher lying on his back, rolling his eyes and muttering something about 'overboard realm travel.'

When I had finally reached my sister and had her in my arms, I allowed myself to comprehend my surroundings.

The four of us lay on a huge platform in the midst of the great eternal abyss of the Void. I would say this place took the shape of an island even, but the biggest difference between the two was that on an island, there was *color*.

This platform took the shape of an island, but it was as if

color was forgotten to be added. Thin, white lines edged most of the curves and creases on the island. They edged along the circumference to form the island's outline—

But, there was absolutely no mass in the island. It was completely and utterly colorless, inside and out. The entire middle of the island was empty, and zero color. The island was entirely matterless, as if the creator had put together the formation of the platform, but flaked out when it came to adding material into it . . . Or maybe the creator tried to, but the Void mercilessly swept away any color or mass that threatened to disrupt its emptiness. The Void wasn't technically part of the game, either. Somehow, a few Katrins were able to slip past the end of the creation, and into a part of the system—

I noticed that the white lines on the ground kept shifting and rippling, like something vibrated underneath it. Like the entire island was just an unstable hologram that lagged a whole lot. It must've not been smoothed and stabilized, either.

The only thing that concerned me was, if the Void wasn't even fully developed yet, then how could it cause such a big change in Katroia? This place was technically a trash can to the system. The island was obviously useless in the creator's eyes—then how could it play such a key role to the resurrection of the Void and open up a new portal?

Ellie stuffed her face into my shoulder and tried her hardest to fight back tears, but when I noticed my shirt dampening, I realized that she was failing.

Asher moaned and rolled over to his stomach so he could push himself off the ground—but when he arched his back, he gasped and fell back down.

"You okay?" I asked, crawling in his direction.

"Yeah, fine," Asher assured me through a strained voice, slowly and cautiously rising back to his feet. He was *not* fine. And this wasn't just from his experience in the Void—he'd been slightly hunching whenever he stood ever since . . . ever since he had been raked by that shadow monster back in the Fallen Realm.

Luke sat back on his knees, his eyes glossy and his expression unreadable.

I dragged three fingers across the frigid ground.

"This place is so . . . empty," I was stating the obvious. Even the air felt empty. It was completely soundless and muffled, like I was reaching a really high summit and my ears needed to pop. I'd never noticed how much air I'd sucked in during one breath in the Overworld—here, I could distinguishably tell the difference between oxygenated air and *empty* air. Like, open your mouth and take a breath right now. Can't you feel the air rushing into your mouth in that breath? Now imagine taking a breath and feeling no breeze inside your mouth—like you're not really taking a breath, but your lungs are still satisfied. *Man,* it's so weird how the laws of life can twist to such far extents in a video game. I wasn't breathing in air; I wasn't breathing anything—but I was breathing, and my lungs were satisfied. Weird.

"So, *this* is what we've traveled eight days to come see," Asher said, staring out into the endless darkness of the Void. I was about to correct him about the number of days we'd been gone, but then I remembered how long everybody had thought I'd been dead.

"Are you saying it's not terrifying enough?" Luke snorted, knitting his eyebrows.

"No—not at all, it's just, *wow,* this is freakishly cool," Asher marveled.

"*Cool?*" Ellie, Luke, and I all shouted in unison.

"Well sure, it's scary, but *look* at this place! Have you ever wondered what it'd be like to be inside the actual game system, on an island that's not actually been completely formed yet—and that's constantly lagging bigtime? Dude, I've been inside a trash can before, but it was *nothing* like this one!"

Ellie and I found ourselves gawking at Asher while Luke sprawled backwards with a dramatic sigh like, *I gave up on this kid a long time ago.*

"Well, we can't judge him for trying to look on the bright side of things," I shrugged. "Wait—you've been inside a trash can before?"

"Sure I have! I had an older brother before, remember?"

"He threw you into a trash can?"

SCREEEEECH!!! A thunderous mass boomed, tearing through the eternal silence and exploding our eardrums, just to add effect.

Asher's playful grin faded to pure horror as he gawked at something upward into the Void. When his eyes widened in shock, I turned around slowly . . . to see a massive navy-purple dragon soaring overhead.

The creature's body reached a length of about ten yards long, with a wingspan of twice that size. Each crevice along its body was lined in white, like everything else in this Void, except this dragon was the only other thing besides us that was fully formed with color. Along its spine, two-foot diameter scales snaked down from its head to the tip of its tail. Its eyes were glassy and shiny, but the fangs hanging out of its upper lip screamed, *this thing's highly venomous!* Especially because they were dripping blood-red venom.

"Oh. My. Gosh," Ellie quavered from my lap. "We're supposed to *fight* that thing?"

The Dragon of the Void screeched again, forcing me to cover my ears to prevent damage.

"Katrins?" It boomed, causing all four of us to flinch so hard we stumbled backward. *"I've never seen a living Katrin before."*

The dragon spread its wings to full length and circled us

repetitively. The creature was five hundred times as big as me and a thousand times more intimidating. The horrific glare it gave me made me want to scream and jump off the edge of the island.

"What are you doing here?" The dragon rumbled, making me jump back into the moment.

Nobody answered it. After, apparently, eight days of promising ourselves that we were going to stand up all brave in front of this dragon and fight it, the words were stolen from our mouths.

"Tell me, little Katrins, is it possible to fall into the portal of the Void on accident?"

"No," Ellie whispered.

The dragon gave us a few seconds of confused, horrific glares.

"Then what are you doing here?"

Why had any of us thought this was going to work? Had we not considered that the dragon was probably a hundred levels over what we could handle? Why hadn't I watched the visions Mom showed me and taken them as a fair warning to turn back to safety?

But I guessed whatever happened next would be worth it if it had anything to do with getting Mom back, so we had no other option but to fight our way through this and see what happened.

You already know what happens, I was silently screaming to myself.

"Tell me, why have you entered my chamber?" the dragon repeated, impatience crawling into his voice.

I rose on two wobbly legs and tried my best to plant my feet as I faced the dragon. "We're here to rescue our families from your Void."

The dragon's eyes slimmed as it stared straight into my daring eyes. It seemed confused at first, but after a few seconds, a few deep giggles escaped from its lips.

"Wait," it snorted. *"You did realize you'll have to kill me in order to do that, didn't you?"*

My head spun when the truth finally hit me after eight days of traveling to this place. All that time, I had shoved aside the fact that we were going to die here. Heck, I even *watched* the four of us die through a vision Mom had shown me. And yet, I ignored the truth and decided to act then, and deal with the consequences later like I always had. Well, in this instance, the consequence was being doled out by the Dragon of the Void.

"You didn't, did you?" The dragon snorted.

"We did," Ellie whispered, immediately flinching for what the dragon would do next.

Fortunately, it only burst into genuine laughter, almost falling out of the air where it circled us. Its laugh sounded like a hive of bumblebees in front of a massive fan. The dragon's strong, majestic wings gave way and it landed hard on the island, causing the ground to quake so hard I toppled backwards off my feet, my pride crumpling down with me.

The dragon used a wing to wipe a tear of laughter out of its eye.

"Oh, that is just too funny," it chuckled. *"Let me clarify this. You four little children journeyed all the way from your little Katrin world to come slay ME?"* it thundered, pronouncing the last word especially loudly as it spread its wingspan as wide as it could reach, billowing over us with a devil's glare.

"We're not . . . just Katrins," I faltered, my voice cracking enough times to make it embarrassing.

"Mmmhm, then what are you?" the dragon challenged.

"A daughter of Maya Kinsworth," I told it. "In case you didn't know, she's . . ."

"Yes, I know who she is all right. A criminal to the Void. Katrins who die and are brought here are supposed to be deleted from the game and forgotten. That no-good mother of yours broke through the veil separating the Void from the system and started messing

with the game!" The dragon snarled. *"And you really think the fact that she can mess with the system scares me?"*

"It should," I retorted, not at all regretting how I was acting toward something a thousand times more powerful than me. I'd learned a long time ago that if you let yourself act scared, it will only make things worse and the chance of you surviving the situation will decrease. And especially now, I could show no fear.

The dragon let out another guffaw before I added, "And this kid is a son of Fore." I laid out my hand in Asher's direction, like I was presenting him to a crowd of people. "And the one next to him is the son of the Enchanter."

So much for presentation. All three of my friends behind me were shaking like the earth was quaking under them bigtime.

The dragon began to snicker again.

"A nice try, but a few children of some higher-level guys aren't half enough to destroy me."

I was frankly impressed with myself for keeping my legs strong as I stood before the dragon, but the more I realized the dragon wasn't an ounce worried for his health, the more my legs started wobbling out from under me.

The dragon laughed and stomped his foot again, causing me to lose my balance again and topple backward. By then, it was gasping for air.

"Ok, ok, enough joking around with you guys. It's been a pleasure laughing with you, really. But I've really been looking forward to tasting live Katrin blood, even if it means killing the fun." The dragon's massive muzzle stretched into a grin. *"But don't worry, kids. Your death will be nice and slow, just so that my enjoyment of this moment will last as long as possible."*

And with another genuine guffaw, the Dragon of the Void leapt from its massive legs and lunged at the four of us, its dark eyes starving and its fangs dripping with fresh venom.

CHAPTER 27

And so, Our Final Battle Begins

If it weren't for Mom, I would have just sat there in all of my misery, gawking at the dragon before it snatched me up and swallowed me whole. Thankfully, I could feel her glitch within me, and I could feel her strength, as I grabbed Ellie and scrambled the two of us out of the monster's range. Luke got away too . . .

But Asher didn't get so lucky. He always seemed to be the unlucky one when it came to the first blow. When I looked back to see if everyone was okay, I saw the son of Fore hanging out of the dragon's mouth, its fangs guarding his escape.

"ASHER!" I screamed, not recognizing my voice. I had no idea how venomous the dragon's fangs were—if they would kill him, or just cause him severe pain.

Asher grunted audibly and thrashed inside the dragon's mouth, clearly in serious pain. I readied myself to sprint over to the dragon and pry its mouth open, but Asher seemed to be able to get out of his situation. He wailed again and stretched out his arms, summoning flames all around him and inside the dragon's mouth.

The dragon winced and spat Asher out into its claws, trapping his arms down and squeezing any energy out of him that would cause him to summon any more fire.

"*Hmm... That smell is oddly familiar,*" the dragon hissed, lowering its muzzle to sniff Asher, who was currently groaning and struggling in the dragon's grasp. "*Smells like shadows.*"

The dragon slowly lifted its other talon and begun to trace it down Asher's chest, tearing the very top of his shirt. "*I see,*" the dragon laughed, eyeing the pitch-black veins that were slowly crawling higher up his chest, nearing his neck—the same veins that I saw crawling up the sides of his face in Mom's vision.

"No," I whispered, as the dragon let off another guffaw and tossed Asher across the island, sending his body rolling across the island's laggy surface and too close to the edge for comfort. When Asher grunted and turned over to see the Void yawning before him, he let out a panicked squeak and scrambled away from the edge.

Ellie let out the breath she'd been holding while Asher's life was in danger—which it still was now, but at least he was on the ground now. She kept scrambling as far from the dragon as possible, but I took my chance to beeline toward Asher and make sure he was okay after being inside the dragon's mouth and claws.

I slid next to my friend. "Are you okay?"

Asher groaned again but managed to crawl to his knees. "Yeah, I'm fine."

"You just burned your way out of the dragon's venomous mouth," I reminded him.

Asher shrugged. "I don't think I actually received any venom since his fangs didn't cut into me." Then he waved his hands all around his blackened torso. "But . . . I'm kind of poisoned."

"Do you have any more potions?"

Asher sighed. "Not for healing shadow wounds."

I let off a sigh and blinked back a tear or two. "Why didn't you tell me about this?"

"You only delay your death," The dragon warned, reminding us all that he was still hungry. *"As I told you, your death will be a slow, painful process."*

I ignored it. "You can still get up and sprint, right?"

"Yeah, it's not as bad as it looks."

But it was.

When I turned around to catch a glimpse of the dragon swooping in for us like an eagle diving in for a mouse, I let out a surprised yelp and laid a hand on Asher, glitching us to safety.

When we rematerialized, I glanced back to see the dragon having an ungraceful, but harmless landing.

Luke, who stood no farther than ten yards from the dragon now, began to wave his arms around in two wide circles. It started slow, but as Luke moved his arms in faster circles, golden dust began to gather in the middle of the circles, slowly spreading into thin disks of golden light.

Once the dragon gained its footing again, it rose to face Luke before me and Asher. *"How dare you threaten my eternal darkness with your little puny light!?"*

It barked, sending visible sound ripples through the air. When Luke's arm circles became faster and more frantic, the dragon howled and lunged at him, its talons extended.

When I saw Luke's legs not budge as the monster lunged at him, I almost screamed some sense into him and glitched him away. Instead, my body refused to obey me, and I had to watch front row what was about to happen to my brother.

When the dragon swiped a claw into Luke, he shielded himself with one of his golden disks, which was now completely solidified. However, it easily shattered into a hundred pieces all

Hannah Jock

around him. Sure, he wasn't hit by the dragon, but the impact sent him careening backward, no matter how hard he dug his feet into the ground.

When the dragon attempted another blow, Luke rolled out of the way and came up on his knees. From there, he hurled his golden disk at the dragon's face like he was throwing a shield, surprisingly pinning it in the face.

"ACK!" the dragon screeched. *"What are you thinking? You think one petty, golden disk can take out the Lord of the Void?"*

The Dragon rose up on its wings and stretched them as far as they could go, symbolizing that this creature was undefeatable. Then, in the blink of an eye, the dragon was plummeting straight down at Luke. Before he could run, my brother was hanging in the air from the dragon's talons, thrashing and yelling in pain and surprise.

The dragon soared up, up, up, as high as it could go before it retracted its claws, throwing him up in the air, leaving Luke freefalling helplessly toward the ground to paint it red.

"Luke!" I cried, and finally my legs obeyed me.

I'd already seen two of my favorite people get snatched up by the dragon, and I wasn't sure if I could watch it again.

I leapt a few feet into the air to add momentum, and then let Mom take me away into a glitch in Luke's direction. Unfortunately, it wasn't possible to glitch through matter.

Instead of glitching toward Luke, my path was blocked by the dragon's enormous body. Mid teleport, I felt my body bounce off of rough, thick scales. The shock paralyzed my body long enough for me to fall, landing flat on my back.

Suddenly, my lungs begged for air. I knew I should have been breathing, but every attempt turned into a wheeze. Alarms banged off every surface inside my head, causing it to throb excruciatingly. And together with the wind knocked out of me, a concussion wasn't exactly helpful.

I heard Luke screaming as he fell in the distance, and I realized he didn't have a ton of space between him and the ground anymore.

The dragon swooped for me again, but I managed to roll out of the way of its claws. It was tedious to do with the air knocked out of me and a throbbing head, but I rolled again and came up standing.

I gasped for air multiple times before I managed to glitch around the dragon to get a sight of Luke. And if it weren't for Mom's reflexes again, Luke would've died.

At the first look, I noticed that Luke was screaming and twisting midair, just six feet from the ground, his eyes closed and ready to embrace becoming a pancake.

I didn't even glitch myself. Mom did. I felt a blue wave of energy ripple across my body, and I blinked over directly under Luke, who was technically on top of me when I landed, but as soon as I felt him touch me, I grabbed him into my glitch and teleported away, breaking his fall and saving his life for now.

The first thing that Luke did when he realized he was okay was gasp and flail out of my arms like a rebellious animal. He flinched when he hit the ground, but no harm came to him after plummeting a hundred feet from the air.

"Kaila," he yelped, without looking up. "Why is everything so close with you?"

I could feel my lungs loosening up for some air. My head still throbbed like an angry hive of bees on a scorching July day, but at least I could breathe again.

"You're welcome," I wheezed.

And without a single second of break time, I heard the dragon's next victim wailing.

"KAILA!" Ellie hollered from across the island. At the sound of my sister's strained voice, I turned my head around so fast it gave me whiplash.

I found myself staring at the Dragon of the Void standing up on its hind legs, holding Ellie tight in its fist and shaking her around like a doll.

"I've got your sister," the dragon badgered, squeezing Ellie tighter in its grasp. She screamed again, but after that, all I heard from her were gasps for air. "Come and get her!"

Okay, you've hit a hard line, I sent into the dragon's mind. Every second I watched my sister having the air squeezed out of her made me so irate, I could have torn apart a mountain.

"*THAT GIRL IS OFF LIMITS!*" I howled at the top of my lungs. Not surprisingly, the dragon didn't even flinch. The next time Ellie gasped for air, an untamable fire sparked inside my chest, shooting pure angry energy through my limbs.

"*You're going to put her down RIGHT NOW!*"

The dragon snorted. "*Or what?*"

I let loose an echoing roar from somewhere deep within my lungs. I didn't even recognize the sound as my own outcry as I leapt off my knees and threw myself into a light-speed sprint.

Whoa, this isn't my energy, Mom transmitted to me.

"*OR THIS!*" I shouted, as I leapt off the ground twenty feet from the dragon and bent the power of the Void to pick me up higher and not let me land—not yet. As all of the darkness bent around me and willed me into an unnaturally high jump, a terrifying howl escaped from my lungs, and I swung an open hand across the face of the Dragon of the Void.

The dragon screeched in surprise as it was sent spiraling out of balance across the island and into a rather hard landing. All I saw out of the corner of my eyes was a purple and gray mess sprawling across the island. But that didn't matter. The dragon had dropped Ellie—and she was in front of me, a ragdoll as she fell toward the ground.

I felt tears burning at the corner of my eyes as I embraced my sister mid-fall and slumped to my knees as soon as we reached the ground. I was afraid too much air had been knocked out of Ellie and she'd be out cold the rest of the battle, but within seconds, her eyes fluttered open.

I didn't say anything. She didn't either. We just stared into each other's eyes, sharing a mix of emotions.

"Kaila, you just smacked the Dragon of the Void across the face," Ellie marveled with disbelief and shock blended into her voice.

"Don't act so surprised. *Nobody* gets to touch my sister without permission," I demanded.

"How comical," the dragon quipped, more cracks in his voice than he probably intended. *"Do you guys still feel that you can defeat me?"*

"Shut up," I retorted, earning a whistle from Asher somewhere across the island.

The dragon's expression transformed from hysterical to dead-serious.

"Oh, it is sooooo on," he growled. *"You ready to play rough? I can play rough!"*

Ellie rose up onto her legs and brushed off her arms. "Mom's trying to tell me something," she whispered to me.

I grinned at her. "Welcome to the club."

The dragon spat venom out of its mouth and licked its fangs for more.

"Who gets the first move?'

Outside of the dragon's line of vision, an immense wall of flames emerged from the darkness, curling around the dragon's back and earning a surprised screech from the immense creature.

When the wall of flames evaporated back into darkness, I spotted Asher standing behind the dragon.

"I do," he grinned, not bothering to pat out the flames licking up his shirt.

Between the flames and the thin red lines that were striped

across his chest and parts of his face, he looked remarkably intimidating. The black poison in his veins was now beginning to inch up the sides of his neck.

Just before the dragon got a chance to bite Asher back, he was pinned in the neck by a thick, golden disk from Luke on his other side.

"I'll take second," he announced, reddening the dragon's naturally navy-purple face.

"*And I'll take third!*" the dragon retaliated, sweeping his tail back at Asher, while swinging a paw at Luke. Thankfully, Luke was able to sidestep his attack while Asher hit the deck fast enough to watch the dragon's whip-like tail sweep over his nose.

I unsheathed *Falethropis* and glitched into the air in front of the dragon's face.

"I really enjoy making blows at this area of your body," I noted, before slicing a gash across the dragon's scaly cheek.

The dragon squealed again and batted me out of the air. Before I hit the ground too hard, I glitched to another area and landed on my feet. I felt like I'd just been hit by a train, but I shook the funny feeling out of my head and charged the dragon again.

"*Do you really think you can defeat me?*" the dragon roared. "*You do realize I'm letting you get your hopes up before I wipe the four of you clean from this island! You've only seen me at ten percent so far!*"

I ignored the dragon and continued glitching around it, swinging and missing blows. I managed to slice a four-foot-long stripe along the dragon's back. But for the dragon, in all of its glory, the gashes probably felt like papercuts.

Ellie stood a few yards from the battle, her eyes focused. She held her hands out in front of her like she was holding an invisible box.

When the dragon pawed me out of the air again, I broke my fall by glitching again—next to Ellie.

"So, what are you and Mom talking about?" I asked her.

Ellie rubbed her temples. "She's trying to hack me a power. Said she can break into some system files—which I have no idea how that's possible in the Void. But anyway, she's going to play with matter, she says."

I raised an eyebrow. "What's that supposed to mean?"

Ellie closed her eyes. "She says if I think past the game I'm used to and start thinking of it as a system, I could learn to shift matter."

My lips slowly parted in awe. "But there isn't even any matter here, is there?"

"Not in this state," Ellie said. "Behind the veil of darkness, there is a split between our worlds. If I can just find out how to get past that veil . . ."

Ellie closed her eyes and extended her arm again, straining her fingers forward like she was reaching for something higher than her arm allowed.

"Think past everything I believe I can see . . ." she uttered, twisting her fingers. "Reach into the split and pull out matter . . ."

I sidestepped over to my sister's side and rested my hands upon her shoulders. "Whatever it is that you're trying to do, I know you can do it."

Ellie smiled at that, still in full concentration, but her fingers not so tense.

She's almost there, Mom transmitted to me. *I can feel the veil churning.*

"*What are you two doing?*" the dragon bellowed, making me jump at the thought that I'd just forgotten about the battle raging on only a few yards away. "*Planning something? It's not going to work!*"

On one side on the dragon, I found Asher's limp body

sprawled across the ground, an oozing gash on the side of his forehead, and the poison creeping up to the point where it was barely reaching the bottom of his face. At the sight, my head turned cold, and I felt my face go pale.

On the other side of the dragon, Luke struggled on the ground, keeping a shaking hand over one of his legs. His teeth were gritted, and his eyes were glassy. He must've broken a leg or something.

"Oh no," I whispered, feeling Ellie grow significantly warmer as beads of sweat began rolling down her forehead.

"Almost . . . there . . ." Ellie managed to say through a strained voice.

"Almost what? Is your mom breaking rules again?" the dragon scoffed, scrunching his nose in utter disgust.

"Apparently," I said.

The dragon snarled at us. *"What is she doing?"*

"Like I'd ever tell you," I snorted, sassing at this dragon like we were just old adversaries poking at each other again.

"Yeah, well, whatever it is better happen fast, because I'm not just gonna stand here while you guys work on . . ."

"I got it!" Ellie sang as I watched the darkness around her arms churn and fold over, shifting matter that didn't exist and curling it over and over.

The dragon hissed.

"How could you even think about disrupting my eternal chamber of nothingness! Are you twisting matter from the split and into my VOID?"

"Apparently," I repeated.

"HOW DARE YOU!?" The dragon thundered, sending a visible soundwave in our direction.

Time seemed to slow down as Ellie swept her arm to the right, churning the darkness to the left and carrying away the soundwaves with it. No expression other than concentration and confusion showed on her face.

"What are you doing?" the dragon again fumed as it charged us, throwing in its whole body to shred us apart with its claws.

Ellie retracted her hand to her chest, closing her eyes, and then pushed outward, sending a tidal wave of pixelated matter purring into the Void. When it hit the dragon, the immense, unstoppable, purple-creature-of-the--Void's-complete-mass shifted backwards by the force emerging from Ellie's hands.

"AAACK!" the dragon raged, as it tumbled across the ground by the impact.

"Error code 381: Spawn nine-thousand, seven hundred twenty-four relocated without command," echoed a voice off the dark walls surroundings us. "Error code 723: Matter from split leaked through Hierld Membrane 21"

Ellie blinked several times, frozen in time for a minute straight. It took that long to process the past minute and a half.

"What just . . . happened?"

CHAPTER 28

Two Down, Two to Go

"*Okay, you asked for it!*" the dragon barked, as it stumbled to its feet, marching at us with pure rage flooding into its face. "*I'm going full out now!*"

The dragon unhinged its jaw and let out an eardrum-banging roar that Ellie never got to deflect. Red venomous flakes spewed out of its mouth that looked worthy of a third-degree burn.

Ellie gasped and swept her arm sideways, getting rid of most of the poison. But a few flakes melted into my skin, triggering a yelp to escape my lungs.

The dragon charged us, and when Ellie didn't move, I grabbed around her waist and glitched us away. Unfortunately, the dragon was fast. Before Ellie and I could comprehend what exactly was around us, the dragon had pounced, giving me just enough time to throw Ellie as far from the threat as possible and scramble most of my body out of the way . . .

But the dragon got a blow at my leg.

I let out a piercing wail as unbearable pain shot up my leg, stealing the energy straight from my arms and allowing me to collapse. I repeated 'ow' more times than I'd like to admit and slowly curled up to hug my leg.

It throbbed so freakishly bad that I worried that the bones inside of it were shattered. Sharp shards picked at the inside of my leg, each shoving tears out of my eyes.

I heard Luke yelling as well and glanced through a blurry vision at a golden mass collecting in front of Luke.

"YOU CANNOT DEFEAT ME!" the dragon screamed for the thousandth time as it took a ground-rumbling step toward Luke, whose golden cloud was now massive.

"YES, WE CAN!" Luke shouted as he pulled back the golden cloud surrounding him to suppress it before releasing it upon the wretched Dragon of the Void.

The dragon inhaled too strongly, the poison from its fangs welled up deep inside its chest, ready to release upon Luke and wipe him out. Both looked equally powerful—except for the fact that Luke had a hurt leg.

Luke yelled with everything inside of him as he thrust his arms out toward the dragon so hard, his feet slid back several feet. The dragon's venomous blast sounded hoarse. Both attackers flew at each other at the speed of sound, each equally powered . . .

And then they hit.

For a second, they sank into each other, as if deciding which one was going to overpower the other. But it appeared their powers were equal, and they sent each other ricocheting back at twice the speed.

Luke tried to catch the golden cloud back into his possession, but his reflexes weren't fast enough. He was swept into the air by his own magic cloud and was blown backward off the island to plummet down into the eternally empty abyss of the Void.

"NOOO!" I roared at the top of my lungs, unable to move or glitch or do anything that could possibly save my brother's life. He was gone. Lost in the Void to have his soul reaped and forgotten forever.

"LUKE!" Ellie bewailed after me.

"I TOLD YOU I WAS DONE PLAYING GAMES!" the dragon screamed in the air, who was able to shoot itself upward fast enough to dodge its own attack. It tucked its wings under its belly and dove down toward my sister, who was sprinting across the island. All I could do was watch as the dragon spun around and swept its tail toward Ellie like a baseball bat, scoring a home run.

My sister let out a guttural cry as she was sent flying in the air across the island in the direction of the Void. I forced myself to ignore the unbearable pain in my leg and glitch to catch her.

Ellie knew I was going to come save her, because the second I touched her, she wrapped her arms around me like a magnet, trembling in my arms again like the little girl I'd seen the night Mom died. The girl that could do nothing but tremble in my arms, cry, and wail about how nothing could ever get better.

But when I landed back on the empty-lagging ground in the Void, her eyes were full of determination.

"We're goanna win," she croaked, inflamed from being batted by the dragon's scaly tail. "Promise me we'll win."

My eyes welled with tears. I knew I couldn't promise that. I'd seen how this was going to go down, yet I ignored it, and promised that I'd defy the inevitable. Now, Luke was dead. Asher was unconscious in the middle of the island, waiting to be snatched and eaten. My leg was broken, and I was helpless. And Ellie . . .

Her eyes grew wide as she spotted something behind us.

"Kaila! Watch . . ."

I didn't catch anything else my sister said. The words were

drowned out by the closest dragon howl I'd heard yet. One that could've done permanent damage to my eardrums.

Ellie yelled something else as she shoved me behind her and extended her arms over me, shifting my matter and causing me to relocate five yards away.

When I looked up, I found the dragon ascending again, a ragdoll body dripping red in its talons. And then the dragon tossed my sister out into the trash can of Katroia.

I almost barfed from the unbearable pain spreading through my limbs as I forced myself to glitch out into the Void, grab my sister, and glitch back to the island with her in my arms. It wasn't until I looked down to see her state that my head grew light and terrifying alarms resounded inside my head.

When I caught a glimpse of my sister, all I saw was a *lot* of red, so I looked away. When I felt my clothes soaking, I screamed.

"Kaila," my sister wheezed, her voice sounding wet in her lungs. I covered a hand over my mouth, screaming at myself to not think about what that meant. "Win . . . this . . . fight . . ." Ellie managed between coughs. Her breaths were so shaky and clotted, I almost dropped her and jumped off the island.

"Ellie," I whispered, my eyes shut. "Please don't die on me. You're not seriously going to die right now, are you?" "Get . . . us . . . back . . ." was the last thing my little sister said before her trembling went still and her heaving chest stopped moving.

"*No,*" I demanded. "Ellie, breathe! Stop lying there and get back up!"

"*She's gone,*" the dragon gibed, a wide grin stretching across its face. "*Two down, two to go.*"

Hannah Jock

CHAPTER 29

I Teach the Dragon a Lesson

"ELLIE WAKE UP!" I cried, my emotions spilling out every time I called her name. "Please, don't leave me now. Not now." I remembered the vision Mom had shown me of how Ellie would die. And that was exactly how it happened.

She'd given her life to rescue mine. She'd seen the dragon lunging at us, shoved me behind her, and willingly gave herself to be crushed in my place.

This was my sister, who'd always been my ray of light during any dreary day. My sister, who'd given me somebody to cry with in bed all day when we had lost our beloved mother. This was Elliana, who'd always have a trick up her sleeve, this time leading us to this Void to rescue Mom. She'd never given up, even as she lay in my arms, taking her final breaths. She believed that I could win this fight, regaining both her and Mom back.

This was my sister, who I was supposed to protect with my life, never letting anything crawl near or they would face my wrath. And *mark my words*, the Dragon of the Void was *going* to face my wrath more than anyone ever has before.

I let loose an earth-rumbling howl as I set down my sister, who began to fade into white flakes. I stood up straight before the dragon, no trembling limbs, no fear in my expression anymore. All I showed was anger. *Deep,* untamable anger that spread energy through my limbs specified to tear apart the wretched Dragon of the Void.

I wanted to swim in the anger; drown in the anger; do anything in my power to scrape up all of the anger that I'd gathered throughout my entire life to hurl at the dragon through a fire hose until it was on its knees, begging for mercy.

"WHAT DID YOU JUST DO!?" I raged, my skin radiating red light. *"TELL ME YOU DID NOT JUST KILL MY SISTER!"*

The dragon's face twisted into an unreadable expression. Then, it morphed into a grin. *"Go on, give me your big speech on how nobody touches your weak little sister or ..."*

"SHUT UP!" I exploded as I called on Mom's energy to mix with my infinite anger aimed at the wicked creature smirking before me. The sight of its face made me want to punch it inside out, rip out its black eyeballs, and stick them up its nose.

"YOU FINALLY DONE PLAYING GAMES? SO AM I!"

I leapt off the ground, screaming in pure rage as I sprinted at the dragon five times as fast as I've ever run before—and that's saying a lot, because I'm pretty fast.

The dragon seemed unsure about this battle, and even took a step back when I unsheathed *Falethropis* with a loud *shiiing*.

"You've hit a hard line, Mr... Now you're gonna pay!"

I let out Katroia's most terrifying war cry as I sprung into the air before the dragon's face again, and as it tried lifting its wings over its face, I swung my sword flat across its cheek with immense power. The Lord of the Void flew backwards, sprawling off the island and into the black abyss. But I wasn't letting it out of my sight until it was dead.

"*I'M GOING TO KILL YOU!*" I seethed, as I glitched out to the dragon, landing on its back. It whipped around, batting at me with its tail, but the dragon could not get rid of me. The whole thing turned out to be a huge fight in the air—the Dragon of the Void using its wings and Kaila Kinsworth in the air by constant glitching, confusing her adversary.

Throughout this entire journey, I had lashed out on hundreds, maybe thousands of monsters on just my mother's reflexes. Mom had taken over my moves, helping my body to wipe out every monster in my path.

But this time, it was my turn to take the power of the Void to my advantage. My reflexes were ten times faster than ever before, but *I* was the one controlling them instead. I was the one making every blow to the dragon, cursing it for every mistake it had made. The constant glitching I'd been using wasn't from Mom, either. She seemed to have leaned back in surprise, astonished by my abilities. While the glitch was mine, the ripples taking me away switched from blue to green, creating a colorful shadow that followed my trail.

I had already hit the dragon twenty times by the time it had three chances at hitting me. Once I was getting bored glitching around the dragon in the air, I gave off another yell as I shot the sinister beast back to its island, where Asher stood back on his feet, flames licking up his body. The poisonous veins had now taken over his face and had turned his eyes jet black. Some of the poison was even beginning to crawl down his arms. And for some reason, he didn't even wince as the flames curled up his bare arms.

"*Thank* you for giving me a turn, Kaila," Asher grinned as the dragon rolled up in front of him. "I was getting bored over here." Suddenly, an immense wall of flames erupted with a few streaks of black shadows wrapped up in the flames.

I winked at him, not realizing how tired I was at this point. I was still incredibly angry at the pitiful dragon, but the battle rage had almost left me, as well as my ability to glitch.

Little bit of help over here, I called to Mom as my limp body fell for the Void. I was able to reach my arms out just enough to grab ahold of the edge of the island. I heaved myself just high enough for my elbows and chest to lean over the mass, but I let my legs dangled off the sides.

Kaila, Mom sent. *That rage was . . . utterly uncontainable. The wave of emotions you let out just completely blocked me out from helping . . .*

It's okay, Mom, I told her. *But I've just drawn some conclusions.*

What? She asked when I didn't finish.

I sighed before continuing.

I cannot change the future, Mom. That's a fact.

Mom kept quiet inside my head.

Buuuuut, you saw me falling into the Void in your vision, correct?

Yeeaaah...

Right, but I had just spent a whole five minutes in the middle of the Void but was able to glitch back to safety. Sure, Asher had limped sometime during this battle with black veins crawling up his neck, but look at him! The visions we saw of the future have come true, but neither of us are dead. So, maybe the visions didn't mean we were all going to die?

When I picked up my head to take a look at how Asher was doing, all I saw was the Dragon of the Void engulfed in a sea of white-hot flames, the fire flapping too loud for me to hear whatever nasty comments Asher had to spit out at the dragon. Sure, the veins in his face were pitch black, as were his eyes, but he wasn't a bit slowed down.

And just when I thought all was well, I saw the dragon sweep its tail around and smack at a black figure in the midst of the flames. When I saw Asher's feet dragging backwards by force, a million alarms sounded in my head.

But then, I noticed that the dragon wasn't up for finishing Asher. Its skin was ashy gray and black and white—anything but purple, its natural color. And the once-horrifying beast that tried so hard to intimidate us and scare us out of our skin now lay flat on the island, its breaths forced and shaky.

Asher, however, was still on his feet, flames curling up and down his body. Fresh blood rolled down his arms, shirt, and face, which also showed a fading expression.

Asher's eyes fluttered and he began to sway. The rest of his face that wasn't black went pale and he tripped over his heels and started to fall backwards.

I glitched to his side and caught him before he hit the ground. His jet-black eyes never shut, but he looked dizzy, like he'd been spinning in circles for an hour straight.

"I feel like I'm floating on clouds," he whispered, his voice deep and hoarse.

Once most of my anger had left me, I remembered how much my leg hurt. During all of the rage, I knew it hurt, but I didn't care. All I was focused on was teaching the dragon a good lesson on who not to mess with. After using a bone-shattered leg so much, I felt like cutting it off would be less painful.

But I left it where it was because I knew that we were going to finish the dragon, creating a way back to the Overworld, where all of my pain would go away once I was in Mom's arms.

"Kaila," Asher wheezed. "Make the final blow."

"Why me?"

"Because it's your job to punish the dragon for killing your sister. Plus, you've totally earned it. You should've seen yourself."

"You should've seen *your*self!"

"I'm in no state to stand, anyway."

"I'm not either."

Asher's eyes wandered to my broken leg, which was now swelling like crazy, and had turned entirely purple.

"Oh," he whispered.

I laughed and rested a hand on his shoulder, making the final decision by glitching the two of us to the dragon's side.

As soon as we reappeared in front of the dragon's face, it gave me a sour look.

"Now what?" it wheezed, its voice quieter than ever.

"Now we get our families back," I demanded, managing to stand up on one leg, while letting the other scream in pain. I looked down at Asher, who nodded back up at me. "I told you my sister was off-limits."

The dragon's face twisted into anger mixed with confusion and hesitation.

"I hope you love your family a lot," It sneered, knowing that its life was at its end. Then, its face softened. *"And this sacrifice better be worth it for all of Katroia."*

"Believe me," I whispered, lifting up my sword over the dragon's head. "It is."

And then I brought down my blade so fast, the dragon didn't have time to squeeze its eyes shut before the sword was impaled into its massive skull, finishing off the Battle of the Void. My spirit-gold sword finally gave way after all these battles and shattered inside the dragon's head. I dropped the hilt, which was the only part of the sword that remained. When it hit the ground, my heart dropped inside my chest and I let my legs give way, dropping next to Asher on the ground.

Suddenly, massive beams of light tore through the dark veil of the Void, striking into the dragon so fiercely, it's body began to implode. With every beam of light that struck him, more of its body withered away. The Dragon of the Void let off its loudest screech yet, for once, not making me flinch. Besides, the soft *shiiing* sounds coming from the light beams seemed to harmonize the dragon's final wail as they overwhelmed it.

I closed my eyes and let out a labored breath, silently praying that the light would take me away before I died here.

And then, all of a sudden, the Dark Veil surrounding us tore in two, allowing a blinding light to flood into the abyss, illuminating the darkness. The darkness didn't stand a chance. It could not overcome the light. It was as if the light was shoving back every bit of black that had ever existed in this place.

And then, as the overwhelming light swallowed me into its comforting presence, I felt a gravitational shift in the air.

***

I found myself floating away through a colorful abyss this time. The fluffiest, cotton candy clouds drifted in the air all around me. Angelic white surrounded everything, erasing every possible trace of sadness, fear, anger, pain, etc. With a big bright smile on my face, I felt as though nothing could ever go wrong again. Nobody could ever be lost to the Void again.

Then, I felt a soft hand slip into mine. I expected to see Mom when I glanced over, but instead, I met eyes with a fourteen-year-old boy with overgrown jet-black hair and coarse front bangs.

"Asher," I whispered, almost not recognizing him without scratches all over him and black veins tracing up his sweaty face.

Asher shot me his movie-star smile. I almost wrapped my arms around him and shed happy tears, but then the little sunshine trip came to an end. The light swept in and carried the two of us away.

CHAPTER 30

A Vision of Victory

When my consciousness came back, I opened my
eyes to see a long progress bar slowly filling with green
substance. Underneath it, a small script was etched into the
white background:

Update in progress . . . 78% . . . 81% . . . 86% . . .

Then, the numbers shot up to a hundred percent, and the
script underneath switched to, *Update Complete! Would you
like to see the changes in your game?* And two buttons appeared
under it.

Then, a strange, slanted arrow popped into the scene and
moved over to the left button, which read, *'Yes'.*

Suddenly, the scene flooded with colors. The first one, I
didn't exactly love. The vision showed me the outside of the
wretched Fallen Fortress. The next part, I *did* love. I watched
with a grin as the treacherous Fortress rumbled from within,
fractures and fissures cracking the walls. Then, the unworthy

building collapsed to the ground, its bricks scattering the ugly surface of the Fallen Realm.

The even-better part was when the entire massive cavern of the Fallen Realm began to tremble, leaving stalactites to crack from the ceiling and splinter into the ground. In no time, the ceiling had collapsed and light from the Split flooded over everything.

The scene shifted to a vision of the Edge. A dozen villages there were shown, in each a massive portal framed with braided bark emerging from the ground. Filling the frame was a thin white sheet leading to the all-new Spirit Realm. When Evelade was displayed, I spotted Zyler strolling through the packed-dirt roads. When he saw the portal rise from the ground, his expression turned ecstatic and he yelled, "THEY DID IT!" Then, everyone came rushing out of their homes to wait with expectation at their new portal, the senators' expressions the most priceless. Then, everybody cheered and began pumping fists before the scene shifted again.

I watched as dozens of Spirit Realm portals emerged in dozens of different places. I watched it happen in our village, making me grin so wide my cheeks burned. Portals kept coming up over and over in different places, somehow never getting old.

And then the screen began to lag the rest out, and everything was bathed in white.

In the center of the white veil, black words were imprinted:

Update Completed! Congratulations, *Kaila Kinsworth and Asher Lolex!*

CHAPTER 31

Welcome Back to
the Overworld

The screen faded white, and as I was being teleported back to the Overworld, I felt as if I was wrapped into a warm comforting blanket of new hopes that lie ahead.

The soft hum of the system echoed in my ears as it worked to shake me awake. I tried to focus on waking up my nerves before I opened my eyes.

And as my consciousness began to return, I noticed first the massive wave of warmth surrounding me—so many arms holding me. So much love and joy and comfort after enduring such darkness and loss. One pair of arms were significantly the warmest, like a heating pad to my skin. I could feel the presence of somebody leaning over me, warming my face with steady breaths that clearly came from a smiling face.

"Rise and shine, my little Kaila Bear," cooed Mom's heart-melting voice—not the suppressed voice from the Void that whispered through a cold filter. These words were warmer than anything around me at this moment. The smoothness in Mom's voice made all my insides turn to mush.

I peeled one of my eyes open, bracing myself for tears at the first sight of Mom's face. So many tears shed over her death—so much darkness and cold feelings inside. No color, no joy . . . and now, in contrast, everything seemed to be double the color and vividness than before, and with twice the joy.

But when I caught my first glance of Mom's soft skin, blushed cheeks, and deep blue eyes, I couldn't fight a tear from slipping out of the corner of my eye.

"Mom," I whispered, not realizing how hoarse my throat was from all of the screaming and holding back of tears over the past 8 days.

"Oh Kaila," Mom cried as she leaned over and hugged the breath out of me. I didn't care. I just kept letting out salty tears and a shaky smile spread across my cheeks.

"Mom," I repeated, my voice more like a whimper. "I thought you were gone forever."

I began to weep harder when I reviewed how hopeless I'd felt about living out the rest of my life without Mom. Now that I had her in my arms . . .

"Mom!" chirped the voice of my little sister, who I'd failed to protect in the Void.

Ellie threw her arms around me and Mom, immediately sobbing. Then Mom began shedding happy tears as well. And then I joined in, wrapping my other arm around Ellie to calm her trembling.

Rich mango-colored sunlight spilled through the windows around the house, wrapping us up in warmth. Everything inside of the house seemed so much brighter than before. Even the shattered glass scattered across the ground seemed to reflect rainbows along the walls, gleaming so bright I couldn't look at them.

The air smelled of blooming lilies and roses and crisp, cool spring air. The clean scent of the pebble-coated river a few yards from our house mixed with the sweet scent that hung in the air, putting me inside a candle every time I closed my eyes. I took steady, unbroken breaths as I listened to the birds perched around our house singing their choruses.

Then, another warm body smashed into the hug and joined in with the tears.

"Luke!" I cried, wrapping my other arm around him. "I'm *so* sorry I failed you guys!"

"Don't even start, Kaila," Ellie interrupted. "If I hadn't died, you wouldn't have gained all that energy you clearly needed to defeat the dragon. You kept your promise."

"Yeah, and while I sunk into the Void, I wasn't at all worried that I was going to be trapped there forever. I knew you would win the battle," Luke added.

Mom wiped a tear from the corner of my eye.

"I never doubted you, Kaila. Of course, you were going to find a way to win me back, so there was no sense in trying to convince you not to try." She smiled down at me. "Oh, how I love you."

Hearing that sentence purr from Mom's lips let the bowling ball I'd been forced to swallow the past nine days finally come up. I felt the pain in my throat evaporate into tears—huge tears that fled out as fast as raindrops. But I didn't cover my face to hide my red cheeks—I embraced the love of my family instead and let my emotions finally spill out. I didn't ever want this moment to end.

"Kaila?" called a female voice from outside. "You're home?"

Everybody froze to watch the door as it creaked open.

"Where did you guys go? We've been searching for ten days..." Captain Freya's voice quickly faded when she saw Mom's rosy smile. "Maya," she whispered.

A long, uncomfortable silence followed that word. "Impossible . . . I—I watched you get sucked into the Tear." Her eyes wandered to mine. "You . . . did something, didn't you?"

My lips stretched into a shaky smile as I nodded. I shared with Freya the entire story, from the break-in to the Enchanted Library to the defeat of the dragon. The whole time I shared, I readied my legs to dash over to Freya's side and catch her if she passed out. Fortunately, she was a good listener and stayed oriented the whole time.

As I nattered on for the next five minutes straight, looking back on the tedious journey we'd endured, I felt a prick of pride crawl into my voice. I still couldn't believe some of the impossible situations we'd survived—thanks to Mom. My voice cracked more times than I'd like to admit as I struggled to share the scary events.

An awkward silence followed the end of the story. Freya's eyes were closed as she rubbed her temples, trying to process every bit of information I'd just shared. It wasn't until then when I realized I should have given her a bit of thinking time in between each event.

The silence was broken when the door swung open again, and a tall man with dark, coarse hair and shadowed features entered the room. He wore long black and blue robes that plunked to the ground and trailed behind him as he walked.

Freya blinked several times when her eyes met his. "Mr. . . Enchanter!?"

The Enchanter nodded. "It's a pleasure," he said with a grin.

Freya never got to process the fact that she was standing in the presence of the Enchanter before four more figures entered the room. One of them was a rugged man dressed in worn clothes, his face smeared with grease and soot—Will, Sherberry's Forgemaster.

Another was Freya's sister Heather, a tall and slim, but deft woman clothed in leather with a sword and bow strapped to her back. Her high hazelnut ponytail was naturally curled, thin strands falling down the sides of her face.

The two other figures of the group were Kaila and Ellie's friends, who lived just two houses down from them. One of them was Kaila's age—fourteen years old with long dirty blonde hair and a permanent smirk spread across her face—Lina. Her little sister, Bonnie, was twelve, with the same blonde hair and blue eyes, but her smile was friendly. Both sisters waved shyly and greeted us, careful not to disrupt our fragile mental states as we clung to each other, our cheeks red and lined with tears.

"Don't worry, guys, I told them the whole story—you don't have to repeat it," the Enchanter told us, a friendly smile planted across his cheeks.

"What . . . are you doing here, my Lord?" Freya quavered.

"Oh please, don't call me that. Mr. Enchanter works. And I came here to congratulate Kaila, Ellie, and my son, Luke. I'll admit it, I highly doubted your success." He lifted his chin. "But here you stand, in one piece as the heroes of Katroia. For that, I give you my thanks. You have fixed a problem, that I had been trying to figure out for years, in just ten days."

I hoped my face wasn't as red as it felt as I thanked the Enchanter.

Once the Enchanter had finished his congratulations, Freya, Will, Heather, Lina and Bonnie rushed forward to give us a proper greeting.

"I can't believe you kids managed to fulfil a quest that a thousand men couldn't!" Bonnie gushed.

"*I* can't believe you broke into the Enchanted Library," Freya said. "But I'm glad you did, because you guys got Maya back . . . and rescued the Void while you were at it," she added quickly.

Lina gave me a long, tight hug. "I was so worried about you—we all thought you were dead. We almost gave up looking for you and were starting to talk about planning for a funeral!"

"Not the first time that's happened," I snorted. "Wait—you guys looked for us all ten days we were gone?"

Lina nodded quickly. "Oh, totally! We didn't stop, well, apart from our meals and defending the village at night."

"I'm sorry," I consoled sincerely.

Before Lina could insist that I shouldn't be sorry, the door flew open *again*. Everybody turned back to watch who was coming in now.

First came a tall man with a mop of jet-black hair on top of his head. He wore steel armor on his torso and legs, and an excited grin played at the corner of his mouth. His skin tone and bright features accurately matched Asher's, as well as his hair and famous grin.

So could that mean . . .

A smaller model of the man popped in from behind the door, his smile as wide as ever as he yelled, "Surprise!" earning a delighted laugh to slip through my lips. It was Asher!

Asher's apparent older brother stepped into the room next—the same grin hung between his cheeks that clearly read, *'I chucked this kid into the trash can once'*. After him followed a younger girl that looked about ten years old. Her head was draped with the longest caramel brown hair I'd ever seen, flowing all the way down to her hips. She focused her two different-colored eyes—one brown, one blue—onto her fidgety fingers as everybody in the room stared at the visitors.

"Asher!" I beamed, extending an arm out so that he could join the hug.

"Did you miss me?" Asher grinned, as he strode over towards us.

"How could I not?" I asked with a laugh as I patted his back. "By the way guys, this is Asher. He played a vital role in the rescue of the Void."

Asher pulled back and introduced his family members.

"This is my little sister, Clara," he announced, pointing to the younger girl in the corner, who was fiddling with the edge of her shirt. "This is my older brother, Jack – the one that threw me into a trash can."

Jack snorted. "Sounds like I'm notorious."

"And I don't think I need to introduce myself," Fore said, snapping his fingers and summoning a ball of fire in front of him that kept changing forms—from a dragon, to a sailboat, to an ugly version of the Enchanter's face. "I think that gives you a pretty good hint."

"Fore," Freya marveled. "What is with the most supreme men in Katroia just walking into this house like we're all simply old friends showing up at a welcome back party?" she whispered over my shoulder.

I just shrugged in response.

"Nothing really surprises me at this point," getting a chuckle from the group.

Fore extinguished the flames in his palm and lifted his eyes up to meet the Enchanter's. "Sup," The Enchanter mumbled.

"Sup," Fore shot back with a wink like, *'It'll take more than what you did two years ago to get rid of me!'*

"So," Clara said. "I made everybody some fresh baked cookies, if you guys want any."

"Cookies!" Ellie sang, jumping to her feet. "Thanks, Clara!"

Clara smiled. "They're all still warm and soft, too!"

The room was filled with joy and love as everybody laughed and shared 'bright side' stories of our epic adventure to the Void. The cookies were the most scrumptious things I'd ever put inside my mouth, and their scent that filled the air was just as delightful. The entire time, I insisted on clinging to Mom and soaking up every last drop of her warmth and overflowing heart of love. I never wanted this moment to end.

But when everybody began to head out a few minutes later, I noticed a playful smirk twisting the corner of Mom's mouth. Before Will left, he returned her smirk and pointed a finger in her direction. "I expect to see you at the forges in ten minutes," he said.

Mom's smile stretched wider as she said, "Not a chance."

When Will left, being the last one, Mom turned back to me and Ellie, tossing her long caramel hair.

"Gosh, after all of that suffocating darkness I've endured in the Void, it would be absurd not to take a refreshing run through the woods, wouldn't it?"

Ellie giggled in delight. "So absurd."

Mom laughed and took my hand into hers and reached for Ellie's with her other hand. I turned and offered Luke a hand as well. He didn't even hesitate before willingly taking it, a totally brotherly smile tugging at his cheeks, showing those cute dimples first revealed in the Fallen Realm.

Now I recall reading in the Enchanter's library that those who survive the Void shall bring back their family. I feel bad that Luke didn't survive long enough to bring his family back, but I am so grateful that Asher and I were able to bring back our families . . . I guess Luke really is family, after all. At least he'll be able to go visit those he lost in the fire, since they've been freed from the Void, and are now in the Spirit Realm.

Mom flashed her beaming smile that could replace the sun as she looked down at both of her girls and her son.

"You guys ready?"

"Best. Day. Ever," Ellie announced.

And with all four members of our family hand in hand again, we took our first step outside together, feeling as though nothing could ever come between us again as we frolicked down the roads of Sherberry Village. The four of us jogged through the central area, earning a few surprised faces as we passed by. Then, we waltzed by the Forges and the armory, headed straight for the woods.

And when we finally stood before the onset and all of its glory, it felt like Mom had never left me. The trees bent down to meet us as we stood before them, beckoning us inside to hear its newest grand symphony. The fresh scent of a stream was carried on the wind and drifted into our nostrils. The birds gave us an exquisite sample of the orchestra ahead as they let off dozens of different tweets and chirps that blended together into a sweet harmony.

Mom laced her fingers through mine, and after giving me and Ellie teary, shaky smiles, she, Ellie, Luke, and I took a step into the superb, lofty forest.

And after we'd leapt over enough streams, moss-caked logs, and rocks, we decided to lay in the grass together, our spirits soaring high above.

"See, Kaila?" Mom laughed as she draped an arm around my shoulders. "Everything will *always* make sense in the end."

My eyes brimmed with joyful tears as I tittered delightfully and threw my other arm around my sister. "We have endless days of joy and sunshine to look forward to. And we know that it's because we have each other—that's all we'll ever need, anyways."

Luke chuckled as he slung an arm around Ellie and the four of us swayed to the rhythm of the wild symphony surrounding us, soaking up the joy that hung in the air. Now, lying on the velvety forest floor with Mom's arm around me and Luke and Ellie curled up nearby, I knew our love was going to stretch on like this forever. And I was going to spend it with my entire family, finally unbroken and with relationships stronger than ever before.

The End
~Hannah Jock

ACKNOWLEDGEMENTS

There are a whole lot of people I would like to thank for supporting me as I chase my dreams of becoming a writer, even at my young age. But first and foremost, I'd like to thank my caring, supportive mother, who has never doubted me and has taken so much of her time to help make my dream become a reality. Maya Kinsworth is a close reflection of who my mom is, only my mom is so much more. I'd also like to thank my exuberant father, who has also believed in me and greatly influenced my writing style.

To Aunt Patti, I could honestly write an essay on how inspiring you are to me. Thanks for editing and revising my book and for giving me the confidence to go through with publishing it. I'd also like to give a special thanks to Tracy for designing a beautiful cover. To Jan Wilson, thank you for being willing to give the book one last detailed comb over to make sure it was just right before having it published. And to all of my friends and family, thanks for believing in me and being supportive in every way you could. I couldn't have done this without all of you.

ABOUT THE AUTHOR

Hannah Jock was just eight years old when she began to feel inspired to write. Ever since then, she's been reading for hours a day, writing flash fiction, and constantly seeking out ways to sharpen her writing skills so that she can become an author "when she grows up". When Hannah was just 12 years old, she decided to put her thoughts on paper and start writing her very first novel, "The Glitch".

Hannah lives in Massachusetts with two siblings, two collies, a loving mother, and an exuberant father. During her leisure, she loves to be outside doing archery, climbing trees, exploring in the woods, playing volleyball, and skiing in the winter.